A Ballad of Phantoms and Hope

K. M. Moronova

Copyright © 2024 by K. M. Moronova LLC

Cover done by K. M. Moronova LLC

Formatting done by K. M. Moronova LLC

Interior character art done by K. M. Moronova LLC

Stock images licensed through Canva

All rights reserved.

No part of this book may be reproduced in any form or by any electronic or mechanical means, including information storage and retrieval systems, without written permission from the author, except for the use of brief quotations in a book review.

This is a work of fiction. Names, characters, places, and incidents are the product of the author's imagination or are used fictitiously. Any resemblance to actual events, locales, or persons, living or dead, is purely coincidental.

Also by K. M. Moronova

Pine Hollow Series (complete)
(Dark Romantasy. Gods/Reincarnation. Why Choose)

A God of Wrath & Lies

A God of Death & Rest

A Goddess of Life & Dawn

Alkrose Academy Series
(Epic Dark Fantasy. Enemies to lovers. Why Choose)

Of Deathless Shadows

Secrets of Alkrose

Stand Alones

The Fabric of our Souls (*Contemporary Dark Romance/Thriller*)

Content warning

The contents of this book may be triggering and disturbing to some readers. This is an emotional paranormal romance with deep discussions regarding death, suicide, and mental illness.
If you are sensitive/easily offended by discussions of mental illness, loss, death and grief then this is not the book for you.
This book includes the following: Physical violence, explicit sex scenes, morbid humor, suicide and the desire to die (explicit), childhood mental abuse trauma, childhood physical abuse (explicit), emotional abuse, explicit death, loss/grief, and trauma bonding.

Author's Note

The Fabric of Our Souls must be read prior to this one. This is a spin off for one of the side characters.

This is not a self help book. Everything is morally grey and not for those who don't enjoy morbid themes. This is a deep dive into emotional and mental illness from _my_ perspective. Not everyone experiences depression/irrational thoughts the same.

This book romanticizes being dead. The main topic revolves around two ghosts who've suffered deeply in life and reflect on their traumas.

988 Suicide and Crisis Lifeline, text or call.

This book dallies with mentally ill characters in a fictional manner. **Harlow Sanctum is a fictional place and in no way, shape, or form are based on real life places or institutions.**

The characters joke about their illness and make light of their conditions at times. **If you are sensitive to**

this aspect please do not read this book. I am not making light of the seriousness of their illnesses but rather expressing what it is like from my own perspective and experience to have depression and mental illness.

For the weary darlings out in the world who seek hope.

Play list

The Night we Met - Lord Huron
In the stars - Benson Boone
This is Home - Cavetown
Atlantis - Seafret
Chem trails - Lana Del Rey
Ride - Lana Del Rey
Oh, what a life - American authors
I'll love you till the end - The Pogues
Everglow - Coldplay
Iris - Goo Goo Dolls
Cinnamon girl - Lana Del Rey
Death bed - Powfu
Until I found you - Stephen Sanchez
Young and Beautiful - Lana del Rey
Skin and Bones - David Kushner
Lovely - Billie Eilish
Train wreck - James Arthur
Bird set free - Sia
Feeling you - Harrison storm
Breathe - Cutts
Let somebody go - Coldplay
Don't let me lose you - Vyen
Beautiful Ghosts - Taylor Swift
Wings - Birdy

Follow you into the Dark - Death Cab for Cutie
Love Story - Indila
Ava - Famy

Saying Goodbye

We're in Boston. It's raining. I'm crying... and I'm so fucking cold.

It takes me a second to recall, but I remember it clearly now. The hospital and my body seizing, succumbing to my wounds.

That's right. I'm... we...

I stare into Wynn's soft brown eyes, drowning in those deep pools of honey.

We are dying.

"Come on, we need to catch up or we'll get left behind."

My eyes flick up to hers and I shake my head. "Not this time, baby. Go on ahead without me. I'll see you two later."

Looking at Wynn makes my chest warm; the cold inside my bones starts to ebb away. She raises her hand

and brushes my cheek gently, tracing my jaw and making my heart come back to life.

"Are you sure?"

I want to say no. I want to beg her not to leave me alone. I *want* to go with them. But tears spill from my eyes as I swallow all those selfish thoughts.

"Yeah. I'm sure."

She vanishes. Liam vanishes.

And I'm left alone in the darkness.

1

LANSTON

"Do not cry," my father would say, calloused and hollow. "I'll hit you harder if you fucking cry. Until you bleed, if I must."

I was being punished for drawing again. My father despised art, said it created foolish minds and derisory souls. He hated me with every fiber of his being—I knew it since I was six. He'd spit at me, glare, and say things and words I didn't yet understand.

But I understood the emotion behind it—the loathing that spilled from his shoulders, the way he carried himself like he could strike me at any moment. I knew the dog was more cherished than me.

The dog received compliments, pets, and delights,

while I received bruises and welts from clothes hangers and shower heads. That didn't start until I was eight, when I became more outspoken about the injustice of his treatment. It only made him angrier, my awareness of his cruelty.

Though I knew he didn't like me, God, did I try my best to change his mind. I wish I had known then that nothing would've worked.

I tightened my jaw the best I could and hid away in my mind, thinking of baseball and quiet places I could sneak off to once this was done. It was the only thing that worked so I didn't break down mentally like I had last time. There was no fighting this fate.

Whack.

The back of my skull was racked with pain. I bit my lower lip, keeping the tears safely tucked away with my sheer will alone. I knew if I cried, it would be so much worse.

Whack. Whack. Whack. Whack. Whack.

I sat slouched in the tub, arms wrapped securely around my knees, waiting patiently for the pain to subside. But he seemed particularly enraged that day, and I had lost count of the blows from the shower head.

His breath was heavy when he finished, and he didn't utter a word as he left.

I remained still for a while, letting my mind come back to itself. The urgency to flee was intense, and I desired to be gone completely.

If Father wants me gone so desperately, why don't I

just go away? I pondered the thought while I washed the blood from the back of my head and continued to think about it as I walked to the baseball field. I thought about it for a long time.

If my existence only brings him misery, then I should go.

But only eight years old, I did not know how to flee. How to go.

As I grew, I came to understand that there are many ways to leave.

When I was sixteen, I tried to kill myself for the first time. People shamed me and said I was selfish and wanted attention. That, if I truly wanted to die, I'd put a bullet in my head. They said I was a coward.

What a nasty, distasteful thing to say to another. Giving me options and ideas? I didn't want to put a bullet through my head. I wouldn't destroy the only part of me I actually liked... my mind. Dark and beautiful, as my grandmother once told me.

I was scared. I wanted to leave—to be a memory. To give my father that peace he so desperately needed from my existence.

It wasn't until much later that I actually got help. In my second year of college, a few people mentioned I should see a therapist. At first, I was offended because *there was nothing wrong with me*, I told myself.

However, the care and gentle ease with which they explained that therapy helps you understand yourself better opened the door for me. It's there that someone told me for the first time in my life: "It's not your fault, Lanston."

"Which part?" I had asked.

"It's not your fault your father abused and disliked you. Nor is it your fault that you have a mental illness."

I cried for the rest of the session. I wept like a child because, for the first time, I felt safe to do so. The therapist wouldn't strike me; she wouldn't hurt me. This I knew.

When she asked me why I was crying, attempting to help me process the emotions, I couldn't speak. I could not even think. All I could manage was to shake my head.

It wasn't my fault?

Then, years later, I changed that thought from a question to a statement, and those words became my daily mantra.

It was never *my fault.*

So why do I still want to die?

I'm a hopeless romantic. Always have been.

I believe in, well, *love.* In its purest form—in the most intimate and selfless light it's meant to be in. And dying young, protecting the two people I cherish more than my aching soul can bear, is an act of love I would do over for eternity if I had to.

I always thought that ghosts were scary or unnecessarily angry at the world. Now I understand that they are just people—hurting in the same ways as we had in life.

Ghosts are sadness and regret. Our hearts bleed as much as the living.

I don't enjoy thinking about the things that hurt. The words that bruise and fester. I've thought long and hard about why I've yet to pass into the great beyond, or heaven, or whatever waits for us after.

And I've come up with only one reason: The dreaded, lousy, *unfinished business.*

Every horror movie I was forced to watch (thanks, Liam and Wynn) taught me that ghosts are hellbent on either getting revenge, because they were wronged in some unimaginable way, or delivering a message to someone they desperately need to reach.

So why am I still here? I have no vengeance in my heart or secret message that needs to be spoken. I've said my goodbyes. Isn't this the part where I just... I don't know, get beamed into the light or something?

Why is my chest filled with so much torment and grief? Why am I still so fucking depressed?

That's the million-dollar question.

I stare out across the empty wheat field where Crosby shot us as I ponder the awful thought. Sometimes, I lose track of time here; you have plenty of time when you're dead to think about things and watch as life goes on without you. I've found that this place is sentimental to me, even though heinous acts unfolded here and two people lost their lives that night.

The breeze is cold—yet early spring flower buds are blossoming on the trees already. I breathe in the smell of the muddy field and think of Perry. Surely, if he can find his peace, I should be able to as well. I wish I could tell Liam that Neil was waiting for him like he'd hoped he would be.

It was cathartic to watch Neil and Perry disappear into what's after, smiling at one another with so much relief, the weight of pain being released from their shoulders. I started keeping a box of notes on things I need to tell the two of them when we meet again.

Liam and Wynn left for Boston five years ago. They visit my grave a few times a year to bring me baseball hats and one-sided conversations that I very much enjoy.

I let out a laugh—fucking ridiculous, really, because who brings hats for a dead man? But I love it when they leave me things. My fingers graze the rim of my new baseball cap they left a few months ago.

It certainly doesn't feel like it's been that long already.

I finally stand and brush off my pants, deciding to head back to Harlow Sanctum early tonight.

You'd think I'd be some big shot here. I mean, for God's sake, the place was named after me, but no, Jericho still runs the show around here. Ever the arrogant asshole who taps on his clipboard like someone who needs their fifth cigarette of the morning.

A new building was built over Harlow, named Never Haven by my darling Wynn and Liam, but for us ghosts, Harlow has followed us into the world in-between. Everything is as it was, comforting and nostalgic. There are many memories that keep this place alive and many ghosts who have kept me company over the past five years.

However, it is rather somber that none of us could properly move on.

Nothing was fair in life—why would it be different in death?

Come on, that's just expecting too much. But at least we suffer together until the bitter end. It's better than being alone. We are together in the dark.

The only thing that has changed is my burdened mind. No longer do I suffer with long nights of staring at a blank ceiling and wishing I were dead. Now, I stare at the same ceiling and wish I didn't exist at all. I think of the misery it would've saved me.

Nothing is fair.

Jericho pokes his head into my room and knocks twice on the frame. "You're back early," he says as he adjusts his glasses and grins at me. His green eyes aren't as weary as they were when we first found ourselves in purgatory. Now they are comfortably filled with hope and purpose once more. I let out a long sigh and stretch my arms over my head, taking my hat off and scratching my hair.

"Yeah, I guess I didn't have as much to think about today." Somehow, that sounds more unfortunate than it should. Wouldn't that be a good thing? Wouldn't that be considered progress because I've sorted at least a few things out? But I keep coming back to *why*.

Why are any of us still here?

Jericho walks in and sits on the edge of my table instead of the chair. I sit up and give him a mildly annoyed look. He looks at my recent drawings scattered atop the surface and blinks a few times at the morbidity of them. The pages are old and tan, with smears of black demons and despairing people on them. But, as usual, he doesn't say anything about the creations I let out of my mind. Sometimes, I think I leave them out so he can see, hoping he'll say something about the darkness he finds within the charcoal sketches.

I don't just show anyone them. But Jericho is like a big brother to me, a fatherly figure I'd been robbed of.

"Really? I'm shocked. You always have depressing things to ponder." He laughs and looks down at his hands thoughtfully before raising his gaze to mine.

He was way too fucking young to die. We all were. I have a suspicion that his unfinished business is being with that woman he was secretly seeing at the Fall Festival years ago. I think he was in love.

Jericho smiles and says, "You know, Yelina and Poppie are going to come with me and a few of the others to the Spring Performance this weekend in the city. You should come too."

My shoulders drop, and I let my body flop back into the bed with a groan. I've become one of those groaning ghosts where all they do is wail and complain. Maybe even scare the shit out of people if they can hear me on the other side.

"It won't be so bad. I go every year and it always manages to be better than the last." Jericho hops off the table and stands above me. "You have to try to find what's keeping you here, Lanston. How sad will it be if you're the last ghost here in the next century after all of us have moved on?"

I scowl at him and he smiles.

"*Fine*—I'll go."

2

LANSTON

I USED TO BE A CITY PERSON—WIDE-EYED AND FILLED with excitement for what the world had to offer. It's difficult to pinpoint what exactly it is that changed my view of the bustling streets filled with people.

Perhaps it's the mundane, sad faces everyone carries. All their youth and energy drained by the lives they carry out.

The misery is palpable.

I'm the phantom here, but they could all fool me with how distant and weary they look. People are meant to be happy, mingle, and laugh. I've forgotten how cold and cruel the real world is. It's easy to be locked away within the safety of Harlow Sanctum. To be in your own sanctuary that protects all the things you hold dear in the world.

However, in the words of Jericho, if I don't leave, I'll never find what's keeping me here.

Birds take to the sky as Yelina and Poppie link arms and rush toward the big pond in the center of the city park. A fountain is at its center, drizzling a steady stream that ripples throughout the pond. I watch a murder of black crows fly overhead with awe before the laughter of the two women draws my attention back down.

Poppie's brown hair is pulled back into a loose braid, strands wisping around her face. Yelina smiles at her, brushing her blonde hair back before she leaps into the pond. Her pastel yellow dress gets wet at the ends and her heels are long gone into the murky shallows and mud. Poppie is only a beat behind her, skipping into the knee-high water. The two of them extend their arms and laugh like two intoxicated fools.

Their eyes catch on the boutique shops that line the main street as the evening lights flick on. They link arms and charge straight for them. Their clothing instantly dries as they set foot outside the pond as if they'd never even hopped in.

Perk number one to being a ghost: You can do whatever you want and not suffer any consequences. We can't get hurt either.

Jericho chuckles low and lights a cigarette, placing it between his lips before stretching and patting my back to follow. "We'd better keep up if we don't want to get left to the wayside," he mumbles, lips half-closed over the joint.

I groan and pull my ball cap down more. Even though only other phantoms can see us, I'm fucking embarrassed to be going to this Spring Performance. Apparently this year's theme is supposed to be one of those sappy, passionate, more of a musical type thing.

The nice thing about tonight, though, is the lovely ambiance in the air. As the sun sets over the mini skyscrapers of the diminutive Montana city, I can only smile as life seems to spark back into all the sad faces around us.

With the darkness of night, the human soul finds solace in being hidden—fewer eyes to interrogate you for the odd joys you hold in your heart. Funny, the things I never noticed before. The things that I wish I would've paid more attention to when I was alive.

But I was always one of those people who couldn't look at others passing by in public. It took a lot for me to look at someone and smile boldly. Harlow was different; I felt safe there. Everyone was similar to me, after all. Broken and fucked up in some way or another.

Out here in the real world, though? I was an utter mess. I suppose it was probably the looks people gave me... For some reason, that bothered me the most. The looks that said I was weird or unlikable for being myself. If my hair was too long or if they didn't like my tattoos. They'd prefer I hide everything about me and pretend.

Draw that fucking smile across my face like every sane person in the world does.

And you better fucking believe I did my best to put on the facade—the show of a century. And as one would presume, people bought tickets to that show of false contentment, of no sad past, no scars.

At least, I did until it didn't work anymore.

One day, I just woke up and couldn't paint a smile on for one more second.

So I stopped looking for approval altogether and stared at the ground instead, because the cement and dirt were at least neutral to my existence. Indignant of those who dare pass judgment on me, I fell into myself. Into the safe recesses of the dark.

My light died a long time ago—flickering with the many exhales of disapproval until finally, with one big breath, it was blown completely out. Like a withering candle left out in the cold, surely to hush and diminish as expected.

I wanted to be so many things.

But most men aren't raised to be emotional. So much cruelty and hardness is expected from us. Perhaps that's why my father was so callous to me—so fucking cold. He didn't know any better, and he fucking hated the softness of my heart. The tears that I shed so effortlessly.

I often wonder if he'd had a shoulder to cry on when he was seven, if he would be a different person now. Heartless assholes aren't born, you know. They're trained into it. Their souls have been drained early and thoroughly by the wicked people before them. Hurt people tend to hurt people.

The cycle. The sad fucking truth of it.

I wish I could've been that shoulder for him to cry on. But I didn't have a shoulder either, not a hug or a warm place to find safety in my darkest of times. And I didn't turn out to be a cold-blooded sack of shit. So where's the excuse? Where's the silver lining?

It's not fair. It was *never* fair, and I suffered for it.

It's hard to let that go—the absolute injustice of it.

I'm still here.

I am still here... and I won't ever get that fucking apology.

At my funeral, my father just stared, cold and empty, at the casket as they lowered my flesh and bones into the earth. Wynn and Liam cried until the sky wept alongside them, but not him. Not my father. He didn't say one word. Shed not a single tear, even for his only son. Even though Mom was dead too, and I was all that he had left.

No. Men don't cry—not men like him.

"You okay?"

I snap my head to Jericho, warm orange orbs from streetlamps hovering behind him, and it sucks me back into the present. "Huh?"

He pulls his cigarette from his mouth and frowns at me. "You've been doing that a lot lately, Nevers." I raise a shoulder and let it drop. He doesn't press me further, even though he gives me that pitying look he always does. "I'm hoping that we'll see fellow phantoms tonight,"

Jericho says, changing the subject. His hazel eyes have that familiar gleam to them. He's a positive-side-of-things guy and I can appreciate how chipper he is.

Five years ago, I was the happy one in the group. My eyes lower to my arm, just above the crease of my inner elbow. The III tattoo grounds me; even if I can't see it beneath my coat, knowing it's there eases me. I think of them every day.

"Why? They're all miserable like we are," I say lifelessly as I shove my hands into the pockets of my black leather jacket.

Phantoms. You'd think we'd call each other ghosts or, I don't know, just people. But the apparent rule is that all dead people stuck in the middle, like we are, typically go by phantoms.

Jericho laughs and jerks his head toward the tall building that has a theater inside. I've only been here once, and it's not fancy or anything. It does, however, have that nostalgic, rustic feel to it. The old bricks are a part of the original structure from the 1800s. The windows and doors are black metal, renovated recently, adding a nice modern touch to the historic building. It's right off the street downtown; bustling cars flash by and people cheer in the bar a few shops down.

"They aren't *all* miserable. You're just choosing to see them that way. Yelina and Poppie are having fun," Jericho mutters as we pass through the doors and slip between the living people.

At first it was hard to get used to them not being able

to feel me as I do them. Although we're shoving our way through the crowd, they can't feel or see us. The things we brush or hold are simply in purgatory only.

"Yeah, well, Poppie and Yelina are still as daffy as ever," I grumble. The foyer is packed, and as hard as I try to hold onto my grumpy mood, it's truly not possible in this environment.

The merch shop is handing out T-shirts left and right as many eager people reach for them. Their faces are alight with happiness and glee. Chanting has already started in the central lower section of the theater, and I raise a brow at Jericho.

"I thought you said this was a Spring Performance?" I shout over the noise.

Yelina and Poppie run through the crowd and link arms with me. "I'm so happy you decided to join us this time, Lanston!" Yelina says with a big smile. I return it and it feels genuine for once. I'm glad they dragged me out of Harlow tonight. The crisp air and new faces remind me how much fun we can still have.

Jericho speaks over the two girls as they chat excitedly around me. "It's unorthodox. You'll see."

God, does this man attend anything that isn't unorthodox?

I let out a breath and nod at him. Whatever, I'm here and I'll try my best to enjoy it.

Poppie holds out a T-shirt for me and I take it. "I thought you'd like the skull one best." She winks at me and I grin. It's a black shirt with a wash-fade design. A skull in the center, not gratuitous or obscene. It's more sad than anything—half broken with a rose coming out the top of the fractured bits.

"Thanks," I say as I take off my leather jacket and pull the T-shirt over my long-sleeve black muscle shirt. It feels like a throwback to high school when this was an actual look. A smile crests my lips as I reminisce on my punk phase.

Jericho looks ridiculous in the oversized black shirt Yelina grabbed him; it has a massive heart with hands tearing it in half. With his black-framed glasses and styled short blonde hair, he looks like he should be in a suit, not wearing a concert shirt.

I ask again because, *come on.* "I thought this was a *musical?*"

Yelina nudges me with her elbow. "You sound like a broken record."

The women have shirts with flowers on them and words I don't bother reading because the lighting is dim, and the noise continues to grow louder around us.

"Oh, it's starting!" Poppie bounces up and down on her toes, Yelina lets out a shriek, and the two of them run off together into the crowd.

I frown—I hate packed spaces. Loud music makes it worse.

Jericho looks at me and laughs like he can see straight through me. "Want to go to the upstairs balcony? I'm too old for the main floor's energy." I crack a smile and nod. Thank God for my dead counselor.

We find a nice empty spot near the back of the third balcony. It's so far away from the stage that you can hardly see much detail of the performance, but it's still loud as all hell back here.

I throw my feet up on the empty seat in front of me and Jericho leans back in his, almost as if he's going to take a nap.

The first half of the show is entertaining; it is a musical but very dark and morbid. I find it mildly disturbing how much I enjoy that part of it. The way the actors are dressed in bleak clothing and murdering one another for things as frivolous as jealousy. Jericho spots a group of female phantoms a few rows to our left and tries to get me to join him in greeting them, but I shake my head.

"Jesus, good thing you're dead, or you'd have like fifteen kids by now," I grumble as he scoots by. He barks out a laugh at that.

"You're dead too, buddy. If you won't live now, then when will you?" he says nonchalantly before he walks over to the ladies. I watch his easy-going demeanor and how naturally it comes to him to start a conversation. The phantoms are all too welcoming and greet him with warm smiles. Their eyes trail over his shoulder and find me, curious if I'll join him, but I look away sharply.

I sink further into my seat, becoming keenly aware of the darkness that cradles me as I sit alone. Yelina and Poppie are below, having a blast and singing along as loud as they can since no one can hear them. Jericho is having fun chatting with other phantoms he'll surely be bringing home with him later.

And then there's me.

In these times of solitude, I think of them; the three of us should be together.

As I'm about to let the dark thoughts of my loneliness take over me, a flash of purple flickers across the stage. I lift my chin and stare, eyes widening, and for the first time since the day I saw Wynn dancing in the rain at Harlow, my heart throbs.

A beautiful woman dances across the stage. She doesn't match any of the cast members wearing drab black clothing; she's wearing a lovely white dress with pink rose petals scattered across the pattern. The tail of the dress is long and wisps beautifully as she leaps majestically from side to side, twirling with each step perfectly in sync with the music. The ends of her dress are torn and tattered, adding a very dreary essence to her languid, long movements.

I stand from my seat and lean closer, mesmerized by her sorrowful motions. Each step she takes makes my heart beat faster and slower at the same time.

She has a pastel purple streamer that she twirls in the air as she dances, and I'm drawn to it like a fish to the lure. *I have to get closer to her.*

I take the stairs two at a time as I sprint down to the main floor, shoving my way through the crowd to get to the front. Yelina and Poppie notice my haste; their brows are raised in question as they watch me race to the stage.

The ethereal woman throws her head back in a graceful final leap toward the ledge of the stage before coming down and placing both of her hands on my shoulders just as I prop myself up on the edge.

My very soul ignites with something I haven't dared to feel in half a decade.

Her purple hair wisps around us as momentum and gravity bring the strands down wistfully, but her eyes hold my gaze as steady as the sun peeking through dappled leaves, bright brown and speckled with glints of alluring green.

She's young like I am, and what a tragic thing that is.

Beautiful, devastating, and very much *dead*.

3

Lanston

The breath ceases in my lungs, moving as if all the locks inside me have twisted. Stagnant air that was once so heavy in my airways is now free to leave but hesitant to do so.

She breathes heavily as the music to "Love Story" by Indila climaxes around us. The song crescendos, the sound reverberates through my hollow chest and raises goosebumps across my arms, then it filters to a fall off—the violins and cellos making their long last strokes over the strings. Her hair falls in kind, and we're left staring into one another's eyes.

This lovely phantom is the very image of tragedy. She

is a ballad of mournful movements, bones, and tattered lace—a symphony unlike any I've endured.

I've lost all sense of myself for a moment, and then I realize my mouth is slightly open in awe. The corners of my mouth turn up into a smile just as her eyebrows firmly pull down, completely demolishing the magic of this moment.

"What do you think you're doing?" she says accusingly, and if it weren't for the red blush spreading across her cheeks, perhaps I'd be able to respond faster, but I'm still so taken with her that I continue to smile like an idiot.

She *tsks* at me and leans back, flicking my baseball cap so it tips up more. The lovely phantom levels me one last look, her eyes lingering on my cheekbones and lips before turning briskly and exiting off the stage.

I adore her ire already.

I start to heave myself up, ready to chase this mysterious woman and find out why I'm so enchanted with her, but two sets of hands come down on my waist and pull me down off the edge of the stage.

"Lanston! What are you doing?" Yelina says, clearly vexed. I don't bother looking at the two women as they pull me down. My eyes are desperately trying to track the mysterious phantom.

Poppie grunts as I fall back on her and growls, "You're ruining the show, for Christ's sake." Yelina helps her up and they both glare down at me.

I push myself up and right my ball cap as I retort,

"We're ghosts—I'm not ruining the show for anyone." The audience is looking beyond us at the normal performance as I expected, and I look at the both of them as if to prove my point. Jericho pushes through the crowd a moment later and looks at me like I'm insane. "What?" I ask, exasperated, and raise my hands up in question.

"That woman *was* the show. We come to see her perform, you jackass." Jericho barks out a laugh and smacks my back.

My jaw slacks and I look at all three of their faces incredulously. "You come here every year to watch a phantom dance amongst the living?"

Yelina laughs like this is the dumbest thing she's ever had to explain. "Of course, Lanston. Did you think we would come all this way just to watch a boring performance? She's the reason many of the phantoms gather here. A small glimmer of hope."

I sit with that for a moment. Even as a phantom she insists on pretending to be alive. Bluffing that this audience of living, breathing people are here to see her. An ache settles deep in my chest.

"What's her name?" I ask, eyes shifting back to the area where she disappeared behind the curtain. My fingers curl into the fabric of my pants as an urge to chase her claws at my soul.

Jericho pulls me closer as the music roars back up around us and drowns out all other noise. He says loudly, "Her name is Ophelia."

Ophelia.

What a beautiful name—sad, too. Why am I so drawn to melancholic things? She has that same look in her eyes that Wynn did. Not when she craved death, no, but when she found hope and all the reasons to wake up again. To pull herself from the depths of the darkness in her mind.

Tears brim my eyes at the thought of my sweet Wynn, and I quickly drag my sleeve across my face before the others can see.

Why is someone with so much hope in their eyes... dead? She shouldn't be here, in the land of the forgotten and lonely. *Why?* It's not fair. Something as beautiful and talented as she. Her marrow isn't done with the world yet; she still has so much left to speak—that much is unmistakable through her performance. Her movements are expressive and boisterous with deeper meaning.

I hear you. I want to shout. *Your cry for life is deafening.*

"Are you okay?" Jericho sets his hand on my shoulder and peers down at me. I shake my head and his grip tightens reassuringly. My lips firm against the trembling that threatens them.

"Oh, Lan," Poppie says with sorrow as her arms wrap around my neck. "You're still having a hard time accepting all this, aren't you? It's okay. We're all not ready to be here, but you need to make the most of it," she whispers against the shell of my ear, and I have to grit my teeth to keep the tears at bay.

Yelina's face softens and she smiles, more for herself

it seems, at a thought that crosses her mind. She cocks her head to the side and offers me her hand as she says, "Should we see if we can find her?"

Jericho adjusts his glasses and smooths back a stray strand of hair before nodding. "A fine idea, Yelina. Nevers would probably enjoy that," he says, like I'm not standing right next to him, but I ignore it.

I want to meet her—something inside me says that I *have* to. There are moments in one's existence when you connect with another in a mere second, something sinks deep into your soul, planting a yearning that may never fade. A song that chills your bones and rattles the blood in your veins.

I must know her.

The four of us exit the building and wrap around to the back. The door is ajar for the performers; two young people share a cigarette near the door and don't blink as we pass by. It's something I'm unsure I'll ever fully get used to, but for now my mind is elsewhere entirely.

"Do you know how she died?" I ask as we walk into the rehearsal area. It looks like a small choir room you might find in a high school, with tiered rows getting higher the closer you get to the back of the room. The carpet is gray and so are the walls. I find most things are gray and dull here. Who's to say if this is how it looks on the living side? It may very well be a colorful room.

Yelina eyes a group of men in the corner who are warming up their voices. She brings her attention to me and my question. Her eyes flicker with thought and hesitation before she says, "Nope. I don't know anything about her except that she performs here every year."

Poppie nods. "Yeah, we heard from a few phantoms the first year we came that a lovely woman danced with her very soul. She always leaves quickly, though, as if in a hurry. So we've never gotten to know her. Rumor has it that she's not very friendly, so we haven't tried speaking with her."

I have a feeling she just uses that unfriendliness as a front. I'd be lying if I said there wasn't a time in my life that I was abrasive to keep myself safe. I had the idea that if I didn't let anyone get close, I'd be safe inside my fortress. And that worked for a long time, but it was also incredibly lonely and filled with sorrow.

"We're all unfriendly at times," I say mindlessly as my eyes flick across the room for her. I frown. "I don't think she's here. Do you think she left already?"

Jericho crosses his arms. "Could be. Let's split up and meet back here in twenty minutes. If we don't find her by then, we should just go on with our night. I met a few nice ladies and would happily introduce you to them, Lanston." Jericho gives me a smirk and raises his brow suggestively. I grimace while Yelina and Poppie simultaneously scoff at him.

"How were you ever a counselor?" Yelina turns her head sharply, but I don't miss the hurt that lingers on the edge of her voice. I think she's been interested in Jericho for quite some time now. But how is a dumbass like him supposed to know if she won't say anything? Jericho seems confused at the ire in her tone and sets his hand gently on her arm. She stiffens and shoots him a warning look.

I raise a brow at their interaction but decide it's not my place to comment.

"Yeah, let's split up. I'll check backstage," I say and start walking toward the loud, distant music.

The hallways are dark, drowned in long black curtains that hang from at least thirty feet high. The ebony floorboards feel light, like particle wood. I suppose most stages are like this though, in order to quickly change them out if needed for certain plays or sets.

I search through the entire backstage, looking in every conceivable spot I can think of before giving up. It's been far longer than twenty minutes, so I'm not surprised when the others aren't in the rehearsal room waiting for me.

Shit, I wonder if they already left and returned to Harlow.

There's no sense in rushing; it's not like I haven't the time to spare. I decide to walk leisurely across the river viaduct near the theater house. This city is quite beautiful, and if there's one thing I truly enjoy about being dead, it's becoming lost within my own thoughts and coming to admire the simple things about the world.

The viaduct is a very tall and architecturally brilliant bridge. A series of arches structure the pillars holding it, creating an alluring look. Lights have been installed along peaks of the arches, illuminating the water far below, while vintage streetlamps light the world above. Wooden benches are laid out every hundred feet or so, with ornate bushes surrounding them.

I take a deep breath and pretend like I'm not a ghost, stopping at the bench in the center of the bridge, this one surrounded by rose bushes, and standing on top of it to get to the higher cement wall. Up here, the universe is silent. It's cold and filled with many stars that no longer speak to me.

My eyes linger on the flickering stars before I look down at the dark water far below.

I find it cruelly ironic. How many times have I stood on a bridge similar to this one? How many times have I wanted to die just to feel numb to the callous world? I wonder, should I jump now, if I'd be able to pass on? I'm already dead, so there isn't really anything at risk.

My foot edges the corner of the cement and adrenaline surges through me. The weary heart inside my chest patters with the dare of it. I shut my eyes and tilt my head back, debating my sanity, considering if it matters.

"You are certainly a curious man, aren't you?"

My eyes flash open, and I look beside me, finding none other than the lovely phantom, Ophelia.

Her purple hair is calmer now that she isn't a whirling dancing goddess. It lies in loose curls behind her, stretching down to her mid back. The breeze slightly shifts her hair over her face and I'm mesmerized all over again. By the hollows of her cheekbones and eye sockets, by the morbidity of her lithe fingers as they delicately caress the rose in her hands. Long black lashes droop heavily as she smells the flower.

I don't utter a word.

There isn't a manner in which I see how I possibly could. To disturb such perfection and raw beauty. She is a wilted rose herself.

Wynn spoke so much of flowers being beautiful in death; I think I finally found that depressing sentiment after searching for five long years.

4

Ophelia

Life is a circus of betrayal and dread.

Nothing good stays and nothing bad ever really goes.

Death is nothing more than a somber replay of it all. An ode to the closing of that very last chapter you perhaps never did get to finish. Is there anything quite as sad as that? A story left unfinished.

Of course, I'm a bitter person.

Ophelia is a nasty woman—a fine excuse of wasted beauty on a rotted soul.

You know what? Everyone can, quite literally, eat shit.

I'm dead. Say what you want, it's not like you didn't when I still breathed air.

I stopped caring about what others thought about me a long time ago. Perhaps that's why I'm stuck here; maybe my bitterness is what allows me to haunt this world.

But something odd happened tonight. A light flickered in the darkness that surrounded me on that stage.

Something different in the last decade of my time spent wandering.

That strange man looked at me with so much pain in his eyes. He was one of the most beautiful men I've ever laid eyes on. His eyes were warm and hazel, enriched with many colors that I'd forgotten were real in this dreary world.

I stop walking on the bridge and glance up. Someone is standing on my bench and moving toward the edge. Panic rushes me and I surge forward to try to stop them from jumping off, but as I get closer, my steps slow, and I realize my panic is senseless.

It's the ghost from earlier.

That hauntingly handsome man.

His face is tilted toward the sky, his sharp features etched like a sculpture, smooth and cold. The black leather jacket he wears fits close to his muscles, and his baseball hat is worn-wash ebony. Thicker, more pronounced black stitches make the hat look vintage.

I circle behind him silently and he doesn't seem to notice. A smile crests my lips as I pluck one of the red roses and step up onto the bench to stand beside him along the edge.

"You are certainly a curious man, aren't you?" I say,

trying to keep any interest out of my voice. I suppose fate finds a way to weave even phantoms together. A beautiful man like him can't be good news. I've lost all the blood in my veins before to one like him. Men are coy like that, seeming entirely innocent before snatching your heart, splaying you out for all to see—spilling secrets that were meant only for them.

He startles and gazes down at me like I'm a sight to behold, those wondrous hazel eyes flickering as he takes me in the same way I do him. His lips are a soft red, like he's cold and in need of warm heartfelt kisses. Light brown locks of hair caress his forehead, peeking down from beneath his cap.

I want to touch his face and run my fingers down each and every groove and divot that lifts over his bones. To feel how soft his skin is and how warm—oh, that's right. Nothing in death is warm. I forget sometimes, especially now as I look at someone who radiates like he does. A defiance of death.

Is his skin robbed of warmth like mine?

Something inside me says I don't want to find out. Certain things are better left unknown. Forever a mystery. I think I'd rather never know.

He doesn't say anything, but there's so much curiosity and warmth in his gaze.

I knew he was strange, but I think I like that about him. He is silence in the form of flesh. He is a damaged soul. He is one who thinks so fervently that he finds his thoughts suffice for unspoken words, perhaps.

I like him.

Men like him hear things that most cannot—whispers of other's hearts. The sadness in his eyes and the dark circles that cradle the gates to his soul elude as much.

My lips curve into a weak smile, and I turn to face the edge of the bridge, clasping the rose tightly to my chest as I lock eyes with him. He looks confused for only a moment, then his brows furrow and horror falls over his lovely face as I tumble backward and down toward the dark, deadly waters below.

A leap I've taken so many times.

Down, down, down. Into the depths.

I hold the rose close to my heart, keeping my eyes on him with little expectations. No one has ever jumped after me before; I mean, why would they? No ghosts who are stuck here are so careless that they'll indulge in the insane, morbid side I have to offer—the leap of hope I take alone.

But he does.

My eyes widen as I watch him jump after me. The lace and rose petals of my tattered dress billow and my hair lashes with the wind, surrounding me in pale colors, while he, above, is a beacon of light.

The way the wind caresses him as he reaches out for me is like a ballad. One that I've danced to a million times over but never quite found the right footing to. His light brown hair is chaos and his eyes are a storm of greens, blues, and dashes of yellow. A parchment of sorrowful words written and scrawled—he reminds me of such a somber, nostalgic song—one of sadness and death.

One never known.

He is a ballad of phantoms... and, perhaps, one of hope.

I stare at his unmatched beauty, unable to break this enchantment we've found ourselves in as we fall toward the dark water.

He jumped—as if he's contemplated the very thought so many times before as I have. And there's something so harrowing about that thought. He craved death once.

Souls shouldn't have to suffer such ruination at the gritty hands of the world. A cold and heartless plane of existence. It took me, and wasn't that enough? I don't know this man, but why did it take him too?

His hands wrap around my shoulders, and he doesn't hesitate to pull me in eagerly, pressing my face against his chest and holding my ghost as if we've been falling for centuries in a timeless dance.

Reaching. *Yearning.*

Listening to the same sad song on repeat and never quite finding the other until now. Until death.

He smells like a cup of freshly brewed coffee and crisp fall leaves.

Our bodies crush the rose between us, but I doubt he cares. He braces for the impact of the water and I let out a meek little laugh just before the water crescendos around us, engulfing our bodies and swallowing us whole.

Darkness follows. The warm orange light on the

water's surface glimmers and sways, satiated and full before it breaks.

My eyes slowly open once we're fully submerged. His eyes are still tightly shut, and I take the moment to study him closely. Water raises his shirt, ballooning it up and revealing his tight stomach beneath. His muscles are lovely in the moonlight.

He slowly opens his eyes and stares into my soul, and then—the most damning thing.

A sad smile.

5

Lanston

Did I just jump off a fucking bridge?

Ophelia's hair is like a wave of soft purple, alluring and shimmering with the moonlight. My lips pull into a smile of their own volition. What just happened?

Then, slowly, my senses return to me and I realize I should be more stern with her for being so reckless. I firm my smile into a scowl and swim up to the water's surface.

Our heads break into the night air and I take in a deep breath, wiping away the water from my eyes before glaring at Ophelia. "What were you thinking?" I grip her shoulders and she lets out a laugh.

My face instantly softens with the light sound of her breathy giggle.

"Have you forgotten that we're phantoms? You just keep getting more and more curious," she says sarcastically and pushes away from me, swimming toward the shoreline.

I follow, forcing my brows together again because she's testing my patience. Somehow, I am both irritated by her and drawn in.

"Ophelia, that's your name, right?" I wade onto the beach behind her and topple over on my back in the sand, my body already growing weary with the exertion. I let my head fall to the right and look at her. She sits close enough to me that I could reach out and touch her if I wanted.

God, I want to.

She holds up her smashed, waterlogged rose and frowns at it, tossing it on my chest before replying, "Ophelia Rosin, and who might you be?"

I grab the rose, ignoring the sharp thorns, and glower at her. "Lanston Nevers," I mumble, and then silence falls around us. What am I supposed to say? At first, I was so taken with her that I just wanted to meet her, but now I can't seem to find the words.

She's mysterious, odd, prickly.

Ophelia pulls her knees to her chest and extends her hand to me. I sit up and look from her hand to her face.

"Nice to meet your ghost, Mr. Nevers. Still new to death?" She smiles like I'm fascinating, and I'm still not quite sure what it is about her that's so filled with whimsy.

I take her hand and her eyes widen as mine do at our connection. Her hand is warm and welcoming, unlike other phantoms who have gone cold.

We say in unison, *"You're warm."*

An urge to pull her to my chest and soak in her warmth cradles my mind. Why is she so warm? Another lovely thing about her that will linger idly in my mind for days to come, I'm certain.

I pull my hand back hesitantly and clear my throat. "I'm not new to death. I've been dead for five years, and please call me Lanston." I offer her a grin as I shake sand from my hair.

Ophelia laughs again. It sounds genuine enough, but I'm no stranger to pretending to be happy for people to like me. She laughs too much and smiles too widely, especially for someone like me who's given her no reason to smile so brightly.

She stands and brushes off her dress. It dries in a moment and so do my clothes. A small reprieve for being a phantom.

"Five years and you're still acting like you can't do whatever it is you want?" She practically scoffs. I push myself to my feet and realize how tall I am compared to her. Her eyes barely reach my shoulders.

"And what could I possibly want to do besides move on to the next phase of death?" I say sadly. It sounds broken and pitiful, but the truth can't be shrouded by pretty words. "I'll never be able to have the things I wanted."

By *things,* I mean the people I wanted.

Silence falls around us and I stare out across the river—the small waves are the only soft noise that grounds me in the moment.

I flinch as Ophelia brushes her hand across my cheek, the warmth and care very much present. My eyes find hers and I fight the urge to lean into her palm. She smiles weakly at me.

"Who says death is the end of us? We're here for a reason, are we not? You are still as much alive in spirit as you ever were." Her lips remain parted just enough to make my throat dry.

"What reasons? I can't seem to find mine. Why am I still here?" I mutter as my gaze returns to the dark water behind her. It laps against the ground with fervor, starved for lost souls.

She shrugs. "We all have reasons, Lanston. Ones that we need to uncover ourselves." Ophelia looks into the distance and starts walking toward the shadows of the bridge.

"*Ophelia,*" I say her name with such utter tenderness. She stops and looks over her shoulder at me, her cheeks rosy, waiting for me to speak. "How did you die?"

Her green eyes are somber. The memory must be like a knife in her heart.

She turns her head before answering me—the warm light of the streetlamps above halo her head as she murmurs, "I was murdered." She pauses and clenches her fists at her sides with anger for herself and her fate, I'm sure, just as I'm enraged on her behalf. "You?"

She was murdered.

My first thought is, *why? Who?*

Who could possibly touch a hair on this enthralling woman's head? No wonder she's guarded, a bit callous. Have I not become those things too? Warded within my own mind and heart... Because life was stolen from me. Friends. Love.

But it was never meant to be mine. That life, as short and lovely and sad as it was. It was never mine.

I was never going to have the things I craved most.

And somehow, I think that might be what's truly keeping me here. The not knowing. I died, not even knowing what I truly wanted. Do any of us actually know? My desires and enjoyments change year to year. What I find fulfilling and meaningful alters after time. I yearn for the answer. *What was I meant for?*

"I was murdered too," I whisper. It sounds so wrong sliding from between my lips. Is it really the first time I've spoken of how I died out loud? The cruelness of it is unfair. Both of us have been left behind while the world remains awake.

Ophelia turns to face me with a look of anguish. "*You?*"

I give her a crooked smirk. "Me."

She stares at me for a while, mournful. Many questions flicker across her expression. I have many of my own as well. But neither of us seem able to ask.

"I'm sorry, Lanston. You seem like a man who still had so much to give." She starts to walk back toward the shadows of the bridge and my legs instinctively follow.

"You do too, I was hoping—"

"Stop," she cuts me off, continuing to walk steadily, but my steps falter. "I don't do the afterlife with others. It was nice meeting you, but this is where our joining ends."

That must be one of her walls. I'm surprised I even made it this far.

"Doesn't that get lonely?" I call after her, shoving my hands into my coat pockets to keep myself in control.

She struts confidently ahead, fisting her small hands at her sides and I can't help but smile at her resolve.

"Heartachingly so," she admits on a pained half-laugh. "But I never get hurt this way." There's a sad truth to her words. To choose to be lonely rather than opening yourself up to others.

I know that pain.

I'm about to say that's a tragic way to exist but in my next breath, all the lights around us are snuffed out and a chill unfurls in the air. Pitch black consumes everything except me and Ophelia. Terror slips inside my veins.

What is this? It's freezing and dark. For the first time since entering the realm of phantoms, I'm afraid.

I stare blindly into the abyss before a hand wraps around my wrist and pulls me urgently. My eyes snap down and meet Ophelia's. She looks terrified as she says in a low, haunting voice, "Don't look back, no matter what you hear."

The sand beneath my feet gives, practically vibrating, as the darkness becomes heavy and terror drives me forward. "What's happening?" I gasp between breaths as she guides us ahead. I don't think she can see any better than I can, but her footing is sure. Has she done this before?

She doesn't respond; all I can see is her lovely purple-tinted hair swaying behind her.

Whispers creep up behind me and chills spread down my spine at the cold that lingers after each hushed word.

What are they saying? I can't quite make it out. My head instinctively starts to turn, curious to find the source of the eerie whispers.

"Don't," Ophelia says sharply, and my neck locks.

"What *is* that?"

She waits a moment, then says, "I don't know, but they whisper awful things. Phantoms that get caught in their shroud end up sleeping for long periods of time, and they aren't the same when they wake."

I open my mouth, but she cuts in again.

"Just trust me, you don't want to find out." Ophelia takes a sharp left and tows me behind her. We quickly step through a door frame and the moment my head passes beneath it, a room forms around us.

Ophelia slams the door shut on the approaching darkness. The eerie whispers press up against the wood, making the door creak and wail. A shudder rolls down my spine. They were mere footsteps behind us. At any point they could've grabbed us. The sounds stop and the cold that penetrated the air is sapped away like it was nothing more than the brisk air of the night.

Ophelia takes a few deep breaths before flipping the lock and sighing as she presses her forehead against the black door.

My first thought is to ask her again what that was about, but the way her shoulders tremble stalls me. So I take in the space instead.

"Where are we?"

I look up and around the place she's brought us into. It's dim, but enough ambient light filters in through boarded-up windows to see most of the room. The ceilings are tall and the space is filled with only tables and plants. Hundreds and hundreds of leafy, viny *plants*.

As my eyes adjust more, it becomes clear that this is no house or apartment; it's an old opera house. A big room, walls black like a gothic church. The seats have been long torn out and replaced with vintage tables and pews. Broken pots and forgotten things fill this place, and it's charming in its own way. The only things filled with life here are the plants, green and soft, making me think of the greenhouse at Harlow that should have been brimming as this place is.

"It's an abandoned opera house," she says in a low tone, timid. Does she think I'd judge her?

"Did you collect all these?" My eyes find hers and she looks away, a blush growing across her cheeks. "I like them," I add carefully.

Ophelia lifts her head and looks at me. Her eyes are half-lidded and filled with dreariness from the day.

It's a silly thing, that ghosts can get tired, but we do. More so than when we were alive. I think it's because of the energy required to exist here in the plane *in-between*. The more we exert, the wearier we become, sometimes drifting off for days to charge back up.

She eyes me carefully and steps around where I stand, nearing the first worn table crowded with terra-cotta pots. English ivy, Boston ferns, pothos, roses. Her hand lowers and she caresses the leaves of a pothos with care.

"Yeah, I did," she says in a cold, closed-off manner.

She did say she didn't like being around other phantoms... I shift on my feet and reach for the doorknob. I hate feeling unwanted and like I'm annoying people.

"I can leave—"

"No," she says meekly, and I pause.

Our eyes linger timidly on one another. I'm trying to figure her out and she's doing the same with me. Then she deflates, worrying her lower lip in a way that draws my eyes and makes me want to brush my thumb over it to quell her woes. "You should wait until morning. Those Who Whisper tend to linger for a while."

My body stiffens at that. I'd almost completely forgotten about them already.

I approach her slowly and stand at her side. When she lifts her chin to look into my eyes, my lungs cease at her intoxicating scent of roses. *"Those Who Whisper?"* I ask, and she nods.

"They bring the darkness with them when they come. I'm not sure who or what they are, but they're bad... of that I am certain." Her voice is small and trembles as she speaks. Chills crawl up my spine at the mere thought of those things. Not knowing what something looks like is often more frightening, because you imagine exactly what you *don't* want it to be.

"I've never encountered them before." My voice is implying.

Ophelia blinks slowly, looking at the door that separates us from the darkness outside. "They only follow me." A mere whisper.

I quirk a brow. "Why?"

Her jaw muscle feathers and she shakes her head. "I don't know." She lifts her shoulder and drops it. "One day they just showed up and they've been trailing me since. Sometimes I go days or even weeks without running into them, but one thing is true, they're always near. Waiting patiently for me to forget and become aloof like I was tonight." She looks at me pointedly. "They almost got me tonight."

The hairs on the back of my neck raise, but I swallow the discomfort.

"Are you scared here? I couldn't imagine being alone." My voice is coarse. The image of her being here alone for days, months, years, a decade, breaks me. I can see her tending to her garden of forgotten plants. This abandoned building keeping a ghost the world has blinked away all this time.

She spreads her arms to the room, smiling and casting away the grim conversation. "I'm not alone. I have all the greenery and knick-knacks a person could ever hope for."

I nod and force a weary grin, glancing back at her door once more. "So you're okay with me staying here for the night? You won't feed me to the dark?" I tease and her guarded exterior lowers; replaced with a lovely smile.

"Tea?" she offers, and I chuckle.

"Coffee, please, and no cream."

6

Ophelia

How did today's events bring me here, drinking tea and sitting across from a beautiful man as he sips on coffee?

His eyes wander around my shack of a home, lingering around the plants and tables that I've collected over the years. We're each seated on a worn sofa; mine is colored maroon, his tan, with an old authentic wood coffee table between us. It has slates of glass for the surface, scoffed and nicked with history. There's an innate feeling of judgment that swirls in my stomach, even though he's shown no evidence of it.

The gothic black walls with coffered edges and chandelier light fixtures definitely don't brighten anything up, but I love these things. This place is me: Broken beams from the rotting roof, drops of rain falling and landing on plants below, and lovely silence. Ebony candles burn and flicker on the windowpanes, tables, and stage behind us.

I'm protective over my oddities.

Because no one else has loved them like I do.

Not the man who claimed to have loved me when I was sixteen, nor the man who possessed me when I was twenty-five. I wrap my arms over my knees and shut my eyes against the memories of my last love. I promised myself I wouldn't think of that man ever again, and yet he still haunts me—a shadow in the back of my mind.

I'm convinced that the living are the ones that keep us here—their desire to hurt us even in death. The knife can forever be plunged deeper, even into corpses.

"So, what's with the purple hair?"

My shoulders tense as I realize I am lost in thought. "Hm?" I look up at him and his soft hazel eyes flicker with curiosity and maybe even some nostalgia. My fingers thread through the long strands of my hair and I force a sarcastic smile. "Don't like off-colored hair?" I ask, not unkindly.

He sets his mug down on the coffee table and leans forward, setting his elbow on his knee and resting his head on his palm as he grins at me like he has a dirty little secret.

"No, in fact, I seem to be particularly drawn to it." His smile becomes distant, and he blinks slowly with thoughts—perhaps of memories of his life or the people in it.

I cup my mug with both hands, enjoying the warmth that seeps into my palms. It's not my place to ask, but I find Lanston oddly comforting and welcoming to such questions.

"Who was she?"

Lanston stares at the floor and his eyes lose their brilliance for a moment. "She was my kindred soul, as lost and sick as I was." It's evident he misses her, but there's something else he isn't saying.

"*But?*"

He looks up at me and leans back on the sofa. His arms rest at his sides. I keep glimpsing the locks of hair that peek out from beneath his ball cap. "*But* she was in love with my best friend. And he loved her the way she needed it." My expression falls and he gives me a weak grin. "It's okay; when you love others more than yourself, it's easy to let it be. I wasn't meant to stay. And that was years ago now." He drags his hand down his jaw; there's a formidable weight of anguish he holds there. In the set of his dark brows, the lightness of his heart.

I frown and nod. "You seem like the kind of guy who would say as much, but doesn't it hurt? Aren't *you* lonely?" I turn his question from earlier back on him, leaning forward to set my mug on the table before I curl back up on the couch across from him. I pull my knees close to my chest and watch Lanston through heavy lashes.

He tilts his chin back and rests his head against the

cushion, shutting his eyes as weariness orbits us. Phantoms grow tired so very quickly. We fade into lost spurts of rest and there's no telling how long we'll sleep. The redness bruising around the bottom of his eyes alludes to how close he is to falling into his dreams.

His voice is raspy and sweet. "Of course, it hurts... I think it always will. But most things that wound your heart like this are worth it. It only hurts because of how precious we hold them. I'm never alone, not really, because I know they will carry the weight of me with them forever."

What a sad thing to say.

My chest already feels burdened with the gravity of him—not wishing to let him go. Lanston Nevers. I don't know that I've ever met a man so filled with somber thoughts and lovely words. His eyes are enough to sink my ship in a dark, starved ocean. That scares me most of all.

"You have someone keeping your memory alive too, don't you?" he asks sleepily. I let my eyes close and think about that for a moment. I think of my cruel stepmother and father. They wouldn't keep my memory alive in a way that's true to how I actually was. Neither would my distant relatives. Not my last love.

"No. No one will think of me." I keep my eyes shut but I can hear him shift on the sofa with discomfort at my words. "I think I prefer it that way. I like being forgotten —it's more poetic and tragic." The corners of my lips lift slightly.

I'm delighted that Lanston was so loved in life, but a sting of jealousy remains in my heart. We all want unconditional love, but it isn't handed out like it is in the movies. You aren't born loved—at least I wasn't.

It's something you must prove you're worthy of. Smile, say yes, and be polite. If you have a meltdown or speak up against your aggressors, you lose the little love you've earned. *Isn't that how it goes?* Well, it was for me. I never quite wholly figured it out. It's a point system of sorts—a cruel game of give and take—constant observation and judgment.

Children must learn quickly, lest their hearts be corrupted like my last love's was. He was created—molded by the hands of evil human beings. Then, set loose upon the world. Upon me.

My love.

His love wasn't unconditional.

The silence is dreary, so I open my eyes just enough to see Lanston staring at me with concern. I restrain the groan at his pitiful expression for me.

"I'll think of you," he murmurs as the last of the candles wisp out around us, leaving our ghosts in the dim moonlight.

I smile and hope he can't see the tears that build in my eyes. "You don't know me, Lanston, and you're already dead."

"I don't need to know you to think of you, Ophelia. You've already imprinted yourself into my mind. You don't give yourself enough credit for how unique you are, how alluring." He leans forward again, and as tired as I am, I sit up to look him in the eyes. My messy hair falls over my shoulders. "Though, I wouldn't mind being able to get to know you."

I hold his steady gaze and pick at the edges of my dress as nerves swarm inside my chest. "You wouldn't want to think about me if you really knew me. I'm not a good person. I'm selfish and awful."

The air is warm between us. Something I haven't felt from a phantom, *ever*. When I'm near Lanston, it's almost like... I'm alive again. Emotions I thought I left in my grave come to life inside my veins. Each breath is increasingly more labored than the last.

"I'm no saint either," Lanston says as he raises a brow and cracks a smile that shows off his perfect teeth.

"I'm not... *good*," I say with a grimace. He stands, makes his way around the coffee table, and motions to the spot next to me for permission to sit. I nod.

Lanston settles beside me; the weight of his presence is all-consuming. My heart slows and speeds at the same time—hesitant and worried about all the things he may or may not feel that I certainly am in this moment.

"None of us are *good*. We're simply human." He leans closer and brushes my hair softly back from my face. "You feel the world more than others do, don't you? You're like me in that sense. Drowning in the expectations and eyes. Would you believe me if I told you when I was alive all I wanted was to die?"

My eyes widen. I thought I saw a familiar sickness in

the way he stood so sadly on the edge of that bridge today. Lanston *wanted* to die? He laughs and nods as if thinking back to his old ways.

"I was unwell, but mainly just... sad. In many ways I think I always will be. Were you sick too?" His question is clear. *Were you mentally unwell?* I want to say, who isn't? Our minds are all so different and ill in alternate ways, yet there is a profound comfort in knowing we are not alone in it.

I hesitate but clear my throat.

"I was raised to keep the dark thoughts inside my head to myself. My family didn't believe in therapy. In fact, it was often used as a threat." I laugh at the concept that they planted inside my brain. "If I was depressed or *off*, they would threaten to take me to the counselors so they could see and confirm how awful I was. I was afraid of that... the eyes of people, the judgment they would pass."

Lanston lowers his hand and holds mine. His warm touch sends shivers straight up my spine. "That's terrible."

I nod. "It is... but I didn't know it then. I was terrified of the world finding out how disturbed I was. How rotten and twisted." I shake my head to keep the tears from forming. "I was very sick and untreated. I wish I had found friends like you did."

He tilts his head slightly and then his eyes light with an idea.

"Would you like to meet some of them? I actually

sorta still live at Harlow." My face shifts and realization dawns over me.

He's from *Harlow Sanctum*.

He dips his chin, reading my expression easily. "So you've heard about that place, huh?"

I lean forward to look closer at him.

"I don't know a phantom who hasn't," I mutter half-mindedly. His smile grows as I study him intently. He doesn't look like he perished in a fire or even has a hint of smoke on his ghost. Every death leaves a tell, even if it's small and hidden away. You can see it if you know how to look for it.

A separate incident followed Harlow's fire, one that made my stomach curl when I overheard it at the bar in town. And the longer I stare at Lanston's gentle eyes, I know it was him.

"You were the man who died by the gunman," I say hollowly. He saved both of his friends that day and lost his life in the process. The entire city was riveted with the aftershocks the story brought, over fifty souls from Harlow and then the murder. It was all anyone spoke about for weeks.

Lanston nods and shrugs. "That was five years ago now. But *anyway*, would you like to meet the Harlow residents? Jericho is my counselor and I know you'd love him."

I shrink back, forgetting that we were discussing our demons a moment ago. He's good at changing the subject —I make a mental note to remember his craft.

"I don't know," I say slowly. Words from the years of torment I faced come whispering back into my mind. *They're going to take you away because you're so fucked up. Freak. You scare people. You're hard to love. Go away. I hate you.*

I don't care about you. I don't care.

That one makes my soul dull completely.

Lanston looks at me and the way his entire heart opens up to me with just one slow nod makes my chest sink. He understands. He knows the fear of letting another see the hurt and the bruises you've hidden so well.

"I promise you'll feel so much better when you say it. And nobody but him has to ever hear it if that's what you want." He holds up his hand and extends his pinky to me. "What have you got to lose, Ophelia?"

"The small, insignificant amount of self-love I've managed to cling to."

His eyes falter, but I raise my pinky and he wraps his around mine. Warmth radiates from between us. I feel safe.

"I promise you won't lose it."

"That's a big promise to keep."

"I never go back on them," he murmurs as we stay connected, sitting in the dark like we're whispering secrets to one another to avoid lingering ears.

His hazel eyes narrow with a smile as I nod and say quietly, "I've never known a man to not go back on a promise."

"You've never met me then." He cocks his head like he's proud and I can't help but laugh.

Our hands drop to our own laps and after a few silent moments pass, I say, "I'll help you figure out why you're still here." Lanston gives me a look of confusion and I quickly add, "You know, since you're helping me."

He leans back against the armrest and smiles. "Are you just trying to say you want to spend more time with me?" He raises a suggestive brow and smirks. "Or is there something you know that I don't about why we're still here?"

I look past his head and out the only window of my opera house that isn't boarded up. The moonlight shimmers across the glass in soft blue hues. It's beautiful to stare at; I often find myself getting lost in it.

"I have a theory," I say.

"Well, let's hear it."

My gaze flicks back to him as I murmur, "A bucket list."

7

Lanston

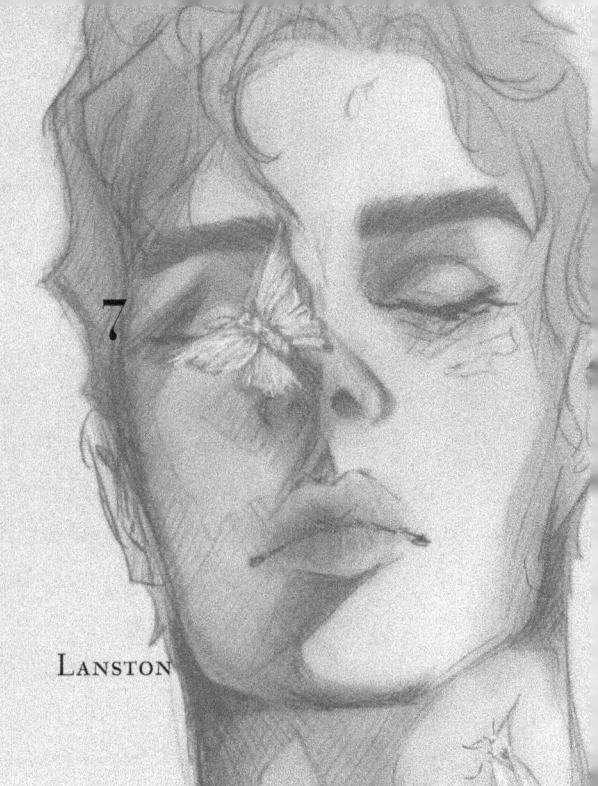

A bucket list.

Why didn't I think of that?

Ophelia fell asleep hours ago, or has it been longer? Time is strange in purgatory. Sometimes, the nights seem to drag on for days. But as I lie on her sofa and stare at the tall, dark ceilings above, I ponder on her theory. Brilliant, really.

A bucket list of things we never got to do. That is literally the definition of *unfinished business*.

I look at her, sleeping soundly on the couch across from me. My hands are cold now that I'm not touching hers. A longing that I haven't experienced in years pulls deep inside my chest. I want to touch her, to run my fingers through her hair and hold her while she dreams. Her lashes look darker against her cheeks.

Slowly, I start making a list in my head: Visiting Paris, sailing one of those fancy yachts you see in movies, stargazing on the beach. But those seem like really stupid things to be on a final bucket list. Is that really all I can think of that I wanted to do?

I groan and press the heels of my palms against my eyes. Are bucket lists supposed to be dumb shit? When I thought of them when I was alive, they didn't seem so silly. Though now, I can't imagine how a trip to Paris is going to send me to the after.

Ophelia lets out a soft sigh and pulls her legs to her chest, shivering at the cold that I seem to be feeling as well. Was I always this cold? It's as if I'm only now realizing how cruel my existence has been without her. I've never been so warm and satiated by another's presence.

I grab the folded blanket at the edge of the couch and approach her quietly, laying the blanket over her and letting my eyes linger over every part of her face.

I wish I were more like Liam. He always knew exactly what to say to women. Even Jericho has a way of clever conversation. Perhaps, once upon a time, I did as well. But in my death, I've found I just want to be silent and listen to the world as it ticks on without me.

She's different though. I don't feel like the world is moving on while I remain stagnant. No, with her, it's as if the world tilts around us—our gravity too immense for the living. We orbit one another, hands reaching and seeking the light.

Her eyes flash open and I flinch because, *fuck*, I'm standing above her, staring at her face like a creep.

"I um—"

Ophelia sits up, her mauve hair tousled on the left side she was lying on. "Careful, Lanston. I'm known to throw men into ditches for touching me." She bristles and a darkness settles over her gaze.

I swallow hard. Jesus, she's like the female version of Liam. Why does that excite me?

"You seemed cold, so I—" I awkwardly motion at the blanket, but as I do, she adjusts her position and my hand brushes her breast. Heat flares across my cheeks and I swear I'm just going to go outside and face Those Who Fucking Whisper instead.

My foot gets caught on one of the coffee table legs and as if things couldn't get worse, I fall ass first on the table and it shatters beneath me. Glass and wood scatter across the floor, loud enough to wake the whole damn city.

Not a second later, Ophelia has me pinned to the floor beneath her. Her thighs are on each side of my torso, one hand to my throat and the other gripping my wrist as if she thinks I have a fucking knife in my hand.

All reason leaves my mind and my eyes widen as I stare up at her. Her breaths are hard and she looks absolutely feral. There's not a lick of fear in her eyes, only searing rage. All her lithe and tender features have vanished.

It only takes me a moment to piece it together.

She doesn't trust men.

I want to be hurt or offended by her brutality in pinning me so ruthlessly, but I know better. I know that it's probably a deep wound she carries, and her hostility is a defensive measure she's developed in response. *It's not fair*. Nothing in this world is fair. I only know what her eyes and reactions allude to.

"It's okay," I whisper, gritting my teeth at the sting the glass brings me as it digs into my elbows. At least all things fade quickly as a ghost, especially pain. It's a mere pinch of what pain in the living world was.

Her expression is stern and pressed, unwavering, yet a soft flicker dances over her eyes.

"I would never hurt you, Ophelia." My free hand reaches up slowly. Pieces of glass fall from my arm and make broken sounds as they collect back on the ground. She puts more weight on my throat and I take a strangled sip of air as she leans in close, her nose pressed against mine. I stare into her sea of darkness, limp and at her mercy.

"Don't do that again."

Her voice is low, lethal in a sense. Chills spread up my spine and I don't dare look away. I have no doubt that she'd leave me in a pit somewhere, as she claimed to have done, doomed to be stuck forever without escape.

She's just as cruel as they say.

And for most people, that might be enough for them to wish to stray from her, but it only draws me closer—my incessant need to fix things and people is something I cannot resist.

Show me the gashes in your flesh that remain fresh.

She's broken in so many ways, but she's strong. Hides her feelings away like they don't exist, but I know they're there. Hidden and locked up because someone had destroyed her at one point in time. Like a titanium locket, she guards herself in the only way she knows how.

I cherish that about her. Cruelness, viciousness, and all.

I manage a crooked grin and say, "Wouldn't dream of it."

Ophelia stares into my soul, searching for the darkness inside me. She mustn't find it because her hands loosen and she sits back, her ass planted right over my dick. I'm not about to do anything to set her off again though, unless I want to end up in a ditch.

She lets out a small sigh and threads her hand through her hair, stroking it back like she's disappointed with herself. "Sorry… I'm not trying to be—"

I start chuckling and she pauses, leveling me a curious look like she can't seem to get a read on me.

"You don't need to apologize. I'm sorry for spooking you. I'd be pissed too if I saw a guy standing over my body in a vulnerable state."

The muscles in her jaw relax and she lets her face fall into that soft, welcoming expression again. "I have a hard time being around others. I know I'm strange and guarded. I'm sorry," she admits as her fingers curl into my shirt. My cheeks warm again. I'm not sure she realizes what she's doing. "For a moment, when I woke up, I thought meeting you was a dream. When I saw you watching me, it reminded me of something else. *Someone else.*"

Apologies after apologies. Someone thoroughly broke this girl.

Where was I? Where was anyone? It hurts me so deep in my soul that there's nothing I can do to take the past away. In some ways, I think the past is all we ever were. There's nothing to be done about it now. Not when you're dead.

I set my hand on my chest, not over her hand, but close. Her eyes shift to my fingers and narrow with anguish. It's then I know she wants to touch me as much as I do her. The air has already lifted several degrees.

"You aren't a burden, Ophelia."

Her eyes widen and she looks like she's somewhere between hitting me or running away.

"You're not strange. You're perfectly yourself, wounds and all. No more apologies." I quirk my lips into a small smile and hope that *I'm* not too odd for her.

She looks down at my hand again and nods, eyes lingering on my skin as if she yearns to run her fingers over my knuckles and trace my bones.

But she doesn't and we're left in the silence and dark.

Both wanting.

8

Lanston

I set my black helmet over Ophelia's head and can hear her soft giggles from beneath. Even though they are muffled, they bring a smile to my face. I notice the ends of her hair are wet but don't think much of it.

"So you've really never ridden a motorcycle before?" I ask as I swing my leg over the bike. She shakes her head. I can't see her expression but the way she grabs at her dress uncertainly sends a thrill through me.

Even though I want to let my gaze linger, I pull it away.

I think of last night again.

We returned to our separate sofas after our encounter. I had a fitful night's rest with a handful of things running rampant through my mind. Yesterday was the first day since being a phantom that I didn't feel so hopeless and melancholic. I didn't think of Liam and Wynn for the entirety of the day like I usually do. My mind was encapsulated by Ophelia. Wholly and entirely.

We rose as the sun did, slowly and with drowsy eyes, and decided to head to Harlow together. A nervous vein has spread through my flesh, worrying over how she'll like the residents I've lived with for so long and if she'll find therapy as helpful as I did.

"Do you want to learn or to ride behind me?" I tease her, thinking she'll sit behind me, but of course she doesn't. My eyes widen as she straddles the bike in front of me, her dress hiked up to her waist and the soft flesh of her ass is practically in my lap.

I swallow hard.

"Well? Teach me."

My brain takes a moment to catch up. "Um, first, you need to learn how to use the clutch and throttle." I show her the parts on the crotch rocket and she observes, memorizing everything I say.

We try a few times, but the first gear is always the toughest. So after she can't get it to catch, she sighs. "Can you get it going and I'll just steer?"

I laugh and lean over her so I can reach the handle; she lifts her foot so I can control the clutch.

"Ready?" I shout over the roar of the engine as I rev it loudly.

She nods vigorously. The excitement is evident in her

motions, and I wish I could see the light in her eyes right now. With my chest pressed so close to her back, I wonder if she can feel the erratic beat of my heart. The way it dips and stutters.

Have I ever felt this nervous around someone? That timid grin that you get from being around someone who lights your heart like a match spreads across my face. The giddiness she releases is contagious.

I take a deep breath before letting the clutch fall and twist the throttle. The motorcycle takes off fast. Ophelia dips down, scream-laughing as we race down the street onto the highway. Her shrills of fear quickly turn into excitement and she sits up more, letting go of the handles and spreading her arms out wide.

It's my favorite sound—the laughter of someone's first ride. The thrill is addicting.

The sun hits my eyes as she turns her head a bit. The helmet shields her face, but I know she's looking back at me, enduring the patterns of my quickened pulse against her back.

Suddenly, I become acutely aware of myself. What is she looking at? My eyes, my lips, my nose? Perhaps I'll never know. She turns to face the road again and juts her ass out more as she leans forward against the wind. Her hand smooths over mine, feeling the throttle and the strength I hold it with.

This is the moment I know I'm in trouble.

The way every cell in my being reverberates and

responds to her. Ophelia is liquid in my veins. Her laugh forever haunting.

Halfway to Harlow, we stop and switch. She sits behind me and I take over driving. Her thighs wrap around me and I look down more than once. The heat of her core warms the bottom of my spine. Ophelia's hands spread across my chest, securing herself firmly at my back.

The ride back is torture. I'm thankful she can't see the boner that tents my pants, and I may take a few alternate roads to prolong our trip to Harlow so the blood can return to my head.

Take it easy, Nevers, I chide myself. She's probably not even into me.

But that thought is hard to enforce in my mind as she lets her fingers glide up and down my sternum. The motions are languid and slow. Her cheek presses to my shoulder and I jolt at the realization that she's ditched my helmet.

"You didn't toss it, did you?" I shout sarcastically, knowing as well as she does that I can just steal one again. Nothing we touch or move actually changes in the living world. We only take fragments of them, small, insignificant pieces like their shadows. Everything is false here. But that doesn't mean it isn't still fun, not any less real for us.

She rests her chin on my shoulder and says, "We don't even need them. Can we stop somewhere first?"

I grin, not that she can see. "I like the way it looks on me. Makes me more mysterious. Sure—where to?"

She laughs. "It's just up this road. Take a left when you get to the forest line."

I follow her guidance and take the narrow road leading into the mountains. The pine trees are closer to the street here, creating a barrier that blocks out all the sounds of the world. Mountains should be visible straight ahead in the distance but the mist is still heavy in the air, blocking out the sun and creating an almost ominous world beneath it.

The motorcycle slows as I let off the gas a bit. "Where are we going?" I ask. This feels more like a horror movie than the basement at Harlow did.

It's so quiet and void of life.

Ophelia's hands are still tightly wrapped around my center as she says nonchalantly, "To my hiding place."

Hiding place? All the way out here?

I open my mouth to ask more questions, but she cups her fingers over my lips gently. Cold air wisps between the gaps and sends chills down my spine.

"You'll see," she whispers against the shell of my ear.

Who are you, Ophelia Rosin, and why has it taken us all this time to find one another?

I want to ask her many things, such as what her favorite music is and where she finds all those abandoned plants she fills her opera house with. When she stumbled upon this place and how she was murdered.

There are so many aching thoughts that burden me. But I keep my lips pressed together, patient.

After a few minutes of driving on the winding forest road, a small wooden sign appears on the right. Ophelia points at it and I turn. The asphalt turns to gravel and the path leads to a small trailhead. A makeshift fence of rotting wood stands in place, along with an overgrown path. Wildflowers and weeds have long since crowded any trail that used to be here.

It's vacant.

There is a stillness here, nothing but the sound of the birds waking above in the boughs, their songs laden with sorrow. Branches snapping beneath the feet of weasels or vixens. For some reason, the sound of them settles the affliction inside me. The anxiety and depression that lingers almost seems hushed here beneath the mist and pines—amidst the whispering trees and the chill in the air.

My eyes close and I let myself become one with this place.

"*Lanston.*" A whisper.

For a moment, I think it's Wynn. The softness and light lilt to it is warm.

"*Lanston.*"

I open my eyes, slowly turning and finding a beautiful rose instead of my pink-haired wonder. Her cheeks are red with the cold spring morning; her eyes are brown and speckled with green, pale against the mournful pines that surround her.

My soul leans, agonizing and wishful, reaching for hers.

I realize that I'm not sad or disappointed that it's not my kindred one. And that's a somber thought in itself—that you indeed can move on from a love that ravished your heart to its entirety. I don't want Wynn to be just a girl I loved once, but when I look at Ophelia, my entire being calls for her.

Familiar and coveting.

Like we've always been destined to meet.

Ophelia tilts her head. "Are you coming?" Her smile is loose and coy.

"Yeah, sorry about that. This place is just so—" I can't seem to find the words to describe it. But Ophelia nods in understanding. Maybe there really aren't any words to describe a place such as this. Even if it is just a forest.

I follow her as she leads us up the steep trail. If I were alive, I'd already be winded by our ascent. The mist grows thick around us and the moisture in the air grips my lungs.

We remain silent as we walk, taking in our surroundings and listening to the trees sway. I think about what she said, this being her hiding place. Who was she hiding from?

As the thought circulates my mind, we step over the final hill and break through the wall of mist. A chill spreads throughout my body, raising the hairs on my neck. The sky looks as though it extends forever, and the soft hues of the mid-morning colors make the clouds dance with pink, yellow, and an orange so fierce and angry one might believe the world to be ending.

We stand side by side at the lookout, fingers dangerously close to brushing against one another, as we stare out into the world that's left us behind.

How bleak it is—yet I'm smiling.

"Why did you hide here?" I ask her finally, softly. It comes out as a mere whisper, yet it's so quiet here above the forest and beneath the stars, that the sound of my voice is startling.

Ophelia looks at me, an ocean of misery in her eyes, and says, "Because no one would ever find me here, where the sky kisses the earth, where I was no longer an ailment to others. Here, I was the goddess of the forest—the only person to breathe the cold air and tell the trees my pain."

I stare out where she has so many times before.

I see it now.

Why I'm drawn to her and crave to know everything inside her mind. It's the sad smile. The almost words that are left unspoken.

"You hid here because you thought about not existing anymore."

Her chin lifts to the faded stars still barely visible in the center of the sky, and she shuts her eyes. I turn my head and look at her. I watch her lips, pulling up into a reminiscent smile as if she is truly happy I heard her wordless confession.

"I hid here... because I *knew* I didn't want to exist anymore."

9

Lanston

Jericho looks perplexed as his eyes drift between Ophelia and me standing in the foyer with rain dripping from the ends of our hair.

On our way back down the mountain, we were caught in a light rain, but it was well worth seeing her personal hideaway. I'm already thinking about when we can return there together.

Ophelia is nervous. I can feel the energy around her shifting as her hands tightly wrap around her arms in an attempt at self-comfort. Her black dress is long-sleeved and drops just below her knees. The rim around her collarbones is a lace pattern that completes her gothic, morbid look.

It fits her so well. Death, I mean.

She wears it proudly, embracing it entirely, not afraid to talk about phantoms and her life here in the in-between. I admire that about her—I can't seem to accept even a fraction of my reality. It's something I reject entirely.

I don't want to be dead. Not yet.

"I was wondering where you went," Jericho says suggestively, and I fight the urge to bury my face into my palms. "Looks like I was worrying for nothing." He casts me a sly smirk. My stomach twists with nerves.

I'll kill him.

Ophelia smiles easily at the counselor, completely dismissing his efforts to embarrass me, and offers her hand cordially. "You must be Jericho. I recognize you; you've been coming to my performances for a few years now, haven't you?" Her voice is light, and her shoulders relax as she seems to find him familiar.

Jericho nods and shakes her hand professionally. "I love your performances. Do you come up with them yourself?" Ophelia's cheeks redden and she nods meekly. "Such talent at a young age. I'm envious."

She shrugs. "Well, I was twenty-eight when I died. That was ten years ago now, so I'm actually much older than I look." She laughs and turns her head just enough to peek over at me.

I smile and say, "Souls don't age. You're forever young; even if you were three hundred years old, I'd imagine you'd still be dancing and throwing men into ditches."

Her face drops and she hurriedly shoots a glance at Jericho, who's already laughing and bringing his heavy hand down on my shoulder to shake me. "Throwing men into pits? What did you do to the poor girl?" he roars, drawing eyes from other phantoms around the foyer.

"Come on, really?" I say under my breath.

Ophelia covers her mouth to hide her smile. "I may have thrown a few sorry ghosts into ditches. Worry not, they deserved it." She lifts her chin and I marvel at her pride. A short silence follows and I'm keenly aware of Jericho studying us together.

"Aren't you two just adorable?" The counselor keeps a brow raised and his smirk only grows with interest.

"*Anyway,* I was hoping you could see Ophelia for a session," I mutter. His smirk fades and Jericho shifts his weight to one leg.

He looks troubled but has a hint of light in his eyes as he murmurs, "Unfortunately, I'm booked for private sessions until next week, but she's more than welcome to join the group counseling this evening. I presume you'll be there anyway, Lanston, yeah?"

Ophelia shrinks, dropping her shoulders and looking a bit disappointed. "I suppose I have all the time in the world, don't I?" she says hesitantly.

Jericho nods thoughtfully, his eyes shifting to me as he claps his hands together, with an idea lighting up his expression. "You should stay here in the meantime.

Harlow Sanctum is always welcoming lost souls. Our rooms are full at the moment, but Lanston has a spare bed in his."

I know what he's doing... My fists clench at my sides and my gaze darts in her direction. He doesn't know about her mind yet—she's not like Wynn. I'm worried she very well might throw *me* into a pit if we're forced into such close quarters.

"Lovely. Show me the way," she chirps and looks up at me from beneath long lashes. The soft brown-green hue of her eyes makes my stomach feel light.

I'm taken aback, staring at her as if she's joking, but she and Jericho start across the foyer and I'm left to follow behind them.

She keeps her eyes ahead, not drawn to or distracted by any of the rooms around us. Jericho stops at my door and pushes it open. It's dark, a cave practically; I tend to keep the curtains pulled closed to help with my wallowing. If I knew I was having my newfound crush over, I would've picked up and left the curtains open.

Shit. She's going to see how empty my death is. Where she keeps her space filled with plants and oddities full of her personality, I keep nothing. I'm a mere shell. In a way, I think I always have been. I don't have many things to define me. Not physical things, anyway.

"I'll see you two later in the group sesh tonight." Jericho winks at me as he passes. I swallow the dread that's building inside my throat.

Ophelia steps into the darkness of my room and

walks straight to the curtains, throwing them open effortlessly and cracking the window to air out the space. I stand awkwardly in the doorway and rub the back of my head as I look around my room with new eyes—my baseball cap shifts on top of my head as I disturb it.

Nothing brings a conscience bias to your own living conditions like someone you're romantically interested in setting foot into your haven. I don't know why I care what she thinks about me, but it's undeniable. I very much care.

My cheeks warm and I pull my baseball cap down further so I don't have to see her expression.

"The bed on the far left is mine... I can give you a tour of the grounds if you'd like?"

She hums with a delightful smile and I can't help but look, peeking from beneath the edge of my cap. Her eyes scour my room, studying each book left piled up on my circular coffee table. Light spills into the room through the slivers in the drapes and illuminates the dust particles as they slowly drift. Drawings torn from my sketchbook are stitched together with hemp string I found in the library. Ophelia seems particularly captivated by them.

I quickly step over and grab the makeshift book of my drawings bound inside. To say I would have an aneurysm if she saw the darkness in my head is an understatement. I never, *ever* let other people see my drawings—not since the art show disaster my father ruined. Not since I completely stopped speaking to him. I never even showed Liam or Wynn this part of me.

It makes me sad—the secrets we keep to protect our hearts. Even against those we love most.

"Just some dumb scribbles," I say, as unenthused as I can in hopes that she won't ask about them.

She peeks over my arm and watches as I place them in my bedside table drawer. "What do you draw, Lanston?" Her voice is void of judgment and only holds a warm curiosity. I think I like that most about her. She's abrasive but so kind about the things that seem to be the most sensitive for others.

As if she understands the grueling eyes of the world.

I was never allowed to draw in my house. Never to dally in things that were artistic or silly. *Be a fucking man.* My father would say. *You'll be homeless and poor if you follow such ridiculous dreams.* My dreams were of art and beauty, of morbidity and lost souls. He could never understand why I wanted to draw such sad creatures on pages, why I wanted to show the world what lived inside my veins.

Let your dreams die. Undoubtedly, if you don't, you'll be miserable.

I wanted to pour the black ink from my heart onto pages and make others feel everything. To allow them to feel what I felt. To experience something they perhaps have once recognized inside themselves as well. And now it is too late. I've wasted what little time I had on earth, not doing anything except letting the illness of my mind take me into the depths. Into the dark.

Until Liam.

Until Wynn.

A tear rolls down my cheek and it pulls me back from my thoughts. I quickly swipe it away with my sleeve, relieved that she can't see it.

"*Ah*, you don't want to know. I draw dark things that come to me in moments of weariness. You know... just to get them out." I shove the drawer shut and turn to her, smiling that cheerful, loose grin I always have tacked on regardless of what's happening inside my head.

Ophelia watches me carefully, considering her words it seems, as she sits down on her bed. "I'd love to see them someday. I'm sure you're quite talented. You'd be surprised at how much I adore dreary, gothic art." She lies back on the sheets and spreads her arms out as she sighs. "I haven't slept in a bed for years."

I tilt my head but recall that her old opera house only has sofas. Phantoms don't need beds, but I guess the old sentiment of them is nostalgic and comforting.

"I'm really not talented... but maybe I'll show you sometime if you promise not to throw me into a ditch." She lets out a short laugh and sits back up. Her pale mauve hair is in loose, natural curls. The color fits her black dress so well, enhancing the olive pigment of her skin and making her absolutely glow. *Ophelia*, I want to say her name over and over until I'm sick of it. *Ophelia. You wondrous thing.*

I want to know every secret in her head. Every last thought that makes her tick.

Ophelia nods. "I can do that. So long as you don't hover above me again tonight."

I bark out a laugh and move toward the door. "Deal. Come on, there's something I want to show you."

10

Ophelia

The air is crisp in the forest lining Harlow Sanctum.

Montana is a terribly cold place, barren most of the year due to the short seasons. It's spring, and yet most mornings are ridden with frost-tipped blades of grass.

But today is warm.

The sun peeks through a break in the gray clouds above and a beam of light casts down upon the misty pines. Lanston leads me through the field surrounding the manor. A whimsical stone path has been laid here; emerald green moss grows between the gray blocks.

I look up and smile as the edge of the forest nears.

"Where does this enchanted little path go?"

Lanston doesn't look back at me as he chirps, "You'll see." His hands are in his jacket pockets. If someone were to see us walking down this path, they'd think we were on our way to a funeral. My black dress and his black jacket and pants certainly fit the bill.

I listen to the birds as they sing different songs than they do in my secret forest. The trees have much to say here; the souls who've walked through long ago have left small traces of their longing. Their voices are soft and tickle my skin. We all leave bits of us as we go, no matter our ignorance of the fact.

Some phantoms never realize the traces are there, but I see them everywhere. In the moss that peppers the shady side of boulders or in the flowers that reach toward the sun—they are there, hiding, small like gems that wish to never be found. Perhaps that's why I don't mind being dead so much. I've learned to embrace my solitude; being alone is something I hold dear. But Lanston's presence refutes the law I've imposed upon myself—his ghost beckons to my own. I've never craved to know someone as entirely as I do him.

I walk headfirst into Lanston's back, grunting a bit from the surprise at his sudden halt.

"*Hey.*" I rub my nose.

He looks over his shoulder at me and grins. "We're here." My eyes lift to the field around us and a small gasp escapes me.

Flowers circle the center area of the field where a few benches have been placed. At its center is a polished black stone about six feet tall with names engraved on it. The top of the stone is jagged in an artistic chip style, while every other side of it is smooth. My eyes are drawn back to the field. Beyond the small, closed white flowers are poppies and lavender. It's a beautiful and quiet place where all the whispering trees that encase it fall into a hush.

"Why are the white flowers closed? They look like they're ready to bloom," I ask as I admire them from afar, wishing to see their petals kissed with sunlight.

"Those are moonflowers; they only bloom beneath the stars," he says softly, reminiscently.

Lanston closes his eyes and takes a deep breath of the floral-scented air. "This is the memorial for all those who perished in the fire," he says sadly, but there's still a smile on his lips.

I walk closer to the pillar of names and find Jericho's near the top. Lanston's too. My fingers linger over his last name. *Nevers*. The stone is cold and instills dreariness in my heart.

"It's a beautiful gravestone. Is this where the missing patients were found too?" I ask and he nods. That story, along with the fire, became all the state's folk could talk about for months. People missing for a decade, their bones found here of all places. It was awful to read in the paper and it feels just as sickening to stand where they once stood.

"All except one. I had to stake out here a few nights but I finally saw Monica, the sole survivor, visiting her friends. I'm glad at least she got away, but she still acts as though she's being hunted down. Always watchful, and I can't say I blame her," he mumbles as if he knows her personally. Who knows, maybe he does, maybe he's studied many people who've come and gone from this place in his hours of boredom.

"Are the other missing patients' phantoms still here? In purgatory, I mean?" I sit on the bench facing the stone pillar and Lanston takes a seat beside me. His scent of pages and coffee mixes sweetly with the flowers.

"No, I think they found their way to the after long ago, but I'm not sure. Some of our fellow phantoms here think they've heard strange things in the music room at night. But I believe that they've passed, either before or after their murders were solved. I'm glad I haven't seen them here though. It gives me hope. That maybe if they can find peace after an unsolved, decade-old murder, then maybe we have a chance too, you know?" His hazel eyes are heavy with weariness. He mustn't have slept at all last night.

I smile. "Good. I'm happy that they moved on. Some souls aren't meant to dwell here." Though I'm not so sure I believe they've really all passed on. The rumors might be worth looking into.

He tilts his head toward me and there's so much sadness in his eyes it hurts. I can tell he's a ghost that isn't meant to dwell. He wants to leave and be at peace, while I wish to stay. We'll never be in existence together for long. It isn't written in the stars.

The first phantom I enjoy being around and he's desperate to leave.

"I've been meaning to ask you about Those Who Whisper... would they follow you here? Are you safe indoors?" Lanston doesn't flat out ask if I'm safe to bring here, because he's kind, but his voice is heavy with it whether he knows it or not.

I grip the black lace of my dress loosely over my knees and keep my eyes lowered. "You're worried about the others."

He doesn't respond for a moment. "Is that why you stay by yourself? It would make sense that that's why you prefer to be alone. You're keeping everyone else away to keep them safe, aren't you?"

I dip my head, not willing to outright admit it. "I wouldn't bring trouble here. You don't need to worry." They don't come around large groups of phantoms. It's usually only when I'm alone and at night when the world sleeps.

Lanston slides his hand over mine and the warmth makes my chest feel tight. "I'm not worried about them, Ophelia. I'm worried about you." His voice is raspy and draws my eyes to his. "When you spend most of your time alone you learn to observe others and see past the mask they wear. You were a bit harder to pin, but I knew right away that you were keeping people away on purpose. Aren't you lonely? Let me help."

I stare at him, surprised.

His eyes narrow with thought and something else I can't quite read.

"What's chasing you, Ophelia?"

"I–I don't know," I say truthfully. "Shortly after I died they appeared, and I've been running from the whispering darkness ever since."

The only place they can't seem to get me is in the old opera house. I credit the plants that I've collected with being what keeps the darkness out. A silly thing, really, but who makes the rules when you're dead? Whatever works, works. Nothing makes sense on the other side. Not the way we can move about the living and still indulge in everyday life. And certainly not in the way we still have thoughts and feelings.

"You said no one wakes up the same after they get touched. Do you know why?"

I look at him and shake my head. "I haven't asked... because they look at me differently when they wake up and I just... I leave. But it's what the darkness tells me that keeps me from inquiring. They whisper terrible things to me, and I'd rather not find out." He nods and takes a deep breath.

"Well, maybe you'll find some answers when you speak with Jericho." Lanston looks back over the field with a soft smile on his lips.

I can't bring myself to tell him that I don't plan on staying long.

The whispers are never far behind and although I

doubt they'd come here, I don't want to risk it. I want to enjoy today for what it is.

"Alright, now how about I show you the greenhouse?" Lanston cheers up the mood with his broad, handsome smile.

I return it. "Lead the way."

The greenhouse is exactly what I wish my opera house could be. Vibrant plants fill the space entirely. Rows and rows all the way to the back. Hanging baskets with long draped flowers keep the roof hidden and the floor is wet from a recent watering.

"Oh my God, I love it here!"

Lanston chuckles. "I knew you would."

I walk up and down a few rows, gliding my fingers across the tops of leaves and succulents before turning and grinning widely at him. He stands at the entrance with a content grin glued to his face. Watching me as if I'm a lost memory.

My smile fades as I realize I've been looking at him for too long. *I can't get attached.* I chide myself. Forcing my eyes to the flowers at the next table, I freeze.

Chrysanthemums.

The flower of death and mourning.

My mood instantly sours. They're the exact same dark shade of red as the ones at my small, private burial. Pain curls inside my chest—a dark and angry beast, restless and starved.

I can still hear my stepmother's hushed whispers to my father at the service. *"Good riddance."*

My murderer stood alone and unnoticed, watching silently. Perhaps the only soul there who was sad and regretful.

"Do you like mums?"

Lanston's voice brings a faint smile back to my lips and I swiftly look away from the flowers, banishing the wilted memories. His eyes are curious and he's standing only a few inches from me now.

I shake my head. "No, I really don't."

A wicked smile. "I fucking hate them too."

11

Lanston

Ophelia looks around the group circle nervously. Her fists are clenched over her knees and she bounces her left leg while we wait for the last few phantoms to show up. Jericho smiles placidly and nods as they take their seats.

I lean back in the simple plastic chair, staring at Ophelia from across the room.

It's unfair to compare this moment to Wynn, but when I stare at Ophelia I see such different things than I did with my lovely Coldfox. Now, I see a woman who is desperate to keep up the farce of being fine. She hides her scars well, but they are there, unscathed and rotting beneath the surface.

Her eyes lift to mine and I offer her a reassuring smile.

Jericho crosses his legs, revealing his black socks that match his suit. He adjusts his glasses as he looks at Ophelia. "Everyone, today we have a new phantom here with us, one you might recognize if you've gone to her shows, Miss Ophelia Rosin."

She dips her head as everyone gives an unenthusiastic "hello."

"Miss Rosin, we like to start these by stating how long we've been dead and why we think we're still here. Care to start us off?" Jericho sets his clipboard across his lap and looks expectantly at her.

For a moment, I think she'll decline, but she surprises me, lifting her chin and straightening her back.

"I've been dead for ten years and I'm still here because I'm not ready to leave. I want to dance; it's been my dream ever since I was a child." She pauses and looks at each and every face in the circle before coming across mine. Her brown-green eyes soften and she says quietly, "I still have so much to give to the world. I want them to know who I am."

"Want who to know? A living person?" Jericho pries.

"Just one person will do. A stranger who will often think of me for any reason other than how I died," she replies with a severe tone. Her brows are pulled tightly together but her lower lip threatens to quiver.

An awkward silence follows and Ophelia takes notice of it. She took a big leap coming here to be vulnerable, and I can see the regret beginning to etch her frown.

She's in denial of her death.

Fuck, we all are, but she's convinced herself that she can still give parts of herself to the living world. A knot forms in my stomach with the sadness that thought holds.

Jericho clears his throat and says, "Surely you know that's not possible."

Ophelia schools her expression into one that's cold and emotionless as she callously questions, "Not possible, how?"

The counselor's face twists with anguish. "Miss Rosin, because you are dead."

"So? Have my performances not affected you in some way, however small it may be? You said it yourself—you've been to my shows for the last five years now." She shrugs and a few heads nod. Yelina and Poppie shoot me a look. They look perplexed that she's here. I lift a shoulder. If they're wondering how I got her to follow me here, I don't have an answer. Sheer luck.

Poppie clears her throat, her voice small and nervous. "Watching you perform has become a beacon of hope for me." Jericho looks at her and his face turns thoughtful. "The way you embrace your existence here so entirely, well, it's beautiful."

Ophelia looks shocked and then smiles. I'm entranced by it. "I might look like I'm embracing it well, but I'm afraid I only hide the sadness in my heart better than most." Her eyes dull as she clenches her hands together over her lap. This is hard for her—it's always hard the first time in a group session.

But there's something to be said for deciding to be so abrasive and outwardly strong, all just to soothe those around you. She suffers inside, like a diseased plant, rotting from the roots—the decay isn't visible on the surface, not at first. But it's such a slow, tragic way to let yourself die.

I want to console her. To know all her hidden demons and wrap her in my arms until the darkness leaves us. We'll banish the shadows that seek us together if we must.

Voices mumble around me, but I'm deep in thought, letting my mind ponder what she could be caging behind that lovely smile. She's a puzzle; her smile could convince anyone. The way she dances and feels the music could trick any observer.

"Nevers."

I snap my head up. The thoughts in my head are silenced instantly. "Huh?"

Jericho levels me that concerned look he's been giving me for years now. He worries about my drifting focus, everyone does. "I said it's your turn. Have you thought more about why you're still here?"

My back straightens and I shove my hands into my coat pockets. "Right, sorry about that. I still think it has to do with... well, you know, dying so unfairly. Sometimes, I wake up in the middle of the day, not knowing how much time has passed or what day it is." I trail off, holding back what I really want to say, but I feel so guilty for even thinking it. I should be with them, the three of us. Why did I have to die?

I'm happy it was me and not either of them, but the sadness and loneliness are too much to bear.

My eyes falter and I glance up at Ophelia. Her rosy cheeks and full lips set an ache in my chest. I don't want to say this in front of her, but I want to be genuine, and I'm not fucking perfect. None of us are.

We are all ruined in some way, bruised and scarred. But those are the parts I love the most in others, so I want her to see mine too. Love isn't conditional. The broken pieces of us should be where we start, not what we inevitably dig up after years of peeling back layers, only to be tired and skeptical.

"I think I'm still here because there are things I haven't gotten to do and experience. I never got to be completely selfish and do what *I* wanted. There are pieces of me out there I haven't found yet, but I want to. There are things people *owe* me."

Ophelia's eyes widen on me and a flicker of hope crosses them, like she's never heard someone be so honest. She leans forward in her chair as if she's clinging to my words. I can almost see the idea lighting her eyes —*the bucket list.*

"I want a goddamn apology from the people who hurt me," I say in a low tone; the pain that spreads across my chest is nothing short of agony. I clench my fingers tightly together. "Is that so much to ask for? *I'm sorry. I love you.*

I'm proud of you. Why? Why won't they say it? Just once would be enough, even if it's a whisper. I–I just..." The knot in my throat grows and I try swallowing it several times to no avail.

"You're angry."

The voice is hers—ethereal and void of emotion.

I blink past the tears forming, looking at Ophelia with torment pulling my brows lower. The understanding and sympathy I find there is comforting, and the pain in my heart subsides a little.

I nod. "I'm so fucking angry. At so many people."

Jericho looks between us. I see something I don't quite recognize flash across his gaze, a realization of some sort.

"It seems the two of you have agendas outside the walls of Harlow Sanctum. Why not explore that? Why not together?" Jericho says smoothly. He's leaned forward in his seat, elbow against knee, his hand covering his mouth as if he can see something of potential in us, as though he wishes to say more but thinks better of it.

Leaving Harlow has always been an option, but this is my home. While the paranormal world is daunting, when I think of doing it with a partner it doesn't seem so bad. The bucket list... it didn't seem like a viable option when I thought of doing the things on it alone, but when I think of the two of us on this adventure... my eyes widen and an ache grows in my chest. My consciousness whispers *"Go. Take her hand and never look back."*

I meet her gaze and it's as if the world has faded

around us. It's only us and the chairs we sit on, staring at one another, a dream growing in my heart. Ophelia looks troubled at the light in my eyes and that dashes those short-lived dreams swiftly.

The room comes back into focus.

After neither of us says anything, Jericho nods knowingly and moves on to the next person. The mumbling starts around me again and I let the fuzzy sounds soften the intrusive thoughts in my head.

I know I shouldn't be triggered by just a look. She didn't do anything wrong. I understand that the thoughts and emotions that well up within me are irrational and stupid. But they are still here existing as horribly as they always have. I just want to not think anymore. To be free of the torment of my own doing.

Can a ghost be suicidal? I still think about it often: the urge to leave.

I rub my forefinger and thumb anxiously over the sleeve of my sweater.

That lingering desire to die is still deep inside me, clawing, ebbing. I didn't understand for a long time, but I think I do now. It's that I want to *feel nothing*.

To *be* nothing.

"*You were never meant to exist.*" Is that where it began? The callous words spoken so cruelly by my father. How long have I yearned to make him proud? I can't bring myself to visit him. He didn't even speak or shed a tear at my funeral. Does he pray for me? That I found peace?

That makes me laugh.

Godless men don't pray, not even for their sons.

The courtyard and field beyond have never looked greener. The cloud cover is low, pressed against the evergreens in the distance and in the branches of the forest. The stones of Harlow are slick and glossy. Moss and fresh blooms add color to the institute, though I'm not quite sure it reaches all the way inside the music room today.

I hold my arms at the elbows, firmly against my chest as I peer around the room. I refuse to admit that I'm still uneasy about ghosts. Just because you've become one doesn't make the unknown any less frightening.

"What did the other phantoms say about this room that made them suspicious?" Ophelia eagerly asks. Her hair is tied back into a ponytail, a few curly purple strands line her face. She turns to glance at me and shoots me a ridiculous grin. "Oh, come on, scaredy-cat."

I glower but lower my arms so I don't look so guarded.

It took her a few hours to decompress after the group session. But now she's back to her normal self, or she's just really good at pretending.

"Are you sure you want to hear them? They're quite frightening," I say darkly. Curiosity blooms across her features.

"Yes, tell me."

"I'll warn you, you'll be too scared to sleep alone."

She laughs and plops down on the floral print sofa in the center of the room. "Try me," she dares and pats the spot beside her.

I grin and take the seat. Ophelia pulls her legs up and ignores the fact that she's in a dress. It takes great focus to keep my eyes from straying from her face.

"Well? Go on," she urges me.

I clear my throat. "As many as fifteen current residents of Harlow Sanctum have claimed to have heard or seen odd and frightening things in this very room." I use my storytelling voice and regardless of her efforts, the corners of her lips pull up at the ends. "Sometimes it's a hushed cry in the cover of night, other times a slam on the keys of the piano. One claimed to see a man running from one end of the room to the other in madness. But it's the sound of the door creaking open all throughout the night that most have heard, the pitter-patter of cold lifeless feet across the corridors and always, *always* leading back to this room."

Ophelia's eyes are wide with attention and I don't miss her shallow gulp.

"What do you think? Is there a phantom trying to stir the pot here?"

She looks around warily as if she's now aware of the dimness of the room. The rain ominously ticks against the window in rhythmic patterns. Her eyes draw back to me and I crack a wide grin.

"Who's the scaredy-cat now?" I taunt her.

Her laughter is instant and she leans forward and pushes me back. I follow the motion, letting my body fall backward onto the sofa. My baseball cap falls off the edge. I stare at the ceiling and chuckle with her.

Ophelia's hands land on either side of my head as she moves over me. Her body doesn't touch mine but she's so close that the heat rolls off her skin and mixes with mine.

"I think you made the entire thing up just to freak me out," she says surely.

My lip twitches. I *wish* I were making it up.

"Sorry, Miss Rosin, I'm afraid I'm not," I say as I lean up on my elbows. She sits back on her haunches, I rise with her and am not aloof to our shoulders touching.

We face the large bay windows looking toward the mountains and thick line of trees, clouds growing angry with the promise of rain. I inhale and catch her scent of roses again. It's subtle, bare.

"Miss Rosin was my asshole stepmother. Call me Ophelia," she tuts, and I can hear the ire in her tone. Though the glance she shoots me is playful and teasing.

I force my eyes back to the forest and clouds, not looking away from the window as I reply, "Okay. Ophelia it is."

A pause.

"Or, rose. I... don't mind being called a rose if you prefer nicknames." There's a vulnerability in her tone. I turn my attention to her, looking so small beside me.

Her eyes trail up to meet mine and neither of us

speaks. Our cheeks are both flushed and before I can open my mouth to say anything, the floorboards behind the sofa creak.

Both of our heads snap back. The air is colder than it was a second ago, but there's nobody there.

We look at each other and both stand as if on cue and walk straight out of the room. The second we're in the hallway, Ophelia bursts into laughter and scares the shit out of me. She takes off running down the hall toward the dorm wing and I hurry to follow her.

"Why are you laughing?" I call after her, laughing too, even though I'm terrified.

She shouts back, "Because what the fuck was that?" I grin at that. She laughs when she's scared.

We don't stop running until we're back in the safety of my room. I block the door with one of my flimsy ass dining chairs before collapsing to the floor and taking deep breaths.

"What are the chances that some phantoms are invisible and can pull pranks?" I huff out between breaths.

Ophelia giggles. "Probably as much a chance as there is for me to have a cloud of whispering darkness following me?"

Our heads brush and we turn toward the connection, our gazes meeting. This close, I can make out each strand of her hair, every lift and dip of her lips. Her eyes are soft and daring, making my cheeks burn.

"I forgot my hat," I blurt out to break the trance she puts me in. I fear if I don't, I'll do something stupid.

"*No,*" she says sardonically.

I restrain myself from reaching up and brushing a strand of hair from her face.

"In the morning then?" I laugh, because we're cowards.

She nods and sits up. "In the morning. When our heads are clearer."

"You going to be able to sleep alone tonight, my rose?" I jest and don't expect her to turn and look over her shoulder at me. But she does. Her eyes are drawn low and filled with desire.

Did I just say *my rose?* My worrying is for naught, as she disregards it completely.

"I don't think I can. Not after a scare like that," she says carefully, studying my features for hints of where my head's at.

My stomach warms and I swallow hard.

"I can put a movie in and whip up some popcorn if you'd like?" I stand and offer her a hand up. She takes it and smiles suspiciously at me.

"What kind of man are you, Lanston Nevers?" She asks as she makes her way to the wall with the microwave and coffee bar. Opening cabinets until she finds a bag of popcorn and prepares it.

What kind of man am I? Is that a physiological question or a simple one? Like when an interviewer asks you, "What's your biggest weakness?" Yeah, because normal people know how to answer questions like that. So I go with my gut.

"I'm a man who never gets what he wants but smiles anyway." I turn on the TV and pull out my bag of DVDs. Slasher and horror films are off the table, so I flip to the section with drama and find one.

The microwave beeps and Ophelia dumps the popcorn into a big bowl we can share. "Why?"

I press play and turn to look at her. "Why what?"

"Why do you continue to smile anyway?" She sets the popcorn down on my bed and walks to her side of the room, lifting her dress up over her head.

My brain stops working.

Heat flares across my cheeks and I sharply look away. "*Ophelia*! What are you doing?" She chuckles and I'm tempted to turn and look just to see her smile.

"Answer the question. Why do you smile anyway?"

I can hear her rustling through my closet. It's a miracle I can even focus enough to muster words. "Um, right. Well, I just figure that if I keep smiling, at least people will think I'm happy. It's better than looking miserable like my father." I pause and tighten my fists at my side. Shit, I should've kept that last part to myself.

"And are you?"

I turn, forgetting why I wasn't looking at her in the first place. Her hair is let down and she's wearing my heather-gray T-shirt. It comes down to her midthigh and I swear to God she's testing me. I've dreamed of having a girlfriend wear my shirt to bed—I shake the thought.

"Am I what?" My voice is low.

"Miserable."

Am I miserable? I have to take a moment to ponder it.

"No." I close the distance between us with a few strides. Her jaw tightens as I stop before her, a breath away. "At least not for the last twenty-four hours." My brows pinch together as I stare down at her.

"Can I tell you a secret?" She whispers.

"Shoot."

"I haven't been miserable since meeting you either."

12

Ophelia

Lanston sits with that statement for a few seconds. I can see the gears clicking in his head and the light flickering through him. His lovely grin kicks up on one side and makes me long to press a kiss to the edge of his lips.

A rarity. The desire to kiss a man you've only just met. Yet, it is the most extraordinary sentiment a person can experience. A rush. A feeling you can sense from the deepest parts of your marrow.

His eyes fall to my bare arms, the first time he's seen past the long-sleeved dresses I've worn, and he finds the butterfly and moth tattoos that stretch over my forearms. A butterfly is chasing a moth on my right arm, a wisp of tattered smoke trailing between them, while a moth chases the butterfly on my left arm, the same threads of smoke tethering them to one another.

His smile brightens a fraction before he sees the scars that hide beneath them. Then I watch as his heart practically stops and a forlorn frown pulls at his lips. Pain, and perhaps many other things, exist within him at this moment. But Lanston, being himself and ever the curious man I've become enthralled with, lifts his hand and brushes his thumb over the tattoos.

"Moths and butterflies, huh?" His eyes soften and he whispers, "Which of them caught who?"

"If the moth catches the butterfly, it will consume it. If the butterfly catches the moth, it will tear off its wings. Which do you think should catch the other?" I say with a maniacal grin. Lanston grimaces at my dark humor.

"Come on, what do they *really* symbolize?" he urges me, smoothing his thumb once more over the ink and sending chills up my arm.

He's so perceptive, unlike so many people who'd known me for so long.

I guess I can tell him.

"They are my take on yearning. You see, the moth is darkness, chasing the butterfly, craving the brightness of it. But when the moth is the one running, the butterfly, being light, chases it in return, unable to exist without the moth, because without darkness there is no light."

Lanston smiles. "That's lovely. And what of the

things they hide?" he says more delicately, his lashes hood those beautiful eyes.

I waver. It's not something I've spoken about before.

My eyes lift to his. Only kindness and understanding live there and I know I'm safe to tell him.

"They can never hide those things for long."

Lanston leaves it at that. He can see the tears starting to brim in the corners of my eyes and doesn't push any further. I find that I'm drawn to his patience. His understanding and care. But it makes me consider all those who weren't kind and patient with me when I still breathed and walked with blood in my veins. Lanston makes me see things differently.

We curl up on his bed and enjoy the movie. Silent and letting the fears from the music room fade. Whatever is in there, it isn't bad. That much was clear. If it was, it would've been more frightening, like Those Who Whisper. But it felt more playful than cruel.

I grab a handful of popcorn and Lanston reaches in at the same moment. Our hands brush. My gaze finds his, lying this close on the bed, our noses nearly touch. My traitorous eyes dip to his lips and lift back to his eyes.

For a delusional moment, I think he'll kiss me.

But when he doesn't, I force my attention back to the

screen. A girl cries in the movie and runs home in the rain. I relate to her in so many ways right now.

I feel foolish for even thinking he'd be sharing the same lewd thoughts.

The movie ends with a happy ending and our popcorn bowl is empty. Lanston eyes his door like he's thinking about getting up and moving the chair.

"Don't even think about moving it." I stand and lift a spare pillow off my bed and toss it at him. He catches it and laughs.

"I wouldn't dare. I was contemplating on adding a second chair."

He sets the pillow down next to his and my cheeks warm. *He meant it when he said I could stay in his bed.*

He notices me in thought and says, "You still scared? Or do you feel better now?"

I want to stay in his bed. I really do. But I can't get attached, so I shake my head. "I feel much better after the movie. Thanks, Lanston." My smile falters.

He deflates a bit but doesn't let it show. "For what?"

"For being so kind."

There really aren't many people like him out in the world anymore. When did we, as humans, become so cold and withdrawn? How many Lanstons did I need when I was alive? More than I can count.

I crawl into the spare bed and pull the sheets up high to my chin, facing Lanston. He does the same, shutting off his lamp and staring back at me—only the moonlight between us again, like back in my opera house.

"*Hey* dreary girl."

I chuckle. "What?"

In the dim light, I can barely make out his sharp cheekbones, but if I shut my eyes, I can see him perfectly in my mind: his soft brown hair and rosy lips. The dark circles beneath his eyes that allude to his restlessness. Yet he's still so profoundly handsome.

"Come with me to the music room tomorrow to catch a ghost and take back my hat?" There's a hint of a laugh in his voice.

"Are you asking me on a date?"

"A phantomly date."

We both quietly laugh as if anyone can really hear us. Two phantoms sharing jokes in the dark. Oh, how far we've fallen from the typical portrayal of ghosts.

"A ghostly rendezvous," I say through giggles.

Pfft. Lanston's shoulders shake with laughter.

I could get used to the sound of such happiness. Such weightlessness from the both of us.

"Put the broom down. What do you honestly expect to do with that?" I nudge Lanston playfully and he gives me an *"I'm not putting down the broom"* look.

"It's better than nothing, isn't it?" He can't even stop himself from smiling.

We're both peeking into the music room, looking for any signs of a hiding phantom. The bay windows let in a massive amount of light; it's almost silly that we are unwilling to enter the room.

"What are you two doing?"

"Yelina!" Lanston shouts; then, after clearing his throat and picking up his faithful broom he'd just thrown, mutters, "Fuck, why would you sneak up on us like that?"

Yelina puts her hand on her hip and gives him *and* me a once over, looking mildly annoyed but more interested in what we're up to. My eyes lift to her shoulders. A wisp of smoke curls faintly before it vanishes, and I know then that she's one of the victims of the fire.

She's a stunning woman. Long blonde hair with an icy tone, not brassy-yellow. Her makeup is the definition of perfection; the dark liner of her eye-wings is flawless and the blush of her cheek bones is lovely.

Yelina is intimidating as hell.

"Why are you two sneaking around and acting like weirdos?" she snaps back, looking into the music room warily.

Me and Lanston share a look.

Are we really going to tell her and risk sounding crazy as fuck?

Lanston shrugs. "None of your business."

Yelina snatches the broom from his hands and is about to fire off another round of insults before another gal strolls into the hallway. She has a lovely pear-shaped face, a button nose, and bright, kind eyes. Her brown hair is pulled back into a loose braid.

She walks right up to Yelina and smiles awkwardly. "What are you two arguing about now?" The way she says it makes it seem like this is very much not a one-time occurrence between them.

Lanston rolls his eyes, and it's the first I've seen it so I crack a wide smile.

Yelina looks at me and I instantly wipe the grin from my lips. She assesses me before speaking to the other girl. "Nothing, Poppie. The two of them are just acting... odd."

Poppie giggles, and I find her much more approachable than Yelina.

In an attempt to thwart any more arguing between Yelina and Lanston, I say sheepishly, "Have you two heard of a ghost haunting this room?" They look at each other before glancing back at me.

Poppie asks, "Are you talking about Charlie?"

I blink a few times. Dumbfounded.

Lanston does too.

"Wait, Charlie, as in one of the missing patients who died, *Charlie?*" Lanston blurts out and both Yelina and Poppie start laughing.

Yelina covers her mouth as she says sardonically, "You two were scared of him? He plays pranks in here all the time. Lanston, I swear Jericho introduced you to him like two years ago."

Lanston's face is blank as he searches his memories,

but he shakes his head. "No way, I would've remembered."

"Ugh, stand up, both of you. I'll introduce you so you can be done with this." Yelina grins cruelly as she steps over us and into the music room. Poppie giggles and offers me her hand.

"I swear she's actually really nice," she whispers so Yelina won't overhear her.

Somehow I find that hard to believe, but I guess I'll find out in time.

Lanston groans as he stands and waits for Poppie to head in before he looks at me and murmurs, "Sorry about them. I really don't remember meeting this guy. But I guess it will be pretty cool to talk to him."

I nod. "Yeah, it's been fifteen years that he's been here. I'm curious to hear what he knows about purgatory and why he hasn't passed. It's sort of sad." I look at the dusty music room and wonder how long it's been his prison. But a more dreadful thought beckons in the back of my mind.

How long can we truly stay in the in-between?

13

Lanston

Yelina and Poppie walk over to the piano and slowly sit on the ebony bench. Ophelia looks around the room for any signs of Charlie as she circles the floral sofa and sits quietly beside me.

Part of me still thinks they're pulling a prank on us.

Though it'd make sense, and of everyone, I'm the least likely to know. I've been avoiding the music room for years. The only memories brought back to me are of Wynn and Liam playing those sad songs they enjoyed so much.

"Charlie, are you scaring the residents again?" Yelina calls out playfully.

Poppie has a content grin on her face, but Ophelia

wraps her hands around her elbows, still not so sure about this. The feeling is mutual.

A key taps repeatedly at the end of the piano—the low-pitch startling Ophelia straight into my lap. My smile is instant and I secure my arms around her to assure her I'm here.

"Charlie!" Poppie laughs and puts her hands on her hips. Yelina offers her hand to the air and a phantom forms—a broad-figured man, probably mid-twenties, with short blonde hair and glasses that make him look intelligent.

Hardly what I imagined he'd look like.

Charlie presses a kiss to the back of Yelina's hand and winks at Poppie. Both girls giggle as he lets his attention wander over to us. Ophelia remains in my arms, seemingly unwilling to budge.

The phantom smirks at us and says, "Sorry about yesterday. I couldn't help myself when I overheard all your theories." His voice is low but filled with an airy weightlessness.

I raise a brow. "Did Crosby really kill you?" The question is harsh and sudden, but I have to know.

Charlie's features fall, turning cold and pale. "Yeah, along with my friends." Yelina and Poppie frown beside him and let their hands rest on his shoulders.

Ophelia slowly rises from my lap and stands before Charlie. The top of her head only reaches his neck. She asks softly, "Why are you still here, Charlie? Do you know how to pass on? Where are the others?"

His lips flatten with thought. Then he nods his head to the chairs and sofa. "Let's all sit down and I'll catch you up."

Ophelia returns to her spot beside me while Yelina and Poppie take the two lounging chairs across from us. Charlie sits on the floor to finish the small circle we've inevitably created.

Folding his hands together in his lap, Charlie says, "The others left after the murders were solved. Anger and rage are what held us here. So, after the bodies were found and Crosby was killed, we were able to pass on. But I can't leave until I find my picture of Lucie. Crosby hid my satchel with everything I cherished. He liked to play cruel tricks on us." His tone fills with grief.

Picture of Lucie? He's stayed all this time for a photo?

"Can't you just go see her?" I ask.

Charlie shakes his head and looks longingly out the windows. "I don't know where she is out in the big world... We were going to get married once I got better. But then I was declared missing for a decade. She probably thinks I ran away and left her and everything behind." He pauses and seems lost in thought. "I just want to see her one last time before I go."

Ophelia's eyes flicker over to me. They're filled with sympathy and I already know she wants to help him. I love that she carries her heart on her sleeve, even if she thinks she doesn't.

"Where have you looked? Where's left?" Ophelia

asks, leaning forward and taking Charlie's hand in an effort to comfort him.

"You'd help me?" He looks at the four of us and we all nod.

I can't help but think how sad it is that his ghost has been reluctant to leave over a simple photo. Can our reasons to linger truly be so small? It must be more than that.

Yelina adds, "Of course, we'll help. It's everyone's goal to pass on, after all."

He smiles and relief relaxes his face. "I've searched Harlow thoroughly so I doubt it's here. I have a feeling he hid it somewhere in Bakersville, but I never knew the places he frequented."

My veins chill like frost slowly freezing a river. I know one spot we can look.

"The lookout," I mumble.

Poppie looks at me. "The what?"

"I know where we can look in town." I stand, eager to get there and help Charlie find the peace he's been deprived of. This may be the answer we've been searching for. If finding it allows him to pass, we will finally have something to work toward.

If the photo works for him, maybe the bucket list will work for me. I hesitantly let my eyes lift to her—she who is so damaged and broken like me. Maybe we can find our peace together.

Ophelia notices my enthusiasm to find the photo.

Her expression softens on me and she stands as she says, "Let's go look."

Ophelia borrows a loose-fitting, cream-colored shirt from Poppie and high-waisted denim jeans from Yelina. The front of her shirt is tucked and she ties her hair back with a cream and pink floral hair tie.

I stare at her as she walks over to me with two paper cups in hand, admiring her tattoos and wondering if I am the moth or the butterfly.

We parked on the main street and decided to indulge while we were here. I've been waiting on the bench I tend to frequent when I feel like people-watching. Five years. It's still so much the same as it was when I was alive. The slow life of a small town, the stress-free grins of the townsfolk who enjoy this quiet place. I envy them and their ignorance of the ghosts that observe their day-to-day lives.

"Here you are, no cream like you so insanely requested." Ophelia hands me the drink, and I grin at her.

"It's an acquired taste," I say like a dignified asshole. She glowers and rolls her eyes before I nudge her with my shoulder. "This is a cute town, isn't it?"

She sips her hot drink and nods as she sweeps the shops with her eyes. "It's a shame all those bad things that happened here tainted its name. I heard that tourism went down and some shops suffered because of it. But the Fall Festival is still a hit."

"You hear a lot of talk around the city, don't you? I'm starting to think I've been roomed with a bar fly." I wink when she glares at me and her expression lightens again.

"I usually hang out in cafés actually. It's nice to see friends getting together after a long time apart or sisters catching a quick lunch between shifts." She smiles, her lips still pressed to the lid of her coffee cup. "It's a good way to get caught up with the latest buzz too, you know?" She looks at me and I nod.

We're so similar, yet so different. I like to sit here on this bench that no one ever visits and wallow in silence, while she spends her time in busy coffee shops just to enjoy the frequency people give off when they're chatting and laughing together.

She's the light. I am darkness.

She's the butterfly, I decide. *I am the moth.*

The real question is, will we catch each other or will we continue to chase one another in a dreary cycle? I suppose time will lend us the answer eventually, but I'm in no hurry. I quite enjoy this journey I've found myself on with her.

As the thought leaves me, I glance down at her and find her soft brown and green-speckled eyes studying my face. She quickly looks away as if I've caught her red-handed and I hide my amusement by taking a long sip from my coffee.

It's all I can think of doing to keep from kissing her. The careful stolen glances that she takes to observe me light my skin on fire and burn into my core. I want to hold her hand and whisper sweet things to her, press my lips against the crook of her lithe neck and tenderly bite her just enough to get her writhing.

Wait—stop. Don't think of that *now*.

I clear my throat. "Well, shall we go to the lookout?" I ask with a shaky voice and hurriedly stand. She's a beat behind me, at my side in the next.

We walk down the main street, passing shops and parlors before the neighborhood district. Then a few blocks until we reach the bottom of the cliffside. The cement stairs have been seared into my memory. I've been here many times, in life and after. I remember every shrub and lamp post, every crack and new ones that have formed over the years.

My eyes always flick to the temporary apartment that Wynn and I stayed in before everything ended. The owner sold the building a few years back and now it's just a storage unit.

I look up the stairway and to the railing of the lookout above. Nostalgia overwhelms me tonight. I'm revisited by thoughts of Liam and Wynn, tattoos and pink hair.

"You okay?" Ophelia's hand smooths down the side of my arm and brings me back to the present. "It happened up there, didn't it?" she asks softly.

I nod sadly and murmur, "Yes, and I've been here

many times since. I just feel so—" I pause because I can't put a word to it.

She gives me a weak smile. "Sad?"

"Yeah... I guess so." It's close enough. But other emotions mingle with the sadness.

"It's okay to be sad, Lanston." She squeezes my arm reassuringly and then walks ahead of me, ascending the steps as she says, "I'm sad too, more than I care to admit."

I follow behind her and try to focus on looking around the underbrush for any sign of a satchel. Though, now that I'm here I think it's stupid that I thought to look here. Where would someone hide a satchel out here without it being found or destroyed by the environment?

"Yeah? Why are you sad?" I ask absently, letting my eyes wander. Somehow, they end up on her.

She stops once we reach the parking lot at the top and turns, giving me an inquiring look. "I'm sad because I wish you hadn't died here, Lanston." She stares off toward the tainted field. "But you did."

A cold breeze ruffles my hair and sends a chill down my spine.

"I did."

"And now we have to make the most of it." Ophelia faces me stoically, the wind moving her hair over her shoulder. "I'm happy to have met your ghost. You are the first person to make me feel..." her brows pull together as she thinks.

"Less alone?" I take a step toward her. The earth

could tilt on its axis and still I would not move from this spot—from where she stands, mere inches away.

Her features soften.

"Like I was never alone," she confesses and closes the space between us. The last threads of the sunset caress our cheeks.

Her lips part and she looks up at me with hooded eyes.

I want to kiss her. Desperately. But I don't want to ruin what little trust we've built between us already. So I give her a mild grin and look around the parking lot. "Let's check around the rock retaining wall and around the lot," I breathe out, sounding disappointed with myself.

She frowns, and I know it then that I made her feel unwanted. *Shit.* I've been out of the romance game for so long now. I open my mouth to say something, *anything*, that might fix the awkward silence that ensues, but she turns sharply.

"Sounds good. I'll look over here," she says coldly.

Goddamnit.

14

Ophelia

There's nothing wrong with me. He's just being polite. Lanston doesn't come off as the kiss-you-hard-on-the-third-day-I-know-you type of guy.

I blow out a breath.

I have to tell myself that a few times as I look for a fifteen-year-old satchel in the dark. We search for over thirty minutes before ultimately joining back at the top of the stairwell. The only source of light is from the lamp posts. Lanston waits, leaning over the edge with his forearms against the railing.

He really is stuck in his past. I observe him before getting closer, trying to picture him before. He seems like someone who used to smile constantly, the light of the party.

A smile pulls at the corner of my lips as I think of something that might cheer him up.

I walk straight by him and start walking down the stairs to the neighborhood below. I cast a look over my shoulder up at him, finding his gaze heavy on me. Confusion pulls at his features for only a second, then he catches my wicked grin and shoves off the rails.

"Where are you going?" he calls after me, but I quicken my pace down the stairs and his footsteps hasten.

It's hard to keep in the laughter that bubbles up from my throat, but I manage as I try to focus on each step. The second my feet hit the ground level of the dark neighborhood, I'm racing off toward the alley.

I slow as I pass a small yellow house with a trashed backyard. There's an old swing set at the center. My feet falter as I take in the familiar setting—the carelessness of the home's appearance and the clutter that's been left to the elements and time.

My family had this exact swing set. The two chain-link swings slowly glide back and forth in the breeze. Lanston's footsteps draw closer, but I don't look at him as he slows. He stands beside me, only his breath disturbing the cold evening air. Warmth rolls off his skin and his lovely scent of torn pages invades my senses.

My jaw sets as I refuse to let my gaze lift from the swings.

"What's wrong?" Lanston dips down, setting both

hands on either of my arms so his face is level with mine. He inspects me for any harm, but when he finds none, he focuses on my eyes.

I force my jaw to unclench and bury my teeth into my lower lip. Why do I find the swing set so upsetting? My gut twists.

He follows my gaze and looks at the swings. His hands loosen but he doesn't let me go. Instead, he pulls me in for a tight hug. I'm so surprised by it that I let out a small gasp that gets caught in the fabric of his sweater. One of his hands braces my midback, securing me close to his chest, while his other cups the back of my neck. He rests his head on mine and my eyes widen.

Tears roll down my cheek and fall on his sweater—I hadn't realized they'd even formed.

"It's okay to be sad, my rose," he whispers, and the sound of his voice is all I can hear in a world so dark.

How long has it been since I've been embraced like this? I let my eyes fall closed and decide that I don't care. I don't want to remember anything except this—only him.

I raise my hands and press them to his shoulder blades, embracing him as endearingly as he does me. The warmth of his chest draws a sensation of security into my heart.

He pecks a kiss on the top of my head and slowly pulls away, grinning sadly and shaking his head. "Want to tell me what's wrong?"

It's impossible not to smile back at a man such as Lanston Nevers.

"I'll tell if you do," I say quietly, as if someone might hear us.

Lanston brushes his thumb over my cheek; heat follows in its wake as my cheeks flush.

"Deal." He looks up at the roof of the house, then back to me. "Ever sit on a roof before?"

I crack a half-grin. "Of course."

"Here, I'll help you up." He doesn't even bother asking as he grabs my hand and guides us over to the side of the yellow house. He lifts me up on top of a garbage can and I manage to climb up from there. Lanston doesn't have any trouble climbing on his own, and he nods to the center of the roof where the peak resides.

We sit together with our shoulders touching, hands gently entwined. I've half forgotten what we even came up here to discuss before he breaks the silence.

"I keep thinking about how I'll never be able to make new memories with them." My heart breaks with the sorrow in his voice. I stare down at our hands joined, fingers interlaced and gently brushing together. "I never got to be anything but the fuck-up son. The friend who died."

I take a deep breath and look up at the sky breaking with clouds and stars.

"I'm certain that's not true," I tell him gently.

He leans his head against mine and murmurs back, "How can you be so sure?"

"Your mind will lie to you more than anyone else will, Lanston. You weren't a fuck-up and you were not just the *friend who died*." I pause to let that sit with him a moment. "You are a *hero*. Why are you the only one who cannot see that?"

He lets out a weary laugh. "Because I don't feel like a hero. I'm just... me. Sad. Depressed... dead."

"I'll remind you forever if I have to," I threaten. He doesn't make a sound, but I can feel his grin against my shoulder.

"I could get used to that."

"I'm sure you could."

"Now you."

My stomach churns and my gaze falls back to the swings below. I think for a long moment, trapped in a place I'd forgotten or rather chose to leave behind.

Lanston shifts, his chin now resting on my shoulder and his lips coasting the tender flesh of my ear. Our interlocked hands on his thigh burn hotter.

"Does it have to do with your murder?" he asks sincerely.

My eyes wince instinctively at that word. "Not really, but I guess it's where it started."

This close, I can feel each breath he takes, drawing cool spells over my skin. I crave this sort of affection. The kind that is patient and attentive. Quiet but so loud in every other sense.

I swallow.

"My parents had a swing set just like that one. A yard just as trashed too. When I was in trouble, my stepmom would lock me out of the house and leave me outside for hours alone. I would sit on the swings for so long that I had indented lines on the bottom of my thighs." The knot in my throat builds and I know I can't swallow it. "After the years passed and I grew older, I'd just leave and go crash at a friend's house instead. But I never forgot about the swings and how long I sat there, wondering why I was so bad. I really tried, you know. I would tell myself, *tomorrow I'll be better. I can change.*"

Lanston lifts his head off my shoulder and I know he's looking at me, but I'm not ready to meet his gaze.

I let out a sad, bitter laugh. "Do you want to know the fucked up part? My being *bad* was stupid shit that kids are supposed to do. I grew to hate the things I couldn't change about myself. The way I craved to sing and dance more than anything. I grew to hate myself."

He squeezes my hand harder and only then do I meet his eyes. They're filled with many words, many apologies that no one else would say when I truly needed them.

"The swings remind you of your stolen childhood," he finally says.

I ponder the statement, then nod.

From up here, I'm beginning to see how small the swings truly are. How insignificant and unimportant, and yet they manage to trigger me in many ways. Loneliness, mainly, I think. The hours of dried tear stains and cold fingers curled helplessly on the chains.

"When I look at them, all the rejection and abandonment return. And all the partial healing I've managed is gone."

Silence.

Lanston springs to his feet. My head snaps up to his, automatically following his motion. The tears that had started to brim in my eyes are swiftly blinked away. He's pulling me up before I can even utter a word.

"Let's fuck up that swing set!" he shouts to the universe, chin raised dramatically, before looking back down at me and scooping me up into his arms, then running down the roof.

I instinctively let out a scream and cling to his shoulders. "Lanston!" I laugh-shout.

But he doesn't stop. He leaps off the roof, laughing like a complete psycho, and lands on both feet with a small grunt. As the cold night air recedes, a playful heat rushes through my veins.

He sets me down and grabs a bat from one of the piles of trash in the yard. "Here—Fuck. It. Up." His smile is bright and void of any thoughts.

"Why? That's insane–"

"I swear you'll feel better."

I consider him for a moment and then sigh, taking the wooden bat from his outstretched hand. "Fine. But you have to help."

He throws his head back and laughs. "Like I'd sit this one out." He winks and grabs a long pipe.

The following five minutes are the best of my entire life. The absolute rush of adrenaline that pumps through my veins is intoxicating. Blood rushes to my head and laughter escapes my lips without any effort. I swing the bat like I've never swung before. The chained swings shatter and break into pieces across the yard.

Lanston laughs beside me, swinging just as hard and breaking the legs of the set. His shirt lifts with each swing and I watch as his muscles flex and move so flawlessly. His spine is defined and one small, round red spot at the center of it stops my heart.

His trace of death.

The sad thought only lasts a second because his maniacal, larger-than-life grin grounds me back into the moment. He tosses his pipe and grabs the bat from my hands, throwing it behind him and reaching for my hand.

I burst into laughter again. "What are you doing now?"

He pulls me behind him, two phantoms running down a dark alley in the middle of the night, and shouts, "We just destroyed personal property! We have to get the fuck out of here."

Lanston knows as well as I do that the swings are intact on the living side. Our debauchery has no consequences, but I play along because this is easily the best night of my life.

We don't stop running until we reach his crotch rocket back on the main street. On the ride back to Harlow, I squeeze him tighter than I usually do with a smile that warms my soul.

15

Ophelia

We arrive back at Harlow with empty hands, but our spirits are high.

Hopefully Yelina and Poppie had better luck searching through the moonflower field, but my expectations are not high.

Poor Charlie. He's been lingering around here for such a long time.

Lanston parks his bike in the driveway; not a single light is on in the manor, making the mist that seeps between the pines in the distance more eerie.

"I knew it was a long shot, but I'm still disappointed we didn't find anything," I say as we walk toward the front doors.

Lanston offers me his hand and a small smile spreads over my somber expression.

"You know, I think I have one more spot we can check. No expectations though."

"Really? Where?"

"Come on, I'll show you." Lanston leads us along the side of Harlow and back toward the greenhouse. We walk by the tables of plants and straight toward the back.

I didn't see the door in the back yesterday with all the leafy ferns covering the area around it. But there it is. The knob is brass and looks rusted and unused. Lanston twists it and has to jostle the handle a few times before it opens.

"Charming," I say, scrunching my nose at the mildewy smell that seeps from the room.

"You have no idea." Lanston's voice is low with distaste as he leads us into the room. He turns on the single light bulb that swings from a cord above. The room is drab and covered with dust—a drain lined with rust at the center of the floor.

"Oh my God, this is disgusting." I cover my mouth and look around warily at the shelves packed with things no one has touched in years—boxes and crates filled with an assortment of papers and random lawn-care equipment.

As my eyes skirt across the shelves, ceasing on a coat rack with jackets hanging by hooks, it looks like there might be something beneath them.

I squeeze Lanston's hand and he looks at me, then follows my line of sight.

"No way," he says, exasperated. He moves toward the coat rack and lifts the first jacket, careful not to get dust or grime on himself. The black coat falls to the floor and the next one is brown, then a woman's small cardigan.

Beneath that is a worn satchel.

We both freeze. Lanston looks back at me with an incredulous expression.

"After all this time, it's been here all along?" I say somberly.

Lanston nods grimly as he lifts the satchel. "The best hiding spots are in plain sight. Crosby came here often to punish Liam."

My stomach sinks with that image. I don't know them, or what the punishment entailed, but the swirls of red on the cement floor make it easy to imagine heinous things.

We hurry back to Harlow, eager to leave the storage room.

The corridor leading to the music room is vacant. All the other phantoms must be asleep at this hour. Though we're much later than we said we'd return, Yelina and Poppie are waiting inside, lying on the floor, with Charlie across from them and playing a game of chess. The fireplace in the corner flickers a warm ambient light over them. Their calm and lovely nature, with half-drunken smiles and glasses of wine, make them paint-worthy. A scene that you'd find in a museum somewhere where only a few people stop to look.

The three of them lift their heads, and I watch as disbelief spreads across their expressions. Charlie pushes himself up onto his elbows.

Lanston crosses the room and lowers to his knee, handing the satchel over to its rightful owner. Charlie is hesitant at first, almost in denial that we actually found it. Or perhaps it's fear of what awaits him should this photo let him pass on.

I sit next to Lanston and Poppie, excitement and uncertainty making my breath uneven and staggered as Charlie slowly opens his satchel.

His brown eyes soften as he seems to recognize the contents inside.

"This is it," he whispers. The silence that follows is thick; none of us dare breathe as he pulls out a pair of glasses, an old book, and then a faded photograph. He holds it to the fireplace light, and tears fall from his cheeks.

"My darling." His voice is weak, pressing the picture close to his chest as if he cannot stand to be apart from her a minute longer.

I admire his devotion and love for her. His love is tireless, even after so many years. My eyes drift to Lanston. His neck is exposed to me and I can only see the back side of his jaw from where I sit. Every bit of him is lovely. I picture what it might be like for him to love me as much as Charlie does his lost lover. Coveting and always yearning for my presence, would he draw circles on my skin with his fingertips? Press kisses along the delicate flesh of my neck?

Lanston must sense my eyes on him because he turns and meets my gaze. He stares right back into my soul, thousands of embers flickering through his hazel eyes. I could kiss him and never know anything else because right now, I'm not sure anything else would matter.

Only him.

Yelina gasps. "Charlie, what's happening?"

The sound of her panic draws both our attention back to Charlie. My eyes widen.

He's disappearing, but he seems entirely at peace with it and wears a comforting smile.

"I'm finally ready," he says. I've never heard a voice so calm. He looks at each of us and shuts his eyes. "Thank you for helping me pass on. Perhaps we'll meet again."

Poppie bursts into tears and takes Charlie's hands. "Oh, Charlie, we will! I'll find you and we can play chess and tell stories like we always did." She drags her sleeve over her eyes. Yelina wraps her arms around her friend and sniffles back her own tears.

Charlie leans forward and grins sadly at them both. "Perhaps, one day. Farewell."

His ghost fades until nothing remains of him, and the four of us are left staring at the empty place where he was a moment ago. It was beautiful and peaceful, so why do I have a pit growing in my throat? Fear slips between my ribs and tangles in my veins like a snake.

How do we know we all get to go like that? What if we are bad? Where do the bad people go? I swallow and try not to let my nerves get the best of me.

The only sound is Poppie's soft cries.

"That's the first time I've actually witnessed someone pass to the other side." I break the silence. The three of them look at me, but no one says a word.

Surely, we must all be thinking the same thing.

What lies after?

Drifting.

That's what I call the strange dissociation we seem to experience here—drawn into our thoughts like the depths of a deep lake. Sometimes, it feels as though weights are pulling down on our legs, making it harder to hear the surface. It is as if we are drowning—slowly and without awareness of it.

It's terrifying to feel as though you're losing yourself bit by bit.

Lanston has been standing by his window for hours now; the sun soon to rise. I watch him with curiosity. His baseball cap is set on the edge of his bed. He's more handsome without it, like a lovely statue that stares into the unknown. The planes of his skin are smooth and hard, and the features of his face are sharp and angular.

He's been somber since we returned to his room. Charlie's passing was heavy for Poppie and Yelina to process too. I wonder how Jericho will take it. Maybe he'll implement new ideas to help phantoms pass on. He's got quite the job here. Unpaid, I might add. But you can tell his heart is in it fully. The way he nostalgically walks the halls in, what I assume are, the same patterns and routines he did when he was alive.

We grow tired of this world here where no one can find us.

We wish to go.

I can see it in Lanston's slouched shoulders. He wants to fade into whatever lies after. A cold and weary thought braces me. *We can never be together. I want to stay.* If there's one thing I know without a shadow of a doubt, it is that I cannot go. Those Who Whisper have told me where people like me go. I won't.

Dreariness thickens inside me and hollows out my heart. Why did I come here... why do I find him so inebriating that I can't step away? *No. I must return home.*

It's better this way. No matter how much I desire to be near him.

I lie back on my bed and let my head fall to the right side. His nightstand is bare, but seeing it reminds me that he slipped his drawing pad inside. I glance his way quickly to make sure he's not going to come out of his drifting anytime soon. His drawer opens without a sound and I pull out the bundle of papers quietly.

The binding is old, the kind that makes you feel like you're in another place in time, scribbling away by candlelight.

I eagerly flip it open and raise my brows at the black, chalky smears across the pages. They are drawings of creatures, forlorn and morbid. The first one looks like an elk with long, entangled horns that curl high above the creature's head. The body is lithe, as if the skin is merely draped over the bones like a thin sheet, with no muscles or flesh to mediate the spaces in between.

A fleshless creature with hollowed, sleepless eyes.

As terrifying as it is, I find a wealth of beauty in it—a sad story left untold.

I hear you. I smooth my fingertips gently over the surface of the page, careful not to smear the black charcoal.

A shadow moves over the pages and I glance up to meet Lanston's weary eyes. There's not a flicker of anger, just understanding of my curiosity and perhaps some vulnerability too.

"What do you see?" he asks, his voice sounding broken and weary.

Our eyes don't break the connection as I say, "I see a tired man. He's barely holding onto himself and he's wearing false skin to hide what's beneath. A facade."

He doesn't respond, but his eyes weaken and he blinks as his jaw clenches.

"But he doesn't need to hide anymore. His feet are already visible; he only needs to take a step out into the world he fears most," I say softly, and something shifts inside me as I watch hope return to his eyes.

Maybe if I'd met him sooner, Those Who Whisper wouldn't have found me.

Maybe I would've asked to make a bucket list with him.

"Ophelia," he says in a deep, smooth voice.

He holds his hand out to me and I stare at his beautiful fingers, calloused like an artist's should be.

"Come with me to explore the world."

Everything stops and my heart breaks. I can't go with him. I'm scared of what awaits me. My eyes lift to his and I find a million wishes in them—my hand moves of its own accord, tracing over his cheek.

"Why me?" I ask breathlessly.

Lanston laughs. "What do you mean why? I like you... and we have fun together. I can't remember the last time I've laughed as much as I do with you," he admits.

I shake my head. "I don't know... I'm not much the traveling type." The corner of his lip kicks up and he pulls my hand, making me stand.

"Well, what if we write out a bucket list? Maybe if you see it on paper, you'll have a change of heart?" His voice is filled with hope, and the dread of letting him down sinks further into me. Like steel bars piercing through organs. He lets go of my hand and reaches for his notebook, flipping to the next blank page before sitting on his bed. He pats the center of the mattress for me to join him. I smile weakly and concede.

We sit in the darkness, with moonlight streaming in and lowered lamps lighting the page. We sip coffee as we make a shitty list of things we wanted to do in life:

<u>Lanston & Ophelia's Bucket List</u>
Go to Paris
Sail a yacht
Ballroom dance
Drink on the beach at night/camp out
Ride a train somewhere new
Visit Ireland's Trinity College Library
Save a stray plant

Seeing our agendas blended like this makes my heart still. It looks like lovers' plans for their honeymoon or dreams scrawled over a napkin quickly in a diner. I think of how much this list must mean to him. To find his peace.

I smirk at the last one. Lanston shrugs as he says easily, "You've inspired me."

My lips curl at the corners and I raise my pinky. "Promise you'll save one?"

His smile is slow and thoughtful, then his pinky meets mine and warmth blooms between us. "Already planning on stealing a watering tin."

Lanston's eyes are etched with red, weariness pulling at him like an intruding storm. I smile through the anguish that drowns me.

I can't tell him that I'm leaving.

His eyes flick down to my lips, remaining there, and finally, he whispers, "Will you stay with me?"

Will I stay?

He falls back against his pillows and then I understand. I grin and nod, pulling the sheets back, cozying in beside him and turning off the bedside lamp. We face each other, foreheads almost touching.

"I meant what I said, you know," he says in a low, hushed tone.

"What?"

"That I like you." His eyes are half-lidded and he has a drowsy grin that's enough to stop my heart.

I shouldn't have come here with him.

"You know I like you too, Lanston," I say quietly, sounding guilty.

He just chuckles a few times and pulls me in closer, wrapping his arms around me and pressing a kiss to the top of my head.

"Promise?"

I swallow.

"Yeah."

It's quiet. His breaths have grown heavy.

I lean back slowly and look up, seeing his lashes flutter with dreams. I inch my way out from beneath his arms and shift until I'm sitting on the edge of the bed. I look back at him, keenly aware that I'm doing exactly what he did a few nights ago that I got mad at him over. His beauty demands attention. The sadness that etches his slumbering features calls to be observed and studied.

"I hope you find everything you deserve in this world," I whisper, my lips so close to his that I fear he might wake. My hushed voice falls upon his dreaming mind, and I tell him, "I'm sorry."

His face is unbothered; he heard nothing, but it still feels better that I said it. "You're such a lovely creature, Lanston. Even though you see yourself as a wolf wearing tattered, thin skin; I see the warm, white coat beneath it. You're only afraid for others to see your beauty. Hush that fear, darling. Let yourself be free."

I press a kiss to his forehead and let my fingers glide through his soft, light brown hair.

"*Ophelia*," Lanston murmurs softly, dreamily.

My smile fades and I brush his cheek one last time before standing and leaving his room. I walk out Harlow Sanctum's doors and down the long stretch of driveway leading away from it. My feet carry me past towns and bridges until I'm standing inside my dark opera house once more.

I can never leave. I am a phantom made to remain, to haunt the abandoned, lonely places of the universe. There will be no dark corner where I am not. For here, I stay.

"I hope he does the stupid bucket list and finds his peace," I whisper to one of my pothos plants. My iPod is a first gen and hardly works, but I turn on my favorite self-loathing song: "Ava" by Famy. Then I step foot on the worn stage and I dance alone.

Alone, as I've always been, as I despise myself for being.

But it's better this way.

16

Lanston

Despair consumes me as I search the grounds for her.

I held her so close last night, but when I woke, my arms were cold and my Ophelia was gone. A chill floods through my veins.

She wouldn't leave like this. *She wouldn't.*

I'm usually good at suppressing emotions, but she knows how to really get beneath my skin and rustle old wounds. Our bucket list is crumpled in my left hand, fisted tightly as I check everywhere I can think of. I end my search in the foyer, reluctantly coming to the conclusion that she isn't here.

Did she wait to leave after I fell asleep? Why does that hurt so much?

Why doesn't anyone I develop feelings for stay?

Snakes coil inside my stomach as rage and sadness war inside my head. I bury my face in my hands. *Abandonment.* My weakness. My forever trigger. It stings almost as much as the fucking bullet that killed me. I ache inside with more emotions than I've felt in years.

She left me.

I'm always the one left behind.

The remaining spring days move slowly. The moon goes through its phases and more phantoms start to leave Harlow.

It's her fault, I think to myself, weary and half-drunk on the rum I'd been saving. My frown grows as I stare at the books piled in the corner of my room. I've read them all four times over and need a visit to the bookstore. I sigh and lean back against my wall; palms braced on the cold tiles of my floor.

Jericho was inspired by Ophelia's notion of the bucket list and Charlie's ability to pass after finding his missing photo—so much so that he implemented it in his program. He wants phantoms to move on and find their reasons, but it only bleeds what's left of Harlow into a shell. The halls have become empty, and the counseling groups now have vacant seats.

Yelina and Poppie decide to stay, but they are among the few that remain. Jericho has developed a look in his eyes, a longing for the world beyond these walls.

I fear he will soon pursue that call too.

It's her fault that Harlow is changing, I think as I browse the bookstore. The shoppers are clueless about my existence and the way I move about them. Each book I pull off the shelf is very much real to me, but when I glance back to the original, it's as if I've never touched it. The notion of my inability to reach the living world claws at my heart, creating fresh wounds where old ones have long since scabbed over.

One book in particular catches my eye. It has a dark cover and a very gothic aesthetic. A smile spreads over my lips as I instantly think how Ophelia would love it. There's a pain that lingers in my jaw as I grind my teeth together. Against my anger toward her, I grab it anyway because I know how much she'd adore it. Just in case I happen to see her again—a thought that both irritates me and fills the void she left inside my chest.

Sometimes, I pretend to check out and pay like a person, but today, I'm feeling rather somber. I leave the bookstore with a handful of books in my backpack and glance over my shoulder to make sure no one truly sees me. They don't. Of course.

My feet carry me back toward the alley that leads to the lookout, but instead of heading to the summit like I normally would, I stop at the swing set that troubled Ophelia so much. Although we completely destroyed it, it's back as it was. It was so the moment we ran away from it that night.

I stare down at the old chains and the plastic seats for a long while before allowing myself to sit down on one. It brings me nostalgia. Of all the times I'd been alone on the elementary school playground and even after hours when I'd run away from home to avoid my father's cruel gaze.

Did she have similar thoughts? Perhaps worse.

I tighten my grip on the chains and push the ground so the swing glides. The air is stagnant, but the small motion soothes something inside me. I glance to the swing beside me. Her absence creates a new hole in my chest. One much louder and more profound than I ever thought possible.

She never seemed to mind my silence, and I didn't mind hers. But her presence is something I yearn for—her soft stolen glances at me and the blush of her cheeks. Her words that no one else can speak.

I miss her.

By midsummer, the sun is hot and the walls of Harlow have started to turn gray. Almost as if the phantoms that resided within it were what kept it in this purgatory. Now it crumbles, a sad image of itself.

I think of Ophelia often, and with thoughts of her come immense anger and pain.

It would be a lie to say I haven't considered checking on her. The yearning to do so only grows. It's unbearable at times; I want to see her and demand answers for leading me on. I want to be cruel for once in my fucking life. But that's not me.

I fist my hands as I aimlessly walk back from the fields where Crosby shot me. The town decided to sell off the land and build apartments over the course of spring; the foundations are already set and somehow, it feels like another piece of me has been stolen away. Forgotten.

This is how the warm evening nights go, played out with melancholic songs of the cicadas and flocks of birds that take to the sky. Ghosts walk beside the world we once knew. My feet are heavy tonight and I stop more than once to rest. I glance down at my hand, where I wish her fingers were intertwined and her thumb would brush over the back of my hand in slow circles.

I close my eyes, trying to will away the thoughts of her. The craving to have her beside me on long walks where we don't say anything. Or ones where we have more to say than we do time to walk.

The asphalt and the quiet road leading to Harlow are at least the same. Today, like most days, I felt like going for a long walk in solitude—something to take up the entire day because I have all the time in the world, don't I? This is who I've become. A seeker of silence and solitude.

My eyes linger over my feet as I trudge down the long driveway. The sun set hours ago. The stars and moon have offered me guidance home and I don't mind their dull light. I think about the alcohol in my room and whether or not it's sadder for a phantom to be a drunk or that it can't kill him.

"Darkness, take me," I whisper to the stars. I smile then because it was Ophelia who made me think to admit things to them. Like she does in her forest where no one else can hear. *Is she speaking to the stars right now too?* I wonder.

Another set of shoes enters my line of vision, black-laced boots.

I halt. A scent falls over me... *roses*. I'm reluctant to look up at her, but I do anyway. More eagerly and tragically than I expected to.

Her face is impassive; I school mine to reflect her lack of emotions. A sharp pulse threads through my veins as my traitorous body responds to seeing her here. My heart aches, throbs, twists, and my stomach flutters with a mix of dread and excitement.

I thought I was angry with her all these months. But I suppose I was wrong.

I missed her terribly.

"What are you doing here?" I ask coldly.

Her head tilts a bit as a loose grin forms on her lips, though her eyes are remarkably sad. "I came to see you."

My brows raise in surprise before I quickly smooth my features. "Why?"

Ophelia nods in understanding at my callous tone; she knows what she did was low.

She shrugs and says, "I wanted to see if you were still here." And then, as casually as she stood there waiting for me, she walks straight by, heading back toward the highway. "See you later, Lanston."

Her voice lingers in the air, drawing that ache in my chest lower.

The muscle in my jaw flexes and I force myself to stay put. I won't turn and watch her leave. I don't know what game she's playing, but I want no part of it.

Ophelia. Cruel and cold, just as the stories of her go.

And yet I lie awake all night, staring at the ceiling and clenching my hand over my chest. Seeing her made the yearning worse—a fresh cut along an old wound that never even began to heal.

Fall always brings me deep nostalgia and pain. It's the season I met Liam. Then, two years later met Wynn. It's the season I died. And now, it's the season when my friends get to visit my grave.

A Ballad of Phantoms and Hope

Even though I know they'll arrive near the middle of October, I consistently linger in the graveyard, waiting and eager to see them. Sometimes I fall asleep out here, especially on the days around the festival.

It's October 2nd, and I haven't seen Ophelia since she paid me that nighttime visit months ago. I linger in the music room, finding that I think more of her now than I do of Liam and Wynn. Her determination to help Charlie was cathartic and drew so much happiness around Harlow. Even though more phantoms leave each day, the overall dread around here is fading. We are finding our peace—well, everyone except me.

But still, I enjoy the silent afternoons of enjoying the sunlight. Yelina and Poppie don't come to this room anymore now that Charlie is gone. I've taught myself how to play a few songs on the piano and even wrote a song, though I don't plan on letting anyone else in the world hear it. But the lyrics are there. It's a good place to thumb through a book and lose time, but as the days drone on, and I continue to glance to the open spot on the couch, I know my missing her will not end.

She haunts me—a phantom haunting another phantom. I've even watched movies about ghosts in my spare time to try and get some insight into the torment I endure with the thoughts of her but, of course, they're all farfetched in comparison to my reality.

So I turn to my romance books and find a bit of solace there. From what I gather, I can either proclaim my love for her like in those sappy movies or pay her a visit to see how she likes it like a petty asshole.

I choose the latter.

My hands are cold and clenched tightly inside my coat pockets as I stroll down the bridge outside the abandoned opera house. I never understood the appeal of stalking, but now I get it. It's fun and entertaining to watch someone. Creepy, I know, but I'm a fucking ghost, so I can have this one thing.

Ophelia hasn't stepped foot outside of her building all day. The longer I pace and stare at other things from the bridge, I begin to wonder if she is even home, and further, how long she had waited to see me the night I ran into her at Harlow. She was clearly leaving when we ran into each other. Did she stay all day? Did she stand until her feet hurt? I think about that for a long time.

Birds swoop through the sunset above. The noisy streets grow louder as night falls and the bridge lamps turn on.

Still, I wait.

I decide to sit on the bench where we met, with rosebushes on each side. The crimson flowers are beautiful, somber, and wilting with the seasonal change. I pluck one and lean back. The thorns are sharp but draw no blood from my forefinger. There is no pain, and after a few seconds, the bloodless wound is gone. My eyes narrow at the spot that should've bled. How strange it is to miss the sensation of something as simple as a prick of a rose.

After some time, movement by the opera house draws my attention. I follow the figure with my eyes and am certain it is Ophelia when I catch sight of her long cream dress laden with lace and sewn flower patterns. I've not known anyone to wear such dresses, except her. It's another thing that makes me covet her.

She's walking my way.

I grin, hoping to take her by as much surprise as she took me.

She walks slowly, alone, her feet bare. Her eyes appear weary, with dark circles beneath them. She's humming a song I can't quite hear, but as she gets closer to the bench, her gaze lifts and meets mine.

Shock physically rolls through her: eyes wide, shoulders straightened, hands clasped together.

"Hello, Ophelia," I say as smoothly as I can. The rose twists between my fingers as I spin it. My nerves won't allow me a moment's reprieve in her presence.

Her throat bobs and she stutters, "L-Lanston. What are you—" she stops, remembering her surprise visit to Harlow, I'm sure, due to the wicked smile I throw her to help jog her memory.

She lets her shoulders drop and laughs. "Don't tell me you waited all day as I had."

She waited all day for me? My cheeks warm and that light sensation pools inside my chest, betraying the rage I want to hold onto.

"Unfortunately," I mutter, scrunching my eyebrows.

Ophelia takes a long breath and tucks her dress against her legs before sitting next to me. Her floral scent is overwhelming and makes me glad I came.

"You look like shit," she says, and it instantly kills all my warm thoughts.

I scowl. "Yeah? Well, you look—" I pause, thinking critically. She raises an uninterested brow. But there's so much there. The anguish that makes her mouth twitch, the darkness in the hollows of her eyes, the pale color of her usual rosy lips. "You look... really fucking tired."

Her smile spreads fast and her laugh soon follows, pulling mine out as well. We laugh together for a moment and it's the best I've felt since I held her in my arms the night she left. Ophelia's presence alone speaks to me. Her laugh is a sound I cherish.

Silence drapes over us like a blanket of stars and broken promises. I observe her in the bleak October light that dims as the sun descends behind the city. Her wavy hair is as alluring as always. Her eyes are filled with less hope, though. The fire she carried in her bones has faded and she sits with a somber slump in her shoulders.

"Why did you leave, Ophelia?"

My voice is the only sound save the soft caws of distant crows.

Her lower lip firms and she dips her chin, unwilling to meet my eyes. It's evident that her heart aches too, but I cannot understand why she is resisting me.

Finally, resolutely, she meets my gaze, her eyes

rimmed with dreary reddened skin. She really does look very tired—of everything, perhaps.

"Lanston... I'm not a good person." I shake my head in denial, but she gives me a pleading look that stops my motion. "People like me don't have good things to look forward to on the other side... we don't get to go where people like you do." Her hands tremble and meet in her lap, firming as she interlaces her fingers.

"*Ophelia.*" Her name is like silk on my lips—a plea.

Does she think something bad awaits her once she passes? How could she believe in such a thing? My chest is sore and I yearn to embrace her, to tell her sweet things, to take away all her pain.

She blinks slowly and then straightens her posture. "You deserve better."

I shake my head. "You are more than you know, more than you'll let yourself consider. What have you done that's so bad, my rose?"

Her throat bobs slightly and her small fists tighten in her lap.

"Can I ask you something?" she asks brazenly.

"Of course."

"Would you rather be physically struck or mentally abused?"

My jaw tightens and a dark, coiling sickness awakens in me. I hate both. I remember not being able to sleep from the bruises that hurt. They kept me awake until dawn sometimes. But the words. Those still keep me awake, even now.

"I'd rather be struck," I say quietly. The admittance is like oil on my tongue.

Her eyes soften and she glances away as she whispers, "I'd rather they hit me too."

I lower my eyes to her trembling hands. I want to set mine over them and provide some solace, but I refrain. "I wish you never had to choose."

She takes a deep breath and narrows her eyes. "I never understood that about people. Their insistence on cruelty through words. The trickery of it. *I didn't hit you this time.* No, perhaps not, but you told me I was the reason you will grow cancer one day. That I will be your undoing just for existing." She pauses and looks at me, eyes so dull it ruins me. "At least when it's a flesh wound it stays there. It doesn't sink any further than my fucking bones. But when they tell me all the reasons why I'm a terrible person or why I'm worthless, those wounds infest my soul. They burn and ache and you know what happens after that? After the initial blow?"

"What?"

"Then it rots. It festers and turns into poison. The first ones aren't so bad. You're able to lie to yourself and bury the decay. But it spreads—it doesn't ever stop and no matter what you try to kill it with, it remains. I'd rather they hit me... because it's easy to hate them for it, but when they make you hate yourself—that's hard. *That never goes away.* It never heals. There will always be that nagging ache in the deepest parts of your heart that whisper to you that you are vile. And you don't know what to believe because you've heard it for so long. Do we not become what we're seen as? Do we not eventually give in to the madness of it all?"

I reach for her hand this time and she only firms her lips and looks at me sadly.

"You are *not* those things, Ophelia."

She blinks slowly. "I think I am. I hurt you, Lanston. And that's all I'll ever do. It's who I am."

I want to scream. At the stars, at anything that bore witness to her pain. Why do the loveliest of souls get stomped on? A knot grows inside my throat. *She's wrong.*

"You should probably get going. It was nice to see you again though. I do love seeing you," she admits as much and lets her eyes trail over all my features, as if trying to commit it all to memory.

Longing makes me bold. "I could stay," I say slowly. I want to stay with her so badly. I'd even sit out here on the bench all night if it meant I could see her tomorrow. The next day too.

A sad smile crests her lips and she shakes her head. "I don't think that's a good idea, Lanston."

It hurts—the ache grows.

"Yeah, you're right." I let out a few sad laughs and thread my fingers through my hair. I stand slowly and let my eyes stay connected to hers for as long as she'll allow.

She breaks our silence. "Will you come to my next performance?"

A voice cries in my head, *that's not until spring.* Is

this her way of letting me know she doesn't want to see me until then? That thought feels oddly crippling.

I nod, forcing a smile. "Of course."

"I'll see you later, then." A hesitant but beautiful smile. I hand her the rose I plucked and she takes it gently, not once breaking our gaze. Her eyes bear misery, and I can't bring myself to make this harder for her.

So I whisper, "Until we meet again."

17

LANSTON

The Fall Festival arrives and Bakersville evolves into a tourist haven.

The press ate up Crosby's slasher-film-cornfield-chase, especially with all the harrowing events that followed. So now, Bakersville has to sell tickets for people to attend, otherwise they don't have enough parking for everyone.

My leg bounces nervously as I sit on my headstone. It's simple—nothing flashy or extravagant. The tall oak trees that guard this place make me nostalgic. The leaves had shed in the last week; a few big windstorms cleaned them out completely yesterday, leaving the graveyard empty of color.

Where are they?

Usually, they've already been in town and have visited my grave by noon, but the sun is already past the midpoint and the festivities are starting.

They've still not come.

I worry my lower lip, pressing my teeth into the soft flesh, and ultimately decide to check the festival.

Main Street is crowded. I'm amazed at how much can truly change in six years. This was a small-town event when I was alive. Seeing it now, it's hardly even the same festival. The vendors have bigger, more modern wooden stands and fancy signs. The cornfield maze is two times bigger than before, and they installed mics on poles that play horror music to make it scarier.

I search the vendor stands and even the bookstore and cafe. The dance is starting soon. Where are they? My worry grows like a tumor inside my gut, heavy and burdensome on my soul. Did something happen?

The dance begins and there is still no sign of them. I walk around every couple just to be sure. That only leaves the maze.

I stand motionless and struck with fear as I stare into the one place I've sworn I'd never return. My heartbeat quickens and the blood rushes to my ears, making it hard to hear.

Swallowing the lump in my throat, I step forward into the corn stalks.

I start walking calmly but after a few minutes, I'm

sprinting through the fields, frantically looking for the two people I love most in the world. They aren't here. My ears start ringing and my vision blurs.

They aren't...

I stop in the center of the maze and crouch down as my emotions get the best of me. Did they forget? Did they not have time this year? My soul aches and weary thoughts run rampant through me.

No. Please don't forget me. Please don't leave me here. I press my palms to my eyes to stave off the tears, but they pool against my skin regardless. Aching and holding all my turmoil. There is no pain greater than feeling left behind. Forgotten.

My stomach curls and I vomit. It's quiet now; the festival ended over an hour ago. I searched for far longer than I should've, but... it seemed so unrealistic that they'd not show up.

I lift my hand and rub the inner part of my arm, just before the elbow creases, letting my thumb brush over my tattoo for the three of us. It was always supposed to be the three of us.

The initial denial of them not being here passes and is followed by guilt. It's not like I can expect them to come every year. They're alive, after all—they aren't waiting around like I am with nothing to do.

Perhaps they've taken the first step into moving on. *And that hurts, I'm not ready.*

My eyes are heavy as I ride my motorcycle back to

Harlow. The sound of the doors closing behind me is loud and echoes throughout the manor.

I think to call out to Poppie or Yelina, even Jericho, but I don't. They shouldn't have to see me like this. I walk slowly and silently down the halls and let my fingertips drag along the chipped, gray walls. Moonlight dapples the floors of the music room. I slip inside and pull one of the blankets around myself. Then I sit at the piano where Wynn and Liam would play such beautiful songs, and I close my eyes and rest my head on the keys.

If Ophelia were with me, would I feel this low? Would it dull the pain in my chest if she were by my side, drawing her fingers over my skin? This loneliness damns me. More and more each day.

The bucket list comes back to mind, and I think about what in God's name is keeping me here as I tap slowly on a single key. The sound echoes through the halls and drowns out the weary beat of my heart.

I think of her name over and over and the ache that lives inside me.

Ophelia.

Ophelia visits me again around Christmas. I'm not sure why, but the burden of my heart outweighs the question.

Do I haunt her as she does me? Perhaps she doesn't have anywhere else to go for the holiday—no one else to haunt and linger near. I observe her from my bedroom window, and she studies me in silence from the courtyard. Our eyes are locked in a winter dance, the silent and steady snow as our witness.

I wait to see what she will do, and she seems to be waiting for me too. After we grow tired of the suspense, she nods her head a bit, then gives a diminutive smile.

Never in my life have I gripped a windowsill so hard. Restraining myself, so as not to run after her and hold her close to my chest. I yearn for her so desperately it festers inside my bones like a cancer—the urge to let my fingertips sink deeply into her soft skin and press my lips to hers.

There's something keeping her from me—Those Who Whisper, her demons, her fear of what lies after. She's trying as hard as she can to keep me at arm's length. But I'm not sure how long we can resist this call from the universe, the pull of the very atoms in our ghosts.

We will collide, this I am sure.

"Come on, you can't stay here alone," Yelina complains as she tugs on my arm. I give her a flat stare and shake my head. She's dressed in a corduroy brown jacket with denim jeans and a hat that says "Adventure" across the top. She readjusts the bag over her shoulder and gives me a pleading look.

"You guys are only going to be away for a few weeks. I'll be fine," I say stiffly, shoving my hands into my hoodie pocket. The truth is, I'm not sure if I'll be okay. I've never been alone for that long before. Even though they've begged me to go with them, I can't find the will to leave. I'm just so fucking tired. No matter how long I sleep, or how long I stare into the dark, rest will not sink into my soul.

Poppie juts out her hip and sets her hand on it as if I'm in trouble. Her oversized yellow coat screams "tourist!" and her suitcase is unreasonably big for traveling. "Are you sure?" she asks sincerely, looking between Jericho and Yelina for their input.

Jericho studies my face with a look of worry, and then smiles. His attire is much less flashy, a black zip-up sweater and black jeans. A small backpack is secured to his shoulders. "He's fine; he just needs to find himself in solace." They both shoot him a glare and he laughs nervously before adding, "Lanston is fine. I know he looks tired, but he's going to attend the Spring Performance again, right?" Jericho's voice has a curious, insinuating tone behind it.

He wants me to see Ophelia again. *I want to see her again too.*

But these past few months have calloused my heart.

I'm so tired, I'm not sure I have the will to leave. All I've done is stare out the windows, watch the snow fall, melt, and observe sprouts begin to rise from the cold, dead ground.

I nod to ease their minds. "Yeah."

I watch from the vacant foyer windows as the three of them leave. Spring winds tussle their hair as they slip inside Jericho's black SUV. He looks back at Harlow one last time, then to me, before disappearing inside the vehicle.

They've long left now, but I remain.

For a long time, I stand in the foyer. This place quickly turned into a haunted mansion in one year. *It's her fault.* My intrusive thoughts say vehemently. The rational part of me knows it's not true, but that's when everything changed. She's made me utterly alone. Everyone's gone to find their way of passing and adventure—everyone but me.

I lie on the floor of the music room the first night that Harlow is empty. Sleep evades me again and my thoughts are consumed by only her, as usual. I tap the floor with my forefinger and stare up at the dark ceilings.

Ophelia Rosin.

The next day, I take my crotch rocket out for a drive. At first, it's aimless; I take turns and roads as they come, but then I realize I'm heading toward Ophelia's hiding place. I park at the old Trail Closed sign and walk up the path; through the trees with their somber whispers.

At the peak, in the dusk, I decide that I will see her

perform. And I won't let her slip between my fingers this time. I'll hold on and bring her to her senses and make her see that whatever is happening between us is not nothing. That we must finish what we started a year ago and embark on our final journey.

It cannot be ignored any longer.

18

Ophelia

A lovely Boston Fern sits at the corner of the sidewalk, abandoned by a tenant in a downtown apartment complex. I crouch down and smooth my hand over the wilted ferns. Sadness draws at my heart in the abandonment of it.

"I'll bring you home," I whisper to it and carry it back to the opera house.

I think of Lanston as I walk across the bridge. It's always him occupying space in my mind and making my chest ache. His curious eyes and the rise of his lips each time he sees me. The lovely kisses his lashes leave across his cheeks.

My eyes skirt over the bench by the rosebushes. Ever

since he visited, I make sure to check the bridge earlier in the day. I've found that I am waiting patiently and hopelessly for my beautiful ghost to return. Even though it is me who left and keeps him away, I crave his presence like darkness wants for light. *I am the moth,* my eyes linger over my tattoo, *he is the butterfly.* His light is blinding.

I have to shake my head to clear the thoughts of him away. He hasn't come, not since then. He didn't come outside when I visited months ago in December, so why would he show up now? I pushed him away and away he's remained. The cold stare he gave me chilled my veins that night.

But one thing is sure. We are tied together. Tethered. Manacled. We cannot part.

The longing hurts worse than any heartbreak I've endured—I think it's because I know he's as starved for me as I am for him. It is I who keeps us apart.

He's not here. My legs slow as I reach my home.

I set the fern next to its new plant family and lie down on my worn red sofa, exasperated from thinking and hoping. Each day he's not on the bridge, I lose more of myself.

My annual performance is tonight, but the thought of him not being there frightens me. Tonight will mark one year since we met—since my world halted and everything I loved about being a phantom ceased.

Because after him, I found that there is nothing to love about being a phantom if I cannot be near him. The fear I once felt so immensely of facing the awaiting darkness has waned. I think I would face the nightmares and the punishments if it meant I could be with him.

I sigh and let my head fall to the side. *What a mess I've made.* A shadow flickers across one of the boarded-up windows. My breath catches in my lungs, stillness and fear rising through my veins.

No one comes out here to the abandoned part of the city. Has the whispering dark come for me in daylight? My heart hammers in my chest and drowns out all reason.

I sit up slowly and wrap my arms around my knees, narrowing my eyes at the door as it ominously opens—a head peers around the corner. Soft brown strands of hair fall over his forehead as he steps inside. His hazel eyes, holding anguish and sadness, find mine and I immediately stand.

"*Lanston?*" I whisper his name in disbelief.

"Ophelia." His voice is low and tense.

Emotions swell in the dusty air between us, flakes drifting slowly in the golden beams of sunlight that stream in through the darkness.

I've run into the arms of many men in my day. When actual air still teemed through my lungs and blood pumped wildly through my veins.

I will not go to him. I will not show him how much I crave to be held in his arms.

You're so eager to be the whore, aren't you? Cold words circulate in my brain. I've heard them so many times before. *Your infected mind will drag him down to the depths with you. You'll be the cause of his ruin.*

Because I'm a bad person.

I suck in my lower lip and press my teeth into the flesh.

Lanston stands with his hands fisted tightly at his sides, staring at me, waiting. *I'm so tired of waiting.*

I open my mouth to ask why he's come here, but the moment my lips part, he swiftly walks toward me, parting the golden streams of sunlight and disturbing the dust. His brows are pulled low, and his arms slowly lift as he stands before me. Lanston's palms are warm and soft, spreading over my jaw and threading his fingers through my hair.

Then our lips reach for one another, almost touching but not quite. His breaths are hard and labored as if he ran the whole way here from Harlow. Sweat beads down his pale skin. I've never seen tendons and bones as lovely as his, beneath the soft of his skin; they magnify the pink of his blush, the red of his lips. My eyes linger on the effortless curls of his lashes.

And he, this beautiful, ruinous man, says, "I cannot rid you from my mind, Ophelia. It's as if you've instilled an illness of your own into me. You are the sole thought that ravages my mind as I lie awake at night. The ceilings make me think of you. The forest. Roses. *Breathing*—I cannot take breath without you eroding my sanity."

Lanston tilts his forehead so it's pressed against mine. Our lips brush against one another, not yet a kiss.

He thinks of me?

His hazel eyes pierce into my soul and rekindle the fire inside my heart.

"You haunt me too, Lanston," I murmur against his lips. Chills spread through my entire body and for a moment, I don't remember where I am. Who I am. Because it doesn't matter, all that matters is us. I see it now. I understand.

"More than anything?" he asks, greedy for my words. My bones fill with happiness, more than I've felt in years.

"Yes."

"Tell me." He breathes against my lips.

"More than dancing and collecting greenery. Every song I listen to reminds me of you. Every glance into the sky, the stars, the sunlight—I see you everywhere, Lanston. I feel you in the breeze that greets my cheeks, the scent of pages and books. You've haunted me from the day I laid eyes on you."

He takes a short breath, eyes arching the way they do when one's heart aches.

"This is the last time I will ask you—" he pauses and swallows, closing his eyes as if making a wish. "Will you come with me? We can find our peace together. I know it in the marrow of my bones. We are meant to be together. We are meant to find our reasons, our tethers to this world, as one. Please. I won't beg for anything, but I will for you."

Lanston keeps his eyes closed. I stare remorsefully at him as tears fill my eyes.

I want to go... so badly I do. But there is darkness chasing me. And nothing good awaits me once we pass from purgatory. Lanston has the purest soul. I know he will have his golden fields and peace, but me? There is only fire awaiting my soul.

I've sinned. I'm not good.

But my heart wins out against the fear that's lived inside me. I want this one last thing. Him, even if it is only for a short while.

"Okay."

Lanston looks up at me swiftly, eyes brimming with hope. "Really?" he gasps.

I nod. A beat of silence wraps around us as he studies my features, his smile bright. He traces the line of my jaw before pulling me in, letting our lips connect as I've longed for them to, as I've dreamed and wished for. The smell of pages and coffee seeps around me. My fingers glide across his neck and jawline, eager to explore his skin with touch and not just my eyes. Lips as soft and engulfing as his should be a sin.

Our kiss breaks, foreheads pressed together. I whisper, "Can you make me a promise?"

"Anything."

I meet his gaze. "Promise we'll go together... you know, when we move on."

His eyes soften and his hands glide down to my neck until they rest on my collarbones. "Together, or not at all."

19

Lanston

Ophelia's opera house is much drearier in the daylight. With the black wooden planks that are weathered and hardly holding together, it's a miracle they haven't torn this place down. The windows are cracked but the plants that line the outside are beautiful. In a sense, her opera house resembles the haunted building it truly is.

Oh, Ophelia, you poetic soul.

It's more endearing during the day, the things she's collected and taken a liking to. Music flutters through the tall ceilings and I lean my head against her sofa to enjoy it. Ophelia has an old music player plugged into a sound system. "Iris" by the Goo Goo Dolls plays somberly through the rafters. I lift my eyes and find her dancing slowly up on the opera stage.

Ophelia wanted to dance one last time on her stage before we embark on our journey. She wears a beautiful crimson dress, long and languid, fluttering softly with her movements. The sleeves come down to her wrists, and the neckline dips low, revealing her cleavage.

Her eyes are closed, and the soft lift of her lips reveals the peace she's feeling. I watch her perfect and practiced movements; her muscles flex against the light, shadows dancing beneath in tandem.

My heart eases and I lean forward on the couch, setting my elbows on my knees as I take her in. Ophelia lifts her gaze and those heavy, beautiful eyes fall on me. Her stare is unsettling, not in a way of discomfort, but in a way I haven't experienced before. Every time she looks at me, I know she sees far more than what lies on the surface. She sees the darkness, the damage. But it's coveting and warm.

Her feet slow and she comes to a stop, offering me a timid smile as she brushes her mauve hair behind her ear.

I rise from the sofa and meet her at the broken stage, extending my hand. My heart flutters when she takes it.

A relieved smile spreads over my lips.

"Let's ride a train first. Somewhere, anywhere, I don't care."

As long as I'm with you, I want to say.

Ophelia takes a deep breath and looks around her

opera house one last time. Afraid to leave it all behind, perhaps. "Will we get to come back? I have plants to care for," she frets.

I grin. "If not, we'll find our new home."

Her eyes grow round with a desire for answers.

"*Our* new home?" she says cheekily.

My face warms, but before I can respond she intertwines her fingers with mine, filling me with the sensation of being pressed close to someone you're not sure you can ever really have. Her lips are soft, begging for affection.

She notices me staring and raises her other hand, gently brushing her thumb across the tenderness of my lower lip. My heart skips four beats and the intoxicating scent of honeysuckles and roses swarms me.

I kiss her tenderly, like two people who've been courting for a century. But there is another craving I'm foreign to that beckons deep within me, a want to bury my teeth into the softness of her skin and be rough—to be as cruel as she can be.

"Do you have headphones we can share?" she asks against my lips with a loose grin.

"Hm?" I blink to focus.

Ophelia grabs her music player, tossing it to me. I barely manage to catch it. "For our train ride."

My cheeks flush and I nod like an idiot, stricken with the thoughts of us lying close, listening to the same songs.

She laughs at me, grabbing her bag filled with clothes and notebooks.

"Where to, Nevers?"

I've never been great at goodbyes, but something deep in my soul is changing. Maybe it's been everyone leaving Harlow. The loneliness that I've had to face. But when Ophelia and I stop at the institution to get my things, I'm relieved to see Jericho's SUV out front.

Yelina helps him unload the vehicle, but Poppie is nowhere to be found.

Their heads lift as we approach and Yelina brightens, her cheeks rosy and eyes puffy. Has she been crying? I park my motorcycle in the driveway beside the car.

"What's wrong? Where's Poppie?" I ask. Ophelia keeps her hands clasped with worry; she must sense something is amiss, too. Yelina covers her eyes and cries; the black hoodie she wears belongs to Jericho.

Jericho approaches me, laying his arm over my shoulders in a side hug, and says sadly, "She decided to stay in Rome. Her family line extends there, and it was important for her to learn her roots."

But I didn't get to say goodbye.

Yelina wipes her tears and says, "She always struggled the most with not feeling that she belonged. I hope that she finds her place in the world and that it saves her."

Jericho lets out a long breath and smiles through the silence that ensues.

"I came to get my stuff; actually, I'm—" I lose the words that I'd rehearsed so perfectly. They evade me as I think of the two of them being all that's left of Harlow.

Ophelia threads her fingers through mine and meets my wavering eyes. "We've decided to pursue our bucket list. Would you two like to join us?"

They both take a sharp breath. Surprised, shocked. But the hope that fills Yelina's eyes, and even Jericho's, is answer enough.

"Well, we'd need to discuss it. How about we collect our thoughts and give our response over supper? Say, in an hour?" Jericho replies professionally, looking each of us in the eyes before nodding.

Yelina wraps her arm around his as they head back into the manor. They seem to have grown closer since their trip. Good. The two of them have been stealing glances at one another long enough. A pang of sorrow hits my chest as I think of Poppie and Yelina being apart. They were inseparable, even in death.

Ophelia lounges on my bed as I pack my art supplies and a few books I haven't gotten to read yet. She watches me curiously. Something flashes through her gaze, questions she doesn't seem open to asking.

I grab my headphones and charcoal pencils as well, thinking it's better to bring things to keep the time between destinations filled.

The hour goes quickly and we don't speak through

much of it. Ophelia seems to have this way about her, an understanding of her surroundings. If one needs comfort or conversation, she is full of things to say and listens generously. However, I'm often silent, fading into my mind and thinking deeply. She returns the act in kind, breathing slowly and staring at the same spot on my ceiling where I've bored holes with my own eyes for so many years.

Our silence is welcome and it's quite nice, in its warm, unforced state.

When I have my bag packed, we meet Jericho and Yelina in the dining hall. The room seems boisterous in the dark, with only four phantoms sitting around a meager candle for light. As if meeting in secret.

"We will join you," he declares with mild temper. I expected him to be much happier or excited about this, but he seems melancholic. He seemed much more enthusiastic earlier when he looked through the bucket list and found Ireland and Paris on it.

"That's wonderful—" Ophelia starts, smiling brightly.

"*But* we will be taking our own excursions." Yelina interrupts with eagerness to speak. "We'll meet you in Ireland and Paris, but apart from that, we have our own agenda." She turns to look at Jericho—Ophelia's and my eyes follow curiously.

His cheeks are red, but he only nods.

"Jericho, isn't this what you've been pushing

everyone to go do? Why do you seem so glum?" I ask honestly.

His mouth firms and his fist clenches over his fork. "Nevers, I've worked here for many, many years now. Since graduating college, in fact. I never got to advance my career or do anything I dreamed of doing." He pauses, eyes searching the table for words before saying, "This place is my home. A home to all of us. Where we laughed, healed, cried... and where we died."

Ophelia's brows pull together with sorrow and Yelina places a steady hand atop Jericho's.

He continues: "But we must leave. We must be strong and embark on this new journey. To find our peace and leave all the death and rot of the world behind us. I am not sad, Nevers. I'm only saying goodbye to the walls that have carried me, *us*, in death for so very long."

I take him in, grieving and slumped. Jericho is the best counselor I've ever had, but even more than that, he is my friend—a guiding light, even in purgatory.

My chair squeaks as I push it out, walk around the table to him, and set my hand on his back. "We will always be a part of this place, even when we are gone. Our laughter and tears permeated the soil itself. It's our turn to carry the meaning of Harlow Sanctum with us. Into the night, into the dawn, into the after."

Ophelia smiles wider than I've ever seen her smile and says, "The world waits for us. You must tell it who you are, Jericho. Shout it if you must."

Yelina laughs, jostling Jericho, and with a somber smile he asks, "It's not too late?"

"We're still here, aren't we?" My rose speaks with fire in her heart. Her voice echoes in my ears and etches unspeakable things into my soul.

I will never forget her words.

We are still here. We always have been, and we always will be.

20

Lanston

Trains aren't as easy to come by as you'd think, at least not in Montana. We're going to have to make it all the way out to Whitefish to catch an Amtrak.

The hybrid SUV we take from the lot of a car dealership is brand new, slick black, and has that toxic new vehicle smell that gives you headaches. I'll never get over how weird it is just to take things as a phantom. It's strange how real it feels, how the salespeople don't bat an eye as I snatch the keys from their desk.

My crotch rocket was hard to part with. In a way, I understood how much pain Jericho had felt over leaving Harlow behind. The motorcycle had been a significant part of my life, but Ophelia assured me we could find another throughout our travels.

Jericho and Yelina were jittering with excitement, hardly sparing time for a swift "see you soon" and exchanging phone numbers so we could be in contact later on, then off they went. Their bucket list is taking them to Hawaii first. Yelina swears a vacation she never got will soothe her ghost.

I only give Harlow Sanctum one final glance through my rearview mirror. Emotions swell in my chest, but I've felt enough heartbreak and sadness within those walls; I won't give it anymore. So, I take a deep breath and smile; Ophelia's hand wraps tightly around mine as we leave the misty mountain institution behind.

Goodbye Wynn. Goodbye Liam. My lower lip quivers but is replaced with hope. My story can begin here. We can leave everything else behind.

I drive.

It's been a long time since I've driven anything but a motorcycle and God, does it feel good to have a steering wheel under my palms again. I prefer a crotch rocket, but I won't fuss about it. Speeding down the interstate and blaring music with a girl in the passenger seat makes me feel eighteen again. Not that I'm complaining about being forever twenty-nine.

Ophelia scowls at me and turns the music down. I don't even know what song it is; so many new artists have come out since I died, but I like the tune.

"You could've told me you were utterly insane. I

would've driven us," Ophelia teases, rolling her eyes dramatically and looking back out the side window.

My brow twitches with her ire.

"Are you so against having fun?" I laugh as I tap the brakes enough for her to jerk forward as she tries biting into her donut. Icing gets all over her upper lip and nose and I have to suck in my lips to keep from belly laughing.

"Lanston!" She shoves the donut in my face, sticky icing smearing over my cheek and hair.

"Hey, I'm driving!" I say urgently, because I'm already steering us off the side of the road going ninety. The dust whirls up behind us and the car nearly tips as I slam on the brakes.

We breathe heavily, icing on both our faces with strands of hair stuck to our noses and cheeks. The donut slides down the windshield slowly, leaving blue streaks in its wake, before flopping on the dashboard.

I look at her, and she turns to look at me. Our eyes are both wide with adrenaline. There is no middle point in which we smile first or giggle; both of us burst into laughter—the kind that makes your stomach hurt and your sides burn.

Tears prick her eyes as she tries and fails to wipe the frosting from her face.

I retrieve some napkins I stuffed into the center console after we picked up donuts and pass her one, keeping one for myself and joining her in trying to get the icing out of my hair.

She's faster than I am.

The napkin I used is completely worthless; I need an entire handful to get the rest off my cheek. I glower at her. My lip still turned up in a smirk because it's way too funny not to laugh at, even though it sucks.

"See what you did?" I tut.

She lifts her chin. "*You* started it."

I notice she still has a dot of frosting on the top of her lip. My hand moves without even thinking. Her eyes widen as my thumb swipes gently over her skin. Her mouth parts a bit and my eyes linger there, admiring every soft aspect of her.

Ophelia sips in a sharp breath and looks away, her cheeks reddening.

"We should hurry, or we'll miss the train," she says, staring out the window and refusing to turn toward me. I narrow my eyes at her. Then I slip my hand over hers. She turns her head, but instead of surprise, I find heat burning in her eyes.

I smile—a simple but charming one. "Don't worry, Miss Rosin, I'll get you on that train." I turn up the radio and it's a song I actually know this time: "Ride" by Lana Del Rey. My hands return to the wheel and I floor it.

She lets out the sweetest squeal as we're ruthlessly thrown forward.

"Lanston!"

But after a few moments, she starts singing along to the song, and I join in. I sneak glances over at her, her wild purple hair blowing in the wind, with the window rolled down. Her feet kicked up on the dashboard and all

I can think of is how beautiful she looks and all the light she emits into my weary soul.

"Tickets, please."

We watch in silence as the conductor punches tickets and passes them back to a family of four. The children look nine and six. The mother is smiling pleasantly, and the father makes an excited face at his kids. They cheer and laugh as they hold their train tickets like new treasures. It's clearly their first train ride.

I smile at their interaction and am envious of the warmth this small family has. Kindness radiates from them; it's not forced or fake.

My throat grows thick with a lump. I'm jealous of the lack of pain in their eyes, the absence of fear, but so fucking happy that they at least get a chance at functionality. To see the world through a lens of love and care.

"My parents didn't love me either."

My eyes snap to Ophelia, wide and shocked. She raises a shoulder, then lets it fall before she pulls out her iPod. Since the train is pretty vacant, we have an entire section to ourselves, but she moves to sit next to me. Our shoulders brush, making my stomach flutter.

I hand her a headphone, not wireless. I grabbed the old-school wired ones on purpose; some intervention is needed occasionally when it comes to the universe. Is it weird that I'm elated that we're connected with the chords of headphones? It satiates the hopeless romantic in me.

"I didn't say mine didn't love me," I respond absently, letting my eyes drift back to the warmth the family fills the cabin with; their laughter is like a disease, spreading and making others grin to themselves.

I love that most, I think.

The disease of love.

"You didn't have to say it. People like us just stick out. We can't hide that part of us. It's the whisper in our gaze, the shadow on our frowns." She doesn't look at me as she talks and then pushes play. Music flows into my earbud, making me smile as I know the song instantly. "Train Wreck" by James Arthur.

My brows pinch together and an incredulous grin pulls at my lips. "Seriously?" I nudge her shoulder and she shoves me back without missing a beat. "You're going to curse this train or something," I say.

She lifts her chin, soft strands of hair falling over her collarbone. "Oh hush, we're already technically haunting it." Her fingers curl against the soft lace of her dress. The black is delicate and mingles well with the maroon rose fabric sewn in. It looks like there really are little roses woven into her dress.

"If we find another dead passenger does that make this a poltergeist then?"

Her mouth opens just a sliver and she scowls at me.

"That's terrible!" The smile she lets slip betrays her words.

"Thought I'd feel out your morbid joke meter." I laugh, shoulders relaxing with the somberness of the song. *I'm a train wreck, that's for sure.*

Ophelia stares at the family across the way. The same envy burns in her gaze. Her brown and green speckled eyes flash at me and I straighten. "Did you ever want children?" she asks, voice cold as stone.

My answer is instant. "No."

"Why?"

I sink into my seat and put my feet up on the ones adjacent to us. My black sneakers blend well with the fabric of the chairs. "I hate the thought of becoming my father. Cold and absent. I know I'm not that way, but still, I worried enough never to want them." My words taste like dirt. It's not worth the breath to even speak of him. "You?"

"Nope. I love being independent and spending all my time on things *I* enjoy." She smiles proudly. Most people would think that's selfish, but I admire her for saying it so boldly—unapologetic and firm in her choice.

And why shouldn't she? Be happy with yourself. You don't *have* to have children just because your parents insist. No one lives your life except you.

"Things like dancing and your unruly plant collection?" I taunt her and she squirms in her seat, trying to get comfortable.

"Yes, and now, apparently, *you* too."

I look at her with subtle surprise. "You enjoy *me*?" Most people get annoyed rather quickly with my dreariness. I prefer to be alone, as Ophelia does, and yet it seems we share this small sacred thing, wanting to bathe in one another's company.

She nods sleepily. Her shoulder bone presses into my arm, but I don't say a word; her warmth consumes me. "I don't want people to see me, but I like that you do. You're handsome, too, so that helps."

I chuckle, my eyes are growing heavier with each breath. "You think I'm handsome?"

She doesn't respond, but the next song, "Jealous" by Labrinth, loads on her music player. I grin like the hopeless romantic I am, leaning back in the uncomfortable train seat and resting my head against hers.

This feels a lot like a love story. Perhaps this time, it can be mine.

21

Ophelia

The greatest discovery in the history of phantoms is the coffee station at the front of this train. I slip behind the workers, who are ferociously serving savage early birds starved for caffeine. I giggle at their furrowed brows and devotion to their jobs. It makes me a bit melancholy that they cannot see me as I sneak by and familiarize myself with the espresso machines.

My years spent as a barista in college are paying off, and luckily, there isn't much to new technology when it comes to making a good espresso. I make myself a white chocolate caramel latte and an Americano for Lanston. Between my teeth are two bagged blueberry muffins.

I walk through the train compartments until I reach

ours, nestled quietly in the back. Everyone riding in this cart has already left, so it's just us now. A tightness coils in my chest as I stop a few feet away from him. His head is tilted to the side and peace draws at the corners of his lips. His high cheekbones make his face sharp and cold in appearance, but I know how soft his skin is, how welcoming and alluring his heart is.

He stirs as I sit down across from him. I place my latte between my thighs and hand him the cup I made for him. He blinks a few times to cast away the lingering sleep and takes the drink with a lovely grin.

"Did you poison it?" he jests as I toss his muffin at him. He doesn't even try to catch it and it lands in his lap. His eyes only shut softly as he takes a sip of the Americano.

Satisfaction leaves his lips on his next breath.

"Perhaps I should have," I say teasingly, taking a sip of my latte without looking back at him. He makes me feel many things that I've sworn off. Love only ever brought me pain. I think of *him*, my last lover, my failing.

I shudder at the thought of him. In my last hours of life, he only brought me anguish. Whether he intended to or not, it was my truth. Sometimes I think it's the memory of him that lures the darkness to me. It can smell the misery.

At least we're moving. Those Who Whisper won't be able to catch up with us for some time at this pace. *I hope.*

Trees and vibrant green grasslands stretch out as far as

the eye can see. It's been raining ever since we entered Oregon. I love how the raindrops look against the glass, bubbling up and clinging until they ultimately fall. Lanston has been reading a book he snagged from the bookshop at the train station in Portland. His hair falls over his forehead as his gaze scours the pages. I watch his lovely hazel eyes carefully studying the words, absorbing each into his imagination.

I often wonder what he thinks—if I linger in his thoughts the way he does in mine.

It's a romance novel.

Now that I think back to it, his room had many stacks of romance books, unorganized and piled carelessly. *Men.* How is it that they can make a messy room aesthetically appealing? Not like messy rooms with laundry on the floor, but the ones that have the curtains pulled shut and their artwork bleeds from the pages into their life. There were torn pages of drawings he didn't love scattered across his table and coffee stains at the edges of his oldest novels.

I think I love those books the most. The ones you can tell were well read and adored, thumbed through like each word was a script, the ones with small notes and underlines—treasures, I like to think.

"What's the story about?"

He doesn't look up at me as he says, "It's a reincarnation tale about finding past lovers." His voice is full of reminiscence and longing.

I think of my own past love and the sting it brings to

my heart. There's not a chance he could be a reincarnated lover of mine.

"I wish to find my past lover," I murmur as I stare out the window, imagining what he might look like if he were real. For some reason, all I can picture is Lanston. His light brown hair and hazel eyes, these he would have in any form. In any life.

Lanston sets his book down in his lap and looks at me. I try not to show that I notice. "I don't believe in reincarnation," he says, as if it is the undeniable truth.

"Why not? It's fun to pretend."

He lowers his head. "We wouldn't be trapped here if it were real."

Trapped. It's odd that we view this middle ground so differently. In a way, I feel like I've been given a second chance—time to accept things before disappearing for good. I think that's what I fear the most, being nothing. All the thoughts and emotions that I've experienced and things I've said... it cannot be for nothing.

"Lanston, why are you so eager to chase what awaits us after this?" I return my eyes to his and watch as his fingers curl around the book stiffly.

He grimaces in anguish. "If I told you, you'd look at me differently." He studies me, trying to decide whether or not to say what he truly feels.

"Tell me anyway," I say impassively.

He chuckles. "You really are like Liam. He was pushy too." I blink and don't bother feeding into his humor. Lanston stares at me with kind eyes, and he says,

"I just want to stop *feeling*. It's an itch I've always suffered, a cold and dark place that I seem to constantly be searching for. A place where my thoughts have long been discarded and everything that's ever hurt me has been shed away like a cocoon. I want to be bare, my skin against the shadows, my bones left to lie still, and to be utterly numb to the sadness that embraces me."

His words impale me like cold steel—drowning me with their pain and weariness.

He's like me.

A familiar soul.

The train cabin remains silent for a few moments. I cannot think of a single thing to say in response to him. I'm the least qualified person to speak on such a matter—the matter of wanting to die.

I'd always been told sick people can't help other sick people. That humans like us, who want to die, are *bad*. We just want attention. *We seek attention.* Surely, if everyone I ever spoke to told me this, it was true, right?

I'm bad... I'm sinful for having thoughts of dying. I'm selfish for wanting not to be here. I'm going to fucking hell if I kill myself. People like me don't go to heaven; they said so. How many nights did I stay awake, praying to a god I did not believe in that I would wake up the next day better? I wanted to be fixed. I wanted to be *good*. I wanted to stop being a disappointment to those who didn't understand the battle I was having with my brain. The chemicals, they said. The chemicals in my brain were wrong.

There was no one as sick as me, I told myself, because that's what was preached to me. *No*, sick people cannot comfort each other because what do we know? But sometimes, there's an inkling in the deepest parts of my marrow. That, perhaps, our knowing we are not bad or alone in our way of thinking does help.

I wish I knew I wasn't the only person who felt like sitting in a dark corner and being forgotten—being dead. Of course, it's odd and abnormal to yearn for such feelings. To not exist. To spectate without being, as we do now. So many people don't understand. They refute the idea with their entirety because their brains process on a normal level. Their chemicals are balanced. Is that really what it boils down to? *Chemistry*.

People like us traverse the world alone because we were raised to believe that we have to.

Smile and pretend.

Smile and pretend. No one cares about your depression. Smile and pretend. Don't let them see what you really are. They'll lock you away if they see. Is that why I ignored it for so long? I didn't want anyone to see me.

But Lanston.

He *wants* me to see him.

He wants me to know that he suffers greatly behind those precious eyes that hold so much warmth and endearment. He isn't bad. He is not at fault for having a broken mind. How could anyone declare such a thing? I've never observed such divine beauty in another's soul—such kindness.

I hear you. All the battles you war inside your head against yourself. I trace his lips with my fingers, and he leans into my hand. *I see you.*

But everything I want to say to him falls short. My words cannot match my thoughts. If I dare speak them, I'll break, and I don't want to dig up buried bones.

So, instead of saying what I truly want, I say, "I'd like to find a place like that, too. I would rest for an eternity, at last." Lanston's eyes flicker, not with surprise but with confirmation. Had he suspected me of being similar to him?

Our waves match evenly in this sea of despair.

"Why are you not so eager then? What is it you fear, my rose?" he says with a sad grin.

Because I'm scared.

I lean back and look out the window once more, pressing my fingers against the glass pane, cold seeping into my bones. "I told you in Jericho's session... I'm not finished here yet." It comes out sadder than I intended it to. What I really want to say is *I want to prove that I'm a good person before facing my end.*

Lanston looks at me for a long moment. We still have so many secrets. So much left unsaid and guarded.

"I'll figure you out one day," Lanston says, more of an oath than a statement.

I smile at that.

"I hope that you do."

22

Lanston

In the last four days of travel, I've found Ophelia to be more inspiring than I initially thought. She tries a new flavor of coffee each morning, determined to experience things to the fullest. I even indulged her a few times, curious to try some of the fancier lattes with cream. I'm reluctant to admit that I finally see the craze behind it.

We explore the compartments, measuring how long it takes to get from one end to the next to pass the time—truly idiotic things, but our laughter rings out loud and true. We find out the hard way that phantoms can indeed still get motion sick. Perhaps it is our willingness to still feel alive that promotes such anomalies as nausea. I hold

Ophelia's hair out of her face while she throws up in the bathroom sink.

At each stop, we find new books and different foods to try. The back of the train looks more like a fortress of piled novels and empty bags of chips, blankets that we stockpiled into a bed.

"How childish my parents would think of me if they could see me right now," Ophelia says with a breathy laugh.

We're pressed close in the fuzzy faux-fur blankets we laid out on the floor. She has a red licorice in her hand and draws it across her bottom lip lazily. Her fingers are slender—the bones beneath create prominent rises in her knuckles. On her side, the dress caves into her midsection and lines her hip bone. I want to smooth my hand over her curves and feel every inch of her skin—the dips and valleys of her beautiful soul. We've kept to just kissing, but our fervent bodies seem to have a more intimate agenda. I'm transfixed for a moment, hardly hearing her.

She gives me a hard stare and I know I've missed something.

"Hm?"

"Lanston!" She pouts and I laugh apologetically. Her body is against me, thighs brushing mine and sharing heat.

"I'm sorry. Something about your parents, right?" I look at her innocently. Her eyebrows flatten, but she lets it go.

"Yeah, they always thought I was childish." She bites

down on the licorice and tears it away, handing it to me for a bite. I eagerly take it.

It's hard not to roll my eyes at the idea of what others consider childish. "Miserable people don't want others to find joy in simple things. That's all it is," I say before taking a bite and thinking to myself that she just took a bite of the same candy. It makes my cheeks warm.

She lets her head fall in my direction. Her purple hair pools in lovely curls, haloing her face. Those brown eyes pierce straight through me.

Our lips are so close I can smell the sweet candy on her. I swallow hard in an effort to redirect my brain before I get an erection.

"They were definitely miserable," she says with a flat expression. Her eyes lower to my lips and I watch the same thoughts cross her mind—of tossing in the blankets, limbs tangled and pressed close against one another. Our skin bare and smooth as we connect, as we fall into one another.

Her cheeks redden and she turns her head away. I reach my hand out and gently grip her chin, pulling her face back toward me.

"What has your mind so lost?" I whisper.

In the dark train compartment, alone, it feels required to speak in a hushed tone, even as ghosts. Her nose is a mere inch from my own. The floral scent that mingles in her hair and smile makes me ache for her in every way a man could possibly burn for another.

She holds her breath, not sure if she should answer. I

wait, and in the few moments that pass, I know I'd wait patiently for anything she'd have to say.

"You talk about what's inside your head so easily... I want to share things with you too, but I can't force myself to say them. Could I maybe write them down for you instead?" She speaks hesitantly like she's expecting to be shut down. I wonder how many times before she's tried to open up and her words and ideas had fallen on closed, cruel ears.

"I'd love nothing more," I say, reassuring her. She lights up and her eyes glimmer like pools of honey. "On one condition."

Ophelia raises a brow in question.

An endearing grin spreads across my lips. The realest one I've felt in a long time. "When you give me a letter, I'll give you a drawing. We needn't ever speak about what we read or see; we only need to accept them."

A short breath escapes her lips and she beams at me. "But should we want to?"

"Then we can talk until the sun rises."

"And if we need more time than that?"

I laugh, taken by this sweet, broken ghost. "Then we'll talk until our voices can no longer carry the weight of our words."

She gives me a daring smile and says, "And if further?"

"When our voices die, I'll trace my fingers across your skin and tell you stories with my touch."

Ophelia is silent, studying my features briefly before

murmuring, "Why are you so kind, Lanston? I'm not a good person." The weakness in her tone betrays all the emotions she refuses to show.

That admittance hurts; it swells painfully inside my chest as death once had.

"Why don't you think you're a good person?" I ask.

She only closes her eyes.

"Maybe I can tell you in a letter someday."

I lean forward and press my forehead to hers. She looks into my eyes before they softly flutter shut. My hand rises over the curve of her waist and I kiss her. A piece of my soul opens, and she reaches right into my chest.

She arches her back to get closer, our kiss deepening as she traces her fingers across my jaw. Blood flows to my core as our tongues chase each other. Ophelia's entire body goes limp in my arms as she surrenders herself to me. Her hands trail down my neck and glide across my collarbones, sending chills up my spine. My cock throbs painfully inside my pants as we tangle in the blankets.

Ophelia lies splayed out on the floor beneath me as I break our connection and start dotting her neck with kisses, nipping her skin enough to draw soft moans from her lips.

"*Lanston*," she cries, threading her fingers through my hair as I slip her dress off her shoulders and pull it down enough to expose her breasts. I draw my tongue over her plump flesh, sucking her nipple into my mouth and swirling my tongue over it.

She writhes beneath me, breathy cries and moans slipping from her mouth. I can tell she wants more and is impatient for it.

A dark chuckle rises from my throat and I raise my head to look at her, finding desperate eyes staring back at me. I lean back up to kiss her and she makes a small, weakened sound as I press my erection against her core.

Her hands slip beneath my shirt and duck into the hem of my pants.

I grin against her lips. "You want more?" She nods, drunk with lust.

She unbuttons my pants and yanks them down. A dry laugh escapes me, and I bury my face in her hair, finding her ear and biting the cartilage gently. She breathes heavily as she frees my dick, quickly wrapping her hand around my girth and eliciting a low groan that rolls from my lips.

"Oh, fuck," I say weakly as she starts pumping me. Her soft fingers pull me all the way to the tip and work me down back to the base in a slow rhythm.

I look down at her, biting her lower lip. Her eyes drip with lust, greedy and wanting me to touch her. Who am I to deny her?

My lips crash down to hers and our bodies move fiercely together, starved from all the moments we'd resisted before. I run my hand down her stomach and lift her dress. She whimpers eagerly and I can't help but grin against her lips.

"Patience, Ophelia," I say, hushed and languid. Her

thighs are warm and she bucks her hips as I squeeze her flesh, inching closer to her core and stopping just before I reach her panties. "Have I told you how beautiful you are, or have I only been saying it over and over in my head?" I ask, breathless.

She nips at my lower lip and that sends a surge of heat through my dick.

"You must've been saying it in your head," she replies, smiling and burying her face into the crook of my neck. "Tell me."

She releases her firm hold on my cock and guides it to her stomach. I groan at the soft sensation of her skin against my tip, lowering my body to the blankets and rolling to my back. She follows the momentum and straddles me, sitting perfectly on my dick—nothing but her thin panties between us.

I look up at her through hooded eyes, high off the ecstasy that builds between us.

She sets her hands on my chest and starts grinding on top of me. I buck my hips involuntarily and fist the sheets. She looks down at me like a goddess, expectantly.

"I can't take my eyes off of you, not even for a moment." It takes a great deal of control to keep my words and tone even as she continues to dry hump me, but I keep my voice steady. I want her to know how much I truly cherish her. "I knew it the moment I laid eyes on you in the theater. Your somber dance and the weight of the world you carried so effortlessly. Your beauty is the kind the world hushes around, to stare in silence and listen."

Her movements slow until she stills. Her hands slide up my chest until she falls to her elbows, braced on either side of my head.

"You say the most beautiful things," she says softly. Our noses are barely touching as she stares down into my soul. "Hopeless romantic or tragic poet?" Her lips kick up in a lovely smile and I laugh, wrapping my arms around her.

"Hopeless romantic."

She nods knowingly. "That's what I pinned you for." Then she kisses me and we roll in the blankets. She lies on her side as I do mine. I push her underwear to the side and find the evidence of her arousal. A groan rolls from my throat as I stroke her clit; her reaction is instant, arching into our fervent kisses more and moaning as she fists my cock again.

We remain in tandem, breathing heavily as our release builds. She strokes me faster and slower until I can no longer see clearly, and I grunt as I come in her hand. She slows and works the tip until my hips stop jerking.

I can tell she's close too, her teeth bury into her lower lip and she gasps as I push a finger inside her. Our lips meet again and I rub her clit until she's quivering in my arms. I don't stop until she cries out with her release and I know she's satiated.

She looks me over one last time before smiling and

tucking her head into the crook of my neck. I smile, too, wrapping my arms around her and pressing a kiss atop her head.

"Dream of me," she whispers drowsily. A warmth spreads into my heart as we lie together, two phantoms on a train and falling into orbit with each other. Do our dreams matter? I hope so.

"I always do."

Ophelia stretches her arms over her head as we finally get off the last train in New York.

I'm hesitant and linger on the last step. I've never been this far in the world, not ever. The East Coast was always a dream of mine, even just to visit. Boston comes to mind, with the two people who mean the most to me somewhere in the forest of buildings and cement. I wonder if they think of me. I try not to linger on the missed anniversary. It's not fair to be upset over it. It's only natural for them to move on, after all.

Ophelia notices my pause and smiles, offering me her hand.

"Come on, we can create new makeshift beds elsewhere if we need to." Her voice is light and airy, lifting the corner of my lips and making me forget the woes that tug at my heart.

"What, like two traveling vagabonds? We can stay wherever we wish, you know. We should stay somewhere nice," I say with amusement. She raises her chin and walks proudly through the platform. It's bustling with people, all wearing blank expressions and bleak-colored clothing. They don't notice us of course. The brick pillars of the platform are larger than I thought possible. It's like stepping into an entirely new world. My expression must give away my awe because Ophelia laughs beside me.

"Pretty amazing, isn't it?" she says with a light flickering across her eyes.

I nod. "This must be how the city folks feel when they come to the mountains of Montana."

Ophelia laughs in agreement. "Yeah, no kidding. Just shows you how used to our surroundings we become."

The awe doesn't leave me as we make our way through the city, armed with hands clasped tightly together and a few stolen kisses.

We end up finding a nice hotel right on the coast. Fancy. One that we could never afford when we were alive. The penthouse is the size of a ballroom, with a full kitchen, four bedrooms, and a living room for entertaining a crowd. But she was right; even though we're surrounded by the finest cotton sheets and luxury beds, we pile the blankets onto the floor of the living room and spread out all the things we've already accumulated along the way. Books, snacks we haven't tried yet, clothing from gift shops, and an entire bouquet of roses Ophelia found at a flower store just down the street. The roses are dark red and still full of life.

Our plan is to set out first thing in the morning and go onto our next bucket list idea. I cross out, *Ride a train somewhere new,* and glance up at Ophelia. She's lying on the ground on her stomach, feet crossed in the air behind her, writing in her notebook with a vintage pen.

<u>*Lanston & Ophelia's Bucket List*</u>
Go to Paris
Sail a yacht
Ballroom dance
Drink on the beach at night/camp out
~~Ride a train somewhere new~~
Visit Ireland's Trinity College Library
Save a stray plant

"Let's sail a yacht to Europe. Then we can cross off Paris and Ireland while we're there," I say as I tuck the paper back into my pocket. I have a good feeling about this bucket list idea. My soul already feels more at ease. Though I'm not sure how much it has to do with the places we visit as much as it does who I'm spending it with.

Ophelia looks back at me from over her shoulder and smiles. "That's a lovely plan." Her eyes glimmer with the mere thought of it. "It's been a dream of mine to dance on the stage of Palais Garnier. It's one of the most famous opera houses in the world."

"The *what?*" I ask, feeling silly for not knowing of it, but then again she's much more of a historical enthusiast than me.

She laughs and pushes herself up to face me. Her black dress, peasant-styled with long sleeves that ruffle at the ends, pools around her legs. "Palais Garnier. You'll see when we get to France. I'd show you a picture, but it will be much more impressive in person."

I try to imagine what a historic opera house looks like; all I can picture are white buildings with massive pillars, like the ones in Roman movies with gladiators.

"Are you going to perform alone?" I rest my head against my palm.

"I always do, but I wouldn't mind a partner for this one if you're up for it." She stares at me, hopeful, and my stomach drops. I wasn't expecting her to ask me.

"Um—"

"I'll teach you!" She quickly cuts me off and stands, grabbing my hands and pulling me up off the recliner I was very much comfortable in.

"*Ophelia,*" I say her name slowly, heavily implying I don't want to learn, but she ignores me and shows me the footing instead.

Reluctantly and with a smile that's all too natural, I move in step with her. One, two, three. One, two, three. Dip, spin. She laughs at my clumsy feet as I struggle not to trip over myself.

"Okay, now take my hands." Ophelia presents her hands to me.

My fingertips glide over her smooth palms. Her skin sends chills down my spine and nervousness threads through my stomach. I don't want to embarrass myself; she's fluid in her steps and motions, while I'm inept.

"Perfect, now this one goes around my waist," she mutters as she sets my left hand on her side. I move closer, closing the gap between us and breathing in her sweet scent. My throat bobs as I swallow, sliding my hand to her lower back.

Ophelia leads, moving in the steps she taught me, and surprisingly, after a few tries we start to move effortlessly. Our feet are in rhythm with one another and when we come to a stop, our breaths heavy, I can't look away from her eyes.

Dancing with Wynn was the only time I'd ever done so. It was nice and I loved every second of it. But with Ophelia, it feels like so much more. As if our hands were molded to fit into one another's—like the stars demand our union and celebrate the ground we move on.

It's intimate and soft.

I brush her hair back, tracing the angles of her face with my eyes. Our lips are nearly brushing. Each breath I take presses our chests together, sending a thick ache through my entire body and reminding me of last night.

But as I lower my head and she lifts her chin, we both freeze.

Whispers.

Her eyes widen and panic spreads over her face. All the blood in my veins turns to ice. I jerk my head back to look behind me and all I can see is darkness; the penthouse is cloaked in shadows, a black hole in the midst of the day.

Has it followed us? All the way here?

"Lanston!" Ophelia screams. The sound of her voice is so piercing it shakes my consciousness. I'm moving in her direction before I can even turn my head completely. She's standing halfway out the window and once she makes eye contact with me and knows I see her, she lets herself fall. Her hair is the last I see of her before I'm leaping from the window after her. I turn enough to see black wisps of shadows clinging near the window's edge where dark coils writhe in anger.

My heart races with thunderous fear. Ophelia looks much calmer now, staring at me with half-lidded eyes and a relieved smile as the wind lashes around her face.

We're falling from a twenty-story building and a different sort of fear consumes me. One that is both exhilarating and filled with terror all at once. Rationally, I know we cannot die, but I don't know what will happen once we reach the bottom. Will we bleed? Will I feel pain?

I despise pain with my entire being.

The ground approaches at an alarming rate, swift and lethal. My instincts tell me to brace for the end, but I only shut my eyes.

The thud of our bodies is vociferous. I only feel a

mild tingling across my skin, like I've been stung by bees but the sensation swiftly fades.

When my eyes open, I find Ophelia lying on her side before me. I'm on mine as well. She looks like she's merely asleep. No blood or broken bones jutting from her skin. Just asleep. Though the tears that form beneath her lashes tell me she's very much awake.

"It's okay," I whisper, reaching my hand to her arm in an attempt to comfort her.

She shifts back, leaving my hand cold in the space between us. Does she think it's her fault that the darkness chases her?

Her head shakes slowly. "It's not."

When I don't respond, she slowly sits up and wipes her tears. I watch as she seals herself away once more inside her castle of safeguards.

And I know she's going to try to lock herself away again.

23

Ophelia

The sky is gray and angry. Clouds grow heavy with rain as Lanston pushes us off the dock. The yacht's engine grumbles, and we start making our way out of the bay. Dark waves lap at the boat, casting spray across my cheeks.

They found me so quickly.

I sit on the bow of the immense and lavish peak of the boat, knees pulled up to my chest, quiet, as the ocean wind greets me with salty kisses.

This was a stupid thing to do. I knew Those Who Whisper would chase me. My gut tells me they'll cross the sea and world just to have my soul.

What if I stopped running?

What if I opened my arms and let them have me? Would they finally cease? It's the not knowing, I suppose, that haunts me the most.

There were no words between us as we ran from the hotel. We'd planned on staying somewhere nice for the evening, but nothing ever truly goes how we intend. Murphy's Law and whatnot.

We decided it was best to find a yacht and sleep aboard the ocean—hoping that this would be safer than resting on land. I glance over my shoulder timidly at Lanston. He stands at the steer, guiding us out of the bay and into deep water. His light brown hair is wind-blown and messy, his hazel eyes alert but weary from our extended day. Still in his state of contentment, he is beautiful. His posture is sturdy and his muscles flex with the grip of the wheel.

He notices me looking and flicks his attention to me, smiling briefly, carefully. I don't return the sentiment. Instead, I turn to face forward once more. I put him in danger by coming, and even though he won't say it, I know he's probably thinking what a mistake this was.

I fist my hand and pound it against my forehead. *Stupid. Selfish.* Why won't the world let me rest? I'm so fucking tired... and just this once, I thought maybe I could have the one thing I actually cherish.

Lanston.

It will be difficult to sleep tonight.

I stare sleepily into the dark waves ahead and think of falling to the farthest depths of the sea, where it is quiet and dark, and the universe can digest me until only my memory remains.

"Here."

My gaze is pulled from the ocean, sparkling in the midday light, and brought to Lanston. He holds out a folded piece of paper and looks nervous.

"What is it?" I ask, taking the paper from him and looking back up at his eyes when he's quiet for a beat too long.

His cheeks are rosy. "Just open it," he says with more attitude than I've ever heard come from his lips. I raise a brow but do as he says.

Lanston shoves his hands into his pockets and leans against the side of the yacht. His eyes are on the distant line where the ocean meets the sky, and I can tell he's anxious. It's the first we've spoken since last night. He tried a few times before we slept; I could tell by his uneasiness and pulled brows, but words evaded him just as they did me. So we didn't say anything. And it was sort of nice just to have his presence with me.

The yacht's master suite is luxurious, and we fell into the plush sheets like two sick pups, sleeping heavily until midday.

I unfold the paper.

The page is almost completely black, with only the shape of a skull at its center. The paint strokes are long and dreary, bringing so much emotion into my chest. The eye sockets are sagged, almost in a sorrowful expression. Red, cream, and gray are mixed and smeared in a perfect blend of color.

I could stare at the image forever. Lanston doesn't look at me once while I study his work. It's raw and dark, but there's so much more to it than just an image. There is a more profound voice wishing to be heard. *What is it you want to tell me?* The question sits cumbersomely on my tongue.

But I've yet to give him a letter; it doesn't feel fair to ask until he has something of me to devour as well. So, with restraint, I tuck the drawing into my pants pocket and thread my fingers through his.

Lanston looks down at me, expression unreadable. I know there is sorrow in his heart. It's in mine, too.

"Can you tell me about them?"

Lanston blinks slowly and a small smile grows. "Who?"

"Your friends. Liam and Wynn. Can you tell me about them?" I lower my chin as he sits beside me. He smiles reminiscently, a bit sad, and nods. The sun's rays reach us as they peek through the clouds, warming my skin and drawing weariness to my eyes. I lower my head into Lanston's lap and he sets his arm around my shoulder, twirling my hair around his finger.

He tells me of the fun and bonding they had in the

short months they spent together. Liam was there longer, but the three of them had only several weeks to fall into the same gravity as the others. But when you find kindred souls, you fall quickly and not sanely. That's how it goes.

I long to have relationships as he did. It's something I've always been bad at. Whether it's because I say the wrong thing or because I'm awkward, I'm unsure. But I enjoy hearing him speak about them, of their adventures and things they'd done.

Perhaps one day, I will shine as much as his fractured soul does.

A week out at sea is lonely. It detaches you from the world.

But we enjoy the silence of it; we welcome the storms that make it noisy and riotous. Lanston's presence is a constant comfort. The kisses we share and the laughter that's returned as the days pass have warmed my heart once more. The nights are my favorite—when my bare skin is pressed against his chest and he holds me adoringly.

He never lets his eyes linger too long when he knows I'm up to something. When he walked into the cabin bedroom of the yacht and saw me writing things down on a crumpled piece of paper, he only stared at me for a moment before turning back around and leaving me to my devices. He smiled knowingly, eager for the letter I promised him.

Sometimes, I wish he'd pry.

He must be curious, just as I am about what he draws.

I crumple the letter I've written him and hide it beneath the side table in the bedroom. He gave me a piece of him so easily, so carelessly, but I'm not sure if I'm ready for him to see how ugly I am on the inside.

Will he look at me differently? That's what I fear most.

I turn and look at him, sprawled out on the sun deck, shirtless and taking in the UV rays. His head is tilted back, exposing the soft parts of his throat. My eyes linger on his collarbones, the smooth line that shapes his chest, and the V that dips below his shorts. He must feel my eyes on him because he turns his head in my direction. Face impassive but curious.

I think of our *activities* on the train and swallow hard. My cheeks flush and I swiftly look away. There aren't many emotions I cannot handle, but the ones of heat and desire that swell between us, the growing urgency of them, are ones I'm scared to face. Lanston is different from any other man I've known. He takes his time, thoroughly enjoying his teasing.

We circle one another. Dangerously. Each waiting for the other to pounce and go for the throat. Once I taste his blood, and he does mine, I'm unsure what will happen next. Our feverish kisses and intimacies on the floor of the train nearly drove us to ruin.

I shake my head and try to think of other things.

It's fun to pretend with him. *Pretend that we're alive.*

And while I'm pretending, I've decided to face my fear of the ocean. A little late, I know. But if not now, then when? It's not like there's anything actually to fear anymore. Phantoms are immune to pain and death, so why do I still hesitate?

I don't bother looking to see if Lanston is watching as I let the soft fabric of my dress slip over my shoulders and pool at my feet. I lift one foot and then the other, slowly stepping closer to the edge.

My feet shift nervously on the bow of the boat, and then I dive in head-first. My fears are thrown to the wind, and my bare skin is vulnerable to the world.

The water's bright surface breaks as it swallows me whole. My body is consumed by the cold, salty water. I'm half tempted to try inhaling it just to see if I can breathe underwater, but I think better of it. Even as a phantom, it doesn't sound so pleasant.

As my eyes open, my mouth pinches with terror. The vastness of the sea is daunting, stretching as far as I can see—deep blue hues and darker as the depths go. Chills crawl up my spine, thinking of everything the sea takes.

I swim to the surface and inhale the brisk spring air. Lanston leans over the railing, his forearms spread along the metal, his hands hanging limply.

He's watching me intently. Feverishly.

His eyes draw fire on my skin, lines that will never fade until he smooths them over with his hands. I become aware of my bare chest and fight the urge to cover myself with my arms. I want him to see me. In the daylight and not just in the dimness of the night.

I avert my eyes and take a deep breath, dipping below the surface once more. My purple hair comes to life with the water and swirls around me.

Lanston.

He consumes my every thought, every breath. Even when we're talking or eating or on the nights he falls asleep before I do, I think of him. While his lashes hide his alluring eyes, and he thinks perhaps of books or the drawings that stain his fingertips black, I think of him.

I feel foolish for it.

You're a bad person—undeserving of a man like him.

My teeth grit together at the words I've heard my entire life. They are irrefutable. I don't want someone as lovely and pure as Lanston to get caught in my gravity of darkness. And yet, as much as I wish to keep him safe from me, I cannot let him go. I'll stay as long as he'll allow.

I open my eyes under water and suddenly find his hazel ones boring into me like anchors, wrapping around my soul and wishing to remain here with me in the heart of the ocean.

Beneath the world, beneath the universe and the stars, it's just us here.

No words to be spoken or places to hide.

Only us.

He lifts his hand to my face and brushes his thumb over the length of my jaw. His other hand hooks around my waist and pulls me closer until our bare skin is pressed against one another. The hard plane of his stomach makes me swallow and the evidence of his desire for me is nestled between my thighs.

I tilt my jaw up to look at him, finding the eyes of a beautiful, yearning soul. I wonder if he sees the same anguish in mine.

His grip on my lower back tightens, but he doesn't move; he just stares at me. Waiting. Watching. Starved for me.

Chills spread up my arms. A thousand reasons why I shouldn't kiss him again race through my mind, but one separate thought is much, *much* louder.

Hold me—kiss me.

Love me.

Our jaws clench simultaneously, and as I reach up with both hands to clasp his face, he pulls in for the fatal embrace. He kisses me hard, not soft and caressing as all the other times had been, but the surprise only adds to the delight that spreads through my flesh. Our hearts are desperate for each other, aching and beating to an erratic tune of carnal desire.

We part, blinking in a daze before realizing we're still underwater. I head to the surface first, pushing carefully away from his chest, and he follows.

Once our heads breach the surface, we connect again.

Our lips crash together, this time more viciously. I can smell his charcoal pencils, coffee and pages as I run my fingers through his wet hair.

"Ophelia," he whispers my name on a breath. It is so languid and raspy that it makes my core ache. Any and all thoughts are distant now. He stole them the moment he touched me.

"Yes?" I breathe against his lips. He leans away and presses his forehead to mine. Our limbs tangle as we bob in the water rhythmically with the waves.

Lanston flexes his jaw, feathering the light muscle that lines the bone. "I can't hide the darkness in my gaze any longer. The things I want to do to you are unspeakable."

My cheeks warm, but I whisper, "What is it you wish to do?"

His brows pull together in thought and a wicked grin lifts the corners of his mouth up. "Do you want me to tell you, or should I show you?" His hands glide down my ribs, sending chills over my skin.

"Show me," I say meekly over his lips. Our foreheads remain pressed together and our gaze unbroken.

Everything about Lanston aches. His mind, his body, his heart.

He lifts my hand from the ocean and presses a kiss to the back of it, salty and cold, before whispering, "Let's get back to the boat."

24

Lanston

Ophelia.

Her body falls against the bed sheets. Our skin dried the moment we stepped back on the boat, and I'm glad for it. The salt is gone from her skin and the cold that the ocean brought to our bones has fled.

She opens herself to me, relaxing and taunting. Her flesh is warm as I spread my fingers across her body, softly tracing every tender curve and dip.

Words seem to escape both of us and I think it's better that way—we are rather talented at talking ourselves out of moments like this one.

I kiss her collarbone, then the rise of her breast. She curls beneath me, eager for stimulation. A grin spreads across my lips as I lower my mouth to her nipple. I stroke her gently with my tongue, kneading her other breast with my palm. She whimpers beneath me and the groan that rolls up from my throat is one I've never known—a hunger so instinctual I fear I may lose myself to it, to her.

The edges of my teeth coast along her nipple. She breathes in sharply and grips my shoulders harder as I tease her. I smooth my hand down her stomach and lower, quickly finding her clit and stroking it in long, languid movements with my thumb.

Her back arches, pressing her stomach against mine and a throb of desire thrums through my core. I release her tit from my lips and look up at her. She's staring at me through hooded eyes, drunk with the pleasure and want that simmers between us.

"Don't fall in love with me, Lanston." Her tone is remorseful. She breathes in sharply again as I push two fingers inside her. Then, voice filled with lust, she says, "Promise me."

That's not an easy thing to promise. We don't get to choose who we fall in love with. It'd be much too simple if that were the case. And I'm already finding it hard to separate from her side. The year we spent longing for one another was not for naught. Our souls are anchored and tied together, tangled hopelessly by all the gods in old lore. They root for us; something does. I feel it down to the very core of my being.

My eyes hold hers and I murmur, "Only you would

ask an impossible thing such as that, my sweet Ophelia. But I don't make oaths I cannot keep."

She moans as I pump my fingers into her. I love watching how she moves beneath me. The raise of her shoulder and the tilt of her jaw. I jolt when she fists my cock—she grips my flesh hard, squeezing and stroking me in rhythm.

"Fine, but you are foolish in doing so."

"I'll be a fool if it's you," I say against her lips. She leans into me and our kiss burns deep into my bones. My entire body feels more alive now than ever before. Our teeth skate over each other's lips and our tongues chase one another feverishly.

I want you. I know you more than you could ever realize. I hear your cries for someone to understand you.

Her floral scent mixes with my musk and we can't seem to stop. I don't want to. She's an ocean I've been swept up in, taken out into the depths where there will be no return. Together, we'll be lost for eternity, and the sound of that is not unpleasant.

We steal moans from each other until we're breathing harder. Her strokes on my dick become slow and she starts to give more attention to the tip. I rub her clit, slick with her arousal, and watch her brows pinch together with pleasure as her mouth lolls open.

She comes hard, riding the last of her waves on my hand as she works me and I'm spilling over her fingers a moment later. My entire body convulses, trembling and eager. My jaw flexes and I moan with the last of my release. She's still reeling, clenching her thighs around my hand and digging her nails into my back.

We unravel. Our breaths are heavy as we roll in the sheets. I pin her beneath me and push her arms over her head. She throws her head back, exposing the soft flesh of her neck to my lips as I press kisses there and tease her entrance with my dick.

Ophelia writhes and wiggles her hips eagerly for me.

"Please," she begs, and I can't help the low chuckle that rises from my chest.

"I'll do anything if you ask me like that," I whisper, pushing the tip in just enough to make us both take a sharp breath. She bucks her hips and takes more of me in and the cry that leaves her lips sets something off in me.

I wrap my hands around her waist, letting my fingertips dig into her flesh and thrust inside her. Ophelia's hands find my forearms quickly, squeezing them as tightly as her core is wrapped around my dick.

I look down at her, moaning and coming undone beneath me, eyes rolling to the back of her head as I pump into her. I've never witnessed anything so beautiful. So lithe and lovely and meant entirely for me.

I let my chest fall to hers, greedy for the skin contact and the taste of her lips, her tongue. I push my hips until I'm flush with hers and I'm sheathed inside her completely. Her fingernails dig into my skin and fire spreads through my veins.

"Fuck, you're so perfect," I whisper into her mouth,

and she laughs against my lips. Urgent kisses between our words.

"Show me those unspeakable things you had in mind." Her voice is liquid and injects me with dark, lustful thoughts.

I grind my hips against hers and she screams out, arching her back again as I fill her up completely. "Are you sure?" I say in a low, dangerous tone.

She nods and bucks her hips like she no longer controls her own body.

I grin mischievously and withdraw from her, pulling her to the edge of the bed where the standing mirror against the wall reveals the two of us, naked and slick with sweat.

"*Oh.*" She breathes out and I watch her swallow nervously.

I offer my hand for her to stand and she takes it, rising smoothly as I sit on the edge. "Turn around and face the mirror. I want you to watch me fuck you."

Ophelia obeys me and faces the mirror, pushing her back against my chest as she slowly lowers herself onto my cock. I guide her hips with my hands wrapped around her lower thighs until I'm completely inside her.

I groan, wrapping my arms around her torso, cupping one of her breasts as I reach down to her clit with my other hand. My eyes lift to the mirror, where I see the two of us connected. A fresh wave of pleasure thrums through me as Ophelia's half-lidded eyes watch my every movement. She bites her lip and squirms in my arms.

"Oh my God," she says as if in a trance, letting her head fall back on my shoulder as I start grinding my hips into her.

My hand slides up her throat and to her chin, focusing her attention back on the mirror. "You have to watch. I want you to see yourself come undone."

The words come naturally to me and I'm both horrified and curious at where these lewd thoughts derived. All I know is that this woman drives me to insanity.

I lower my lips to her shoulder and watch as my thrusts become her undoing. Her orgasm hits its peak as I buck my hips one last time and our bodies tremble together as we climax. She shudders and goes limp in my arms as my dick throbs inside her with my release.

Exhausted, I fall back into the sheets, holding her securely in my arms and adorning her cheek with kisses.

"I really like you, Lanston," she whispers, like it's a forbidden thing to say.

I smile and brush her hair back away from her face. "I *really* like you too, Ophelia." *So much more than like you*, I want to say, but I won't press her.

She looks dreary in the dim light of the yacht's bedroom. The shades are pulled, making it seem like night is upon us. Perhaps it is; I've lost track of the time. She does that to me. Steals things as fickle as time.

We roll to our sides to face each other, and I admire her brown-green speckled eyes. She watches me in silence as I watch her. My soul feels naked beneath her gaze.

"What are you thinking about?" I whisper. The words hang between us and settle into the sheets.

She studies me a few moments more, then blinks slowly.

Ophelia sits up and leans over me. Her waist is warm against mine as she reaches below the nightstand and pulls out a cream-colored letter. The envelope is wrapped closed with twine, and a single dried red rose is tied down to it, thorns jutting out between the threads.

My chest grows heavy and I take a moment before saying anything. She sits back on her haunches, naked and bare to me, like a goddess of the sea. Her long hair covers her breasts as she stares down at the letter with a pained frown.

"I'll read it outside," I say softly. She looks up at me, more tired than I think I've seen her. Darkness collects beneath her eyes and I wish I could take all these demons from her. Maybe one day I can.

She nods with a small smile and holds the letter out to me—trusting me to get to know the parts she doesn't show anyone.

I wait until she falls asleep. Nestled in the bed, worn out from our mischief.

By the time I reach the sun deck, it's pouring rain.

The darkness of the clouds bruises the sky, making the sea angry and drawing out large swells of waves.

If I weren't already a phantom, I'd be terrified. The ocean has always frightened me. It swallows anyone whole, never to be seen again or found.

I sit at the end of a lounging chair that barely borders the edge of the canopy shielding against the rain. Water flicks up against my shins and the cold droplets ground me in this moment while the sky weeps.

The minutes pass as I hang my head, staring dully down at the dried rose. *Ophelia.* Do I have the strength to read something from your heart? I only gave her a laughable picture I drew, one of the pain I endured inside my aching soul. But she's written down things that are explicit, black and white. True to her. Can I really read them? Is it okay for me to?

My back is arched, elbows set against my knees. I lift my head and look out into the storm. The sun peeks through in some places, breaking the darkness and shedding a few beams of gold down onto the angry gray sea.

I can read it with love—with understanding that perhaps only I have for her.

The twine twists as I untie it and set it down beside me. The rose remains laced between my fingers as I carefully unfold the letter.

Lanston,
You've inspired me, so I'm telling you a story—my story. In it, you will read many sad things, but my hope is that you

will perhaps find answers to the questions that flicker through your eyes when you look at me.

I knew long ago that I was unwanted. It wasn't one slight glare but many. Should a five-year-old know the sting of a belt? I knew it well. You learn quickly how to hide, how to plead, and, most of all, how to shut out the world.

It wouldn't be fair to say I'm a nice person because I'm not, not really. I know I'm cold and distant. It's the fail-safe that keeps my mind taped together in its fragile state.

Remember when I told you I was murdered?

It's not pretty—the thorns are sharp, and they will pierce you.

This is the beginning of the end—the story of how I died. Will you hear it?

I lower the note, crinkled where my thumb has pinched it. Seeing that my emotions must have gotten the better of me, I loosen my grip.

Who killed you, Ophelia, and why?

The rain eases and the sky shimmers with the last of the cold droplets. Ophelia's note is snug in my pocket, waiting to be read again and again. Her rose still between my fingers, piercing my skin and drawing a slight sting.

Her thorns are prickly, but I'll keep the cuts they leave forever.

25

Ophelia

The bed dips as Lanston finally returns. The sun set long ago and the waves have been mild since. I dipped in and out of sleep for a few hours but now stare at the small window showcasing the glassy ocean lit up with the stars. With no lights out here, it's as if the entire universe calls to us.

"Are you awake?" he asks quietly.

I turn and look at him from over my shoulder. "Yeah."

Lanston grins, taking my hand and pulling me up. The sheets fall to my lap and my bare breasts are exposed, but his eyes remain soft on mine. He smooths the back of his hand over my cheek and whispers, "I want you to see something."

He hands me a black shirt. I think it's his, but it's too dark to tell. I slip it over my head and follow him out onto the sun deck.

Air escapes my lips as I stare up at the night sky. There isn't a cloud in sight tonight. The air is crisp, our breaths visible.

The sea reciprocates the stars, making it look like we are sailing across the universe, across all worlds. Could we sail into the stars? I wonder.

"This is beautiful," I say with a hushed voice, because the stars can surely hear us.

Lanston nods and smiles at me. His eyes aren't as dark as they were earlier. I swallow the image in my head of him reading my letter.

"Do you see the light on the horizon?" He moves to stand behind me. My skin pebbles with goose bumps as his hand skates over my arm. He rests his weary chin on my shoulder, and I follow his other hand as he lifts his finger to the line where the sky meets the sea. It's almost indistinguishable in the darkness, but the light that brightens the small area of the sky makes itself known.

"Is that Ireland?"

He nods against my skin, leaning his head on mine. "We'll stop in Dublin first and look at the castles, taste their potatoes, and see their libraries."

"And museums?"

He laughs; his chest is light against my back. "Of course."

"And their parks and art?"

Lanston wraps his arms around me, pressing his lips to my temple. "All of it for you, my rose."

Our first destination is a clothing shop. We agreed that we wanted to have the entire experience, so we must dress the part. Lanston finds tight black jeans with dress shoes and a collared shirt matched with suspenders, while I manage to get my hands on a floral dress with a cream base and white lace over it with sewn flowers.

It's a dress I could never afford. The fabric is unbelievably soft and looks ethereal in the light. I thought it might feel special wearing something so unobtainable, but I find that I only long for that fleeting feeling to be filled again by the next thing that's out of reach. Isn't that how it goes? It's never truly enough.

Lanston leans against the brick wall of the dressing room. He hasn't noticed my appearance yet, so I decide to tease him. I sneak out the other end of the dressing room and circle back, watching him from his right side, intending to scare him.

His hands sketch quickly over the page he's marking up with black. The charcoal pencil flicks across the paper knowingly as his hands make the darkness in his mind come to life.

I abandon my idea of taking him by surprise and fold

my hands behind my back instead, properly, how a woman in a dress such as this should behave according to social standards. My footsteps are light, and I approach his side in silence.

He doesn't even glance up at me as he mutters, "Here I thought you were going to try and scare me." My cheeks burn. When I don't reply, he finally lifts his eyes to mine. Whimsy flickers through his features. "Want to see?"

I nod and lean over more to peek, but as I do so, Lanston shuts his notebook and shoots me a ridiculous grin. Light brown locks of hair drift over his forehead and in the next moment, he's making a break for the shop's doors, fleeing from me.

"Hey!" I shout, half flustered and partly laughing as I give chase.

Not one person on the crowded streets of Dublin looks our way. They cannot see us, but I'm as real as I ever was, taking in the crisp spring air and feeling the rush of emotions as I chase my cherished one down cobbled roads.

"Lanston, stop!" I laugh, breathing hard and trying to keep up with him.

He glances back at me and holds up his drawing notebook. "Come on, I've always wanted to be chased by a pretty girl," he shouts back.

I'm not a phantom in this moment; I'm just a woman in an expensive dress running after a handsome, flirtatious man in a foreign country. The freshness of the air and buzz of the street lightens my heart.

Lanston can tell I'm starting to slow so he eventually stops at a vibrant park in the center of the city. Artwork lines the entire fence surrounding the park. Artists stand proudly next to their pieces and speak with people who've wandered close enough to listen, mesmerized by the creative minds the city has to offer. I've heard of this place, Merrion Square.

I find myself pulled in, unable to look away from all the lovely pieces from different walks of life, straight from each artist's heart.

Lanston gives me a heartwarming smile, one that makes me ache for all the years I've not known him, all the lost smiles I didn't get to see. His breaths are staggered, but the eagerness in his eyes shines so bright. He explains before I can even ask how he knew this was here.

"I overheard some ladies talking about the art here while I was waiting for you to get dressed," he says through inhales.

A laugh escapes me. "So you made me chase you here, did you?"

"Wasn't it fun? To run through the city and feel the cobblestones beneath your feet? To be free of eyes that would normally keep us from being our genuine selves?"

My gaze softens on him. I still can't figure him out. He's a wonder. I crave to see the world through his eyes and feel everything as he does. "Yeah, it was," I admit. The ache in my chest grows.

"Shall we?" He offers me his arm. I hook my arm

through his, and we stroll through the park, taking in all the paintings and drawings with awe. We stop at a few, looking longer at some black-and-white paintings that bear endearing brush patterns.

Lanston leans in and studies the techniques, intrigued by the styles. Maybe he'll try some of them himself later.

I wish I could've paid for some and told the artists how lovely their work is. It would be nice if they knew two phantoms were admiring their art. By the time we finish the loop, I'm sullen with reminiscent thoughts. Lanston untangles his arm from mine and goes to stand by the black fence that lines the park.

I'm entranced by an elderly couple walking slowly through the center path of the park. Their wrinkled hands are clasped tightly and the peace of their expressions as they silently traverse the park brings a small smile to my lips.

They know each other so entirely, it's evident. The old man buys her a flower and a painting of trees, a vibrant green like the ones around us now. She smiles at him, joy so pure yet quiet—it touches me.

I watch them until they leave and then realize I've forgotten myself. Where did Lanston go? How long was I watching? I look from side to side. The sun is setting and I'm alone.

As panic dawns over me, I turn completely, looking back at the fence and finding Lanston sitting between two other artists—a weary smile lifting his lips as my eyes connect to his.

He fits here amongst the dreamers. One of his suspenders has fallen over his shoulder, and the cream-colored shirt he wears beneath it is baggy and already stained with charcoal. With his notebook in hand, he tears out a page.

"I've just finished," he mutters cheerfully.

My brow arches as I approach him, standing an arm's length away. His cheeks are red; nervous energy fills the space between us.

"Are you going to show me this time?" I tease.

Lanston grins before he turns to face the fence; he tapes the paper to the steel and glances back at me again with those piercing hazel eyes. "You can't laugh."

I nudge his shoulder as if I'm offended. "Why would you even think such a thing of me?" He seems reassured by that and steps aside in one fell swoop.

Air invades my lungs and ceases the pulse in my veins.

His drawing is... of me a moment ago, as I watched the elderly couple.

The woman in the image stands alone, people blurring around her as if they are the real ghosts and not her. The dress is vivid, with flowers and lace blowing in a breeze. The woman clutches her dress slightly between her fingertips—not in a violent way, but with yearning. Most of all, I notice how anguished her expression is, the tears not shed but brimming in her eyes.

The pain she experiences while watching love reach its earned end—the way it's meant to.

He really does see me.

A knot builds in my throat. I've never seen such talent, someone who puts every emotion and feeling they have into a piece of art. And into knowing another soul.

Tears spill down my cheeks and I hastily wipe them away before letting my eyes find Lanston. He watches me in silence, understanding all the emotions that wash over my weary mind in this moment.

Because, well, I've never seen how sad I truly look to others.

When I look at myself in the mirror, I'm compelled to smile. It's what we're taught, isn't it?

Smile. Look pretty. *Smile.* Even if it hurts, smile.

"You see me," I whisper, words I've never spoken.

His face remains emotionless, studying my expression as he replies, "I see you as clearly as you see me."

I hesitate. Does he despise the sorrow I carry, the melancholy that holds me fiercely in its dark embrace, as everyone I ever confided in did?

"Do you see the ugliness that lurks beneath my skin?" I choke out the words as tears continue to fall.

Lanston's face crumples in anguish. "No, Ophelia. I do not see any bad, ugly things. Not in you, my rose. You are the most precious of things, holding far more beauty than I could ever describe to you."

My cheeks warm at his words, as do his.

I take a moment to straighten myself, sniffling the last

of my tears away before gracing him with a wide smile. "Hello, sir. I would like to buy this picture, please." I pull out my wallet, filled with more money than I've ever made in life.

Lanston tilts his head with amusement and lifts the paper from the fence, extending it to me with that charming smile he so easily steals my heart away with.

"It's on me."

I laugh and shove a few hundred-dollar bills in his hand. "I insist!" I say loudly, snatching the drawing from him and throwing money his way. He leans in and narrows his eyes at me. I scream as he scoops me up in his arms, lifting me from the ground swiftly and spinning us in a circle before running off with me in his arms.

Our laughs echo through the streets, bustling with cars and people.

No one can hear us.

Our laughter is a lovely sound, louder than the life surrounding us could ever be.

26

Lanston

How can it be that you come to know someone more than you know yourself? I would know her in any life, this I am certain. I don't believe in such things, but should reincarnation be real... I'm beginning to think Ophelia is my eternity. We would find each other in every life or death, even as phantoms. We would know, just as I do now. Our souls call and beckon, waiting for the inevitable joining of us.

She looks at me the way Wynn used to, but more. She unshackles me and helps me spread my wings, encourages me to find the light I seek, joining me in my adventure. She is a spark of desire and uncontainable affection.

I'm a hopeless romantic. This I know. But I never knew it was this little rose I'd been searching for.

Ophelia stares up in awe at the towering ceilings of St. Patrick's Cathedral.

As she observes the architecture, her mouth falls open—more than once. I chuckle to myself at her reaction to this place. It is beautiful yet chilling in a way.

The air is heavy beneath these old stones. A mildewy and aged scent lingers, much like how I anticipated a place as old as this to smell. The stained glass windows are breathtaking, letting in colored lighting and dappling the floors with the rainbows of a worshipped god.

"This is... I don't know. I can't even express it," Ophelia says as she slowly makes her way up to the choir. A priest readies his sermon and many tourists gather in the pews. The aisles aren't very spacious and the old wood creaks beneath the weight of the visitors.

We walk past the priest and up into the restricted portions of the building.

It's dark up here, the stones aren't as clean, and the air is thick with dust and moisture. I follow Ophelia, sparing glances at the large paintings that grace the walls.

"It feels off up here," I say, knowing that I'll sound like I'm afraid of dark, decrepit places. And, well, *I am*.

She doesn't turn to look at me as she says, "Oh, don't be a baby. No one gets to see these parts of the cathedral. Where is your sense of adventure?"

I give her a sarcastic grin. "I don't have one."

Ophelia laughs and holds her hand out behind her,

open and waiting for me. I set my palm in hers and let her lead the way.

"What if this place is haunted?" I ask slowly, humorously. Cold ebbs into my bones as we continue through the restricted area. That stops her right in her tracks. Ophelia turns and gives me a sour expression.

"Really?"

"Well, obviously not *us*, but what if there are unfriendly phantoms lurking around?" My eyes trail through the dark corridors, and I swear I see movement in the far doorway.

"Why would you assume they are unfriendly?" I shrug and she sighs. "Maybe *we're* the unfriendly ones."

I wait until she turns to face forward again before rolling my eyes. A flash of white races across the hall from one door to another. We both freeze and I set my hand on her shoulder.

"Let's get the fuck out of here," I whisper-shout, already turning on my heels. Ophelia brushes my hand off her shoulder and walks steadily toward the room with a phantom. "Ophelia!" She ignores me.

I curse under my breath before following after her; fists curled at my sides with fear as my breaths become hollow and short.

"Hello?" Ophelia says softly. Her voice is like silk, enticing and kind, anyone should answer to such a lilting sound.

We both stop at the doorframe and stare into the large, empty room. A thin, tall ghost dances alone. Her white hair reminds me of starlight and as she slowly twirls, arms lifted slightly, she grins nostalgically. Perhaps she is remembering her partner.

"Hello, phantoms." The dullness of her voice skates across my spine. Her steps are light and I notice she wears no shoes—only the rag-like white dress that drapes over her shoulders. "Far away from home, aren't you?"

Chills crawl up my spine. How'd she know?

When neither of us replies, the woman stops dancing and faces the windows that overlook the well-tended gardens below. Rain steadily pitter-patters over the grounds, thickening the air. I have to blink a few times when the mist starts to appear around the woman.

The way she holds herself is so melancholic.

She does not face us as she speaks. "What is it you want?"

Ophelia looks at me, and I shake my head. *You're the one who wanted to chase her*, I want to say.

Clearing her throat, Ophelia says, "We are only passing through."

The phantom lifts her head a bit but still does not turn in our direction. "A journey? What could two ghosts possibly be traveling for? Don't you have a manor to haunt?"

I press my lips into a thin line, trying my best not to laugh. This woman must be long dead to think in such archaic ways. Must phantoms haunt places?

"A bucket list," I intervene, "of things we could not do while we were alive."

The woman pauses. Considering us. Then she turns her head only enough for us to see the side of her face. I tremble and resist the urge to recoil. The nerves in my body shoot fleeing sensations through me.

Where are her eyes?

The woman has only a mouth left; her long white hair seems to weep beside her sorrow. Ophelia tenses at my side as well, taken by the revelation of her missing features.

"You've never seen one like me, have you?" the phantom says gently. I'm sure it's not hard to place the reason for our sudden silence.

We both shake our heads, almost like children. We don't wish to be rude, but we're also shocked.

"Be glad for it and pass on to the afterlife. Lest you become like me."

Ophelia hesitantly steps a bit closer. I want to pull her back, but I keep my hands firmly placed at my sides.

"How do phantoms regress to your state?" she asks boldly.

The phantom holds up her hand, the light from the window spilling through her bones. She says placidly, "I've been here far longer than any ghost in Dublin. I suppose I began to notice the change after the first few centuries."

Centuries? How terrible. My brows pull closer with pity for the ghost. To be stuck here in the in-between for this long is a cruel fate.

"Can we help you in any way?" I ask. If we helped

Charlie, then we might be able to help her too. However, I don't know anything about the city and I'm sure neither does Ophelia.

The woman turns back to face the window and, with a deep breath, her shoulders sag. "There is one thing."

Ophelia lights up and shoots me a quick, eager look over her shoulder.

"I haven't left this cathedral in over three hundred years. You see, there was a man I once loved. He would bring me roses and sing to me. After I died, well, I don't know what happened to him. If you could find out for me, I think that might bring me a great deal of relief. Peace." She lifts her head once more. I think she's looking at me, but it's hard to tell with only impressions on her face where her eyes *should be*. "My name is Elanor. Please, find my Gregory Briggs."

It's a task I wasn't expecting her to say. I glance at Ophelia and she has her chin held high, tears brimming but not yet falling. Ah yes, my rose is a hopeless romantic as well. Her heart must be breaking for this old, forgotten ghost who dances in the dark, alone and away from the world. Even her face is forgotten.

"I will find what became of him," Ophelia says, not as a statement but as a promise. Elanor seems pleased by it and resumes her forlorn slow dance.

We see ourselves out of the cathedral and don't speak until we're a few blocks away, slipping inside a warm bakery for an afternoon cup of tea and croissants. We help ourselves to the food without a blink from the staff or customers.

The water has long since dried off my clothes, but Ophelia's hair is still wet. I wonder why she takes so long to dry sometimes. A drop trickles down her face and drips from her nose. I frown and reach over the table with a borrowed scarf from the gal behind us.

Ophelia's cheeks are red, and she smiles at me innocently as I dry her face and hair.

"Thanks," she murmurs thoughtfully before sipping on her tea.

I lean back in the wooden chair and take her in. Trying to get a read on this woman is like trying to solve the world's hardest math problem. And I'll be the first to admit that I was never any good at math.

She solves it for me.

"How are we going to find Gregory Briggs? We didn't even get a time period to search for." Ophelia sullens and takes another long sip.

I laugh and take a bite from my croissant. "Ophelia, we can't possibly find him. The poor phantom will need to find her peace some other way."

That earns me a scowl.

"We'll find a way."

I swallow thickly, feeling the heat in my veins. I hate confrontation, even as mild as this is. "Ophelia, where would we even start? You said it yourself: you cannot stay in one place for too long. Those Who Whisper might catch up to us again and we've already been here for the full day." I try to say it kindly and with reason, but she looks troubled.

"I saw so much of myself in her, Lanston. I don't want to leave without giving her *something,* even a small piece of information that might help her pass on." Her eyes dim and she stares down into her mug.

She's right, we have time for at least a quick internet search or rummage through the old libraries.

"How about we look while we're at Trinity College then?"

Ophelia's eyes meet mine as she lifts her head. A lovely smile spreads over her lips and I allow my eyes to linger there. I'd do anything to see her smile like this forever.

27

Ophelia

Trinity College. It is a beautiful campus with many, *many* tourists. I'm not sure how the students get anything done here with the buzz. The grounds are filled with curious eyes. Gardens greener than you've ever seen and the smell of fresh rain—I could stay here for days, just observing the flowers and students. It's the perfect place to crack a new book and jot down notes.

Lanston crosses Trinity College off the bucket list and grins. "We've nearly completed half the list." He looks up at me, curiosity and affection dancing behind his eyes. "Do you feel closer to crossing over?"

I shake my head. "No. You?"

He shoves the paper back into his pocket and

breathes out a long sigh. "No, but I also have no clue what that would feel like." His lips arch into a smile, but I don't miss the tension that pulls at his jaw.

He's worried we'll cross everything off the list and still be stuck here.

That's a valid fear.

I feel it too.

But at least we'd still be together. I think and look over at Lanston as he studies the architecture of Trinity. His lips are red with the chill in the air, eyes bright with curiosity. *At least we'll still be together.*

I smile at the thought, however fleeting it may be.

We venture inside the library, slipping between tourists as they stare in awe at the impressive room. No, it's more than a room; it is a great hall, grander than any I've ever seen. The bookshelves are tall, nearly twenty feet or so. There are two stories of shelves. The ceilings are drafty, made of wood that arches beautifully with a rich brown stain. Each section has a ladder that looks entirely too thin to use. Sculpture busts of people who died a long time ago rest at the end of each row. The center of the room is made up of multiple glass cases in a perfect line. Each holds artifacts and things you'd find in museums.

Lanston traces his fingers along the glass display cases and looks up at the books, admiring the knowledge this place keeps tucked away. The ache in my chest grows as his eyes dim a bit.

"You can still do something with your experience

here, you know," I say softly, staring down at my intertwined fingers. He glances my way and I find a flicker of hope in them.

"Like what?"

"Anything you want." I reach into his satchel and place his notebook in his hands. One of his suspenders has slid over his shoulder and he truly looks like himself right now. The messy, disorganized man that he is. His light brown hair is disheveled and those hazel eyes warm on me.

"Would you let me draw you again?"

I raise a brow and grin mischievously, folding my hands together over the crux of my lower back as I walk casually away from him. "You never asked to begin with, *Nevers*," I say sarcastically, and I can hear him chuckle to himself. The smooth sound of his voice sets embers alight inside my chest.

The thought of falling in love as a phantom seems ridiculous. I've already had my chance at love in my short life, and it didn't end well.

I take the spiral staircase at the end of the hall up to the second story of ancient books. It smells like dusty pages and old, creaking wood up here. The silence of the library, though filled with at least a hundred people, is deafening.

My eyes find Lanston quickly. He has selected a pillar to lean against, his eyes studying the shelves and ladders as his hand draws furiously. His brows pull together with focus.

How could such raw, beautiful talent and passion go unnoticed? I stare in awe as he works, admiring every emotion it strips from my soul.

I want to share things and bleed as he does. But first, I need to finish telling him my story; otherwise, I'm unsure he'd fully understand.

The longer I watch him, the sadder I become.

Who staved off his dreams of being his true self? Who wasn't he good enough for? The adoration and inspiration that fuels his lovely mind should've been enough. I wish someone would've told him that his art didn't belong hidden in his room at a mental rehabilitation center. It should have been broadcast and shouted from the rooftops. *Look. I existed and these are the things I felt inside. These are the images I drew for the world to witness, to feel alongside me.*

I wish I could've been that person for him. I wish we were alive. I'd show everyone here what he can do.

I let out a soft sigh.

My eyes drift over to a row of books labeled with different religions. There is a framed image by the section of a woman surrounded by demons; fire consumes her and the pain in her expression is palpable.

Weariness drags into my lungs as I stare at the torture depicted so mercilessly.

Is this what I fear? *Where the bad people go.*

Is this why I'm still here?

We stay at the library for the rest of the day, watching people come and go—ignorant of the phantoms that observe them. I search for Mr. Briggs in history books, but I can't find a thing about the man. It stings my heart, but perhaps that phantom stuck in the cathedral has already forgotten our promise. She seemed aloof enough. Selfishly, I hope it's the case. As Lanston mentioned, we can't stay long, but it doesn't stop the guilt.

I spend the remaining time writing Lanston the second letter of my story and fold the pages into my pocket. He uses up at least five pages in his notebook before finding me and letting his shoulders drop with weariness.

"Ready?" I ask, letting my head fall to the side a bit as fatigue tugs on my eyes as well.

He nods and offers me his hand.

We find an empty dorm room on Trinity's campus. The bed is stripped bare, the closet vacant. Lanston sets his coat over the bed and lies down, lifting his head expectantly for me to follow.

I linger in the doorway, rubbing my thumb over the pages I wrote for him to read tonight. We haven't spoken about the first letter. Nor his drawing.

But I want to watch him read it tonight. I have questions about his picture too, the hurt behind it. The story that it drew breath from.

Lanston quirks a brow and sits up. Both his suspenders are off his shoulders now and he looks serene in this state of disarray. The dim light catches on the swell of his lips. "What's wrong?" he asks.

The letter feels heavy in my hand as I pull it from my

pocket. His eyes lower to the pages and a smile awakens over his sleepy features.

"I want to watch you read it."

He doesn't say anything. Instead, he reaches over the edge of the bed and into his bag. A torn page is already folded and he finds it quickly, giving me an innocent grin. "Guess we had the same idea."

28

Lanston

Ophelia sits beside me. Our legs touch and share warmth between us.

"You first," I say nervously and pass her my torn page. One of the things I love most about art is that it's very open to interpretation. I needn't explain all the darkness behind it. People feel or see what they want—what they need to see.

She gently takes the folded page from me and stares down at it as if it holds the universe's secrets. Long lashes hood her eyes.

I watch patiently as she unfolds it, eyes greedily taking in the charcoal smudges and crosshatch shading.

Her face is impassive and unreadable. My legs become restless, waiting for her to say something, anything.

I drew this one from a place of rage. It has sat in my lungs, heavy and suffocating, for years.

A boy sits curled up with his arms wrapped around his knees. His eyes are the focal point, encapsulating his fear and incomprehension of why he is so thoroughly beaten. The skin around his cheekbones is bruised, darkened, and heavily shaded. A tall, dark figure looms over the boy—the taker of my soul.

Ophelia looks for much longer than I thought she would. She reaches for the boy's face and gently smooths her finger down the paper as if she can comfort him. Then her eyes lift to mine, forlorn.

"He is just a boy." A statement, not a question. Her voice is weak with pain.

I nod, biting the inside of my cheek to quell the unwanted tears. Her face is sullen. Somber thoughts reveal themselves in the ache in her gaze and the way she curls her fingers.

She looks back down and brushes the page again. "I wish I could tell him that whatever it is he's done, it was never deserving of this. I wish he knew that."

Something old and mistreated in my heart cracks when I hear her say that. How I longed for another to see me, the sad boy, the unloved child. To look and see the misery in my gaze. To say, *I will help you.* It never came. No one wanted to see me, not until Liam and Wynn.

How many times did I call out for my mother, *Please*

help me. Why do you allow this? And to my father, *Please stop. I'm sorry I exist.*

It hurts.

It rots the inside of my brain like a disease.

Ophelia reaches for me, grabbing my shoulders and pulling me in eagerly, desperately. Her embrace releases the tears that I've kept hidden away. The warmth of her hands spreads into my aching soul and finds where I'm still so cold.

"Can you tell me more about the boy? I'd love to hear his voice, even if he's a grown man now. Sometimes, we just need to release the broken parts of us. Unchain them and let them be free," she whispers against the shell of my ear, her soft lips brushing my skin. I wrap my arms around her slowly, fisting the back of her shirt and pulling her closer. My tears stain her shoulder, and she lets them.

Ophelia hums a song I recognize as she strokes the back of my head in slow, affectionate strides. The song is "Death Bed" by Powfu. I let my head fall against her and she squeezes me tighter with her other arm, pressing a tender kiss to my neck.

It's easier to confess things when you're not staring into the eyes of a person you care for dearly. I don't want her to look at me differently, but I don't want to hide from my demons anymore. I've done that long enough.

"It was usually my humor that made him angry." I start and Ophelia stills; her hand rests softly on the back of my neck for a moment before resuming the languid strokes. "But then, as I got older, it became more things that I couldn't help. It wasn't the trouble I caused or even the bad things I said. He hated *me*. He hated my characteristics. The way I loved to learn literature and art. The hope that glimmered in my eyes as I dreamed of a life better than his. The way I smiled so easily without the weight of the world weighing me down." I pause, thinking deeply, remembering the awful looks he gave me. "I think he hated that most."

Ophelia pulls away only enough to look into my eyes. Her nose brushes against mine as she gazes into my soul. I'm scared to find pity there, but I'm met with understanding and a well of rage.

"Your father was a lousy piece of shit. A jealous asshole for your ability to be happy." Her voice is the most angry I've heard it, and it makes my eyes widen with surprise.

"I didn't know you could curse," I chide her, but she dismisses it completely.

"You deserve so much love, Lanston. I hope you know that."

I lie. "I know."

She furrows her brows and fists my shirt, pinching my skin with her emotions on her sleeves. "Don't lie. You... You are the most beautiful soul anyone could know. I see the bruises that have long since healed across your pale skin from abuse, the lingering thoughts of death that you bore upon yourself because you wanted it to end. You tried to die. Many times."

I tried to die. I admit to myself, tears quietly

streaming down my cheeks—*many times*. My eyes lift to her arm, seeing the butterfly and moth chasing each other, hiding many things beneath them that she won't say. Not yet.

"I know that ugly pain. It yields no mercy for us, does it? I know that illness as thoroughly as I know you. It is cancerous and grows beneath a blanket of flesh, hidden because it's not pretty. When you try to speak about it, people quickly hush you. They don't want to see the ugly, bad things inside us. The sickness that takes many of our kind. It steals them away in the night and we wait. *We wait.*" She pauses, taking a few deep breaths as her eyes finally brim with tears too. "We've waited for so long. To be heard. To be listened to. To be understood. We've waited for the light. For the morning that seems to be just out of reach. And yet, we're always reaching, aren't we? Swaying wearily and always dreaming for that day to come."

I press my palm to her cheek as she lets those heavy tears fall. She leans into me and I whisper, "I'll tell you a secret, my rose."

Her eyes are blurry with tears, but she waits for my words.

"We are the light."

Ophelia's eyes widen and then nearly shut as a fresh wave of emotions overcomes her. The ends of her hair are wet; her body seems colder. I run my fingers over her skin, comforting her the best I can.

"Together, we are no longer a small, insignificant

candle against the dark pillars of the world. We are an inferno—a growing, living beast that demands to be witnessed, to find our kindred souls," I say gently.

She studies my features before murmuring, "Like phoenixes—the symbol of rebirth after tragedy." The corner of her lip lifts into a hopeful grin.

I return the sad smile. "The real question is if we'll ever truly fly."

Her eyes flicker with long-lost flames. "I hope so." She hands me her letter.

She swallows and a worried crease appears between her brows.

"Are you sure you want to stay while I read it?"

Her nod is firm.

I grab her hand and pull her into my lap. She relaxes against my chest and sighs with relief at our connection. Our fingers interlace and I hold her lovingly—how a phantom as precious as her should be held.

Lanston,
Hey you, where did we leave off? Oh yeah, the beginning of the end. The sick game death likes to play before we ripen.
Where do I start my story? I guess where it begins... when I was five, my cousin died by suicide. I didn't understand the gravity of that yet, but my family said horrible things about her after her funeral. They said she was selfish and

was going to hell for "committing the ultimate sin." That she would burn for what she did.

Even at a young age, I thought to myself how unfair it was of them to say. She was a kind person, that is all I remembered of her, but I knew that she wasn't bad. She was the most generous and caring human I'd known.

But I also remembered the things they said about her. I kept it locked away in a compartment in my brain for the day my brain started to turn on me too.

Patrick was the first boy I fell in love with. He wasn't very nice, but we dated for a few years until I turned seventeen. That's when I learned how much a person could wound you without a weapon. He cheated on me with some tall blonde and that was the end of it. A betrayal that I'd carry with me for the rest of my life.

"You aren't a good person. You know that. It was bound to happen," my stepmother told me.

Little did I know that someone else had their eye on me, on my suffering, like a reaper drawn to rot, waiting patiently for me to ripen. Someone watched me until I fell into ruin.

My murderer was always close. Always near.

I wish I'd known.

The pages fold as I loosen my grip around them. Ophelia doesn't lift her head from my chest. She breathes evenly, surely hearing the falter of my heartbeats.

"How did you die?"

My question is raw and her body tenses. When she doesn't reply, I take it as her answer that she's not ready to talk about it. But then she slowly lifts her head and sits back on her haunches to look at me.

"I'll tell you, I promise I will. But you need to hear the full story first. Otherwise, I'm worried you won't understand," she says meekly, keeping her eyes lowered on her hands.

I give her a small nod. "When you're ready."

We sleep with our hearts pressed together. My arms wrapped around her shoulders and her face buried in my chest.

I dream of her drowning, her hair swaying in the waves. I'm startled awake, breathing heavily, but she's here, sleeping soundly in my arms.

Lowering my head back down to hers, I lie awake and stare into the dark. Too afraid to close my eyes and dream of her demise.

Ophelia holds down her beige sun hat as a gust of wind threatens to lift it from her head.

"Which pub were we meeting them at?" I shout over the howl of the Cliffs of Moher. My eyes are narrowed at the smartphone we brought along with us in case we needed to contact the two of them.

"It's called Old Stones, in Galway." She hangs over my shoulder and points to it. Her lips brush against my cheek before she pulls away, and I grin.

"I can't wait to see Jericho and Yelina. I hope they've made more progress than we have," I say. It's been a little under a month since we've last seen each other. Time has never moved as fast as it does when I'm with her.

Ophelia laughs. "I hope they haven't. That would mean they won't show up and we'll be left waiting all night." Her genuine smile lifts my spirits.

The cliffs are wet and cold like much of Ireland is. The clouds bear low in the sky, meeting the earth and rocks. The greenery of the world here is bright and loud. Much more breathtaking than the photos, but it's fucking cold.

We explore the castles along the roads to Galway, taking giftshop knick-knacks and finding new books and notepads to bring with us. Funny, the things we cherish most on our journey aren't at all expensive. They are things of the heart.

Galway has those cottagecore streets you love looking at on Pinterest. They have tightly packed townhomes, two-story shops, and music. Everything closes early so people can flock to the pubs.

Ophelia's excitement is uncontainable, and honestly, so is mine. We walk up and down each street, taking in everything we see, going into each shop and trying pastries or sweets. By the time the sun begins to set, we head to Old Stones. The pub is packed to the brim.

Anywhere else, my anxiety and stress would be through the roof, but here, the people are cheerful and loud. Boisterous energy with laughter and dancing fills the air, quickly bringing smiles to both our faces.

"I should've dressed more casually," Ophelia says loudly through all the hollering and singing. Her dress isn't fancy by any means, but I see what she's saying: jeans and a T-shirt would've been more appropriate. Though, no one can see us, so it doesn't really matter. But it doesn't hurt to feel more like we fit in.

"You look fucking amazing," I blurt out without really thinking and her eyes widen. Her cheeks redden and I decide to just roll with it. "You already know I think you're the most beautiful woman in the world." My smile hurts.

Ophelia opens her mouth to reply, but we're interrupted by a woman clamping down on her. Ophelia shrieks before registering that it's Yelina, and the two burst into laughter.

I look up and find Jericho coming in for a bear hug. "Are you guys ready to have the night of your lives?" he shouts. I accept his ridiculous hug and chuckle.

I say back, "As long as we aren't going to end up wasted and stupid."

29

Ophelia

A few hours in and Lanston is drunk, singing on the small stage with Jericho's arm wrapped around his shoulders. The two of them sway, each with a beer in hand.

Yelina makes it back to our corner table and slides another cup of draft beer toward me.

"I've never seen him so… himself," she says as she leans back in the booth. She sighs, shaking her head at the two men as they start singing the next song, "Oh, What a Life" by American Authors.

Lanston's drunken eyes meet mine and he grins at me like he'll never look away.

"Really? What's different?" I ask without breaking my gaze on him.

Yelina laughs and props her elbows on the table. "Him *singing*? Are you kidding me?" She takes a swig from her mug. "I think he's got it bad for you. The question is, how do you feel?"

That grabs my attention. I look over at her and find analyzing eyes. Yelina's chin is perched on her palm, elbow against the table as she smiles at me.

I take a moment. I love him. More than a heart could bear, I love him. He's everything I've ever wanted in a man, in a partner to traverse the cold world with. Side by side, we wade through the dark.

Yelina smiles as if she can read my thoughts and says, "What's keeping you from telling him?"

"This is going to sound stupid, but I'm not deserving of someone like him. I can't follow him into what lies after like we're planning." My lips feel cold as the words come out. I haven't told him this, and I'm not sure why I feel so comfortable to discuss it with Yelina. But part of me just needs someone else to know.

Her head tilts and she frowns. "Why not?"

"Because I'm not going where good people go... and he is." I leave it at that.

She stares at me for a long moment. The laughter in the bar is quieter now; the evening has stretched into the late hours.

"You're right."

I meet her gaze once more. "Hm?"

"That is *stupid*. You're the one who's been babbling on about how *it's not too late to do things*. Fix your fucking faults then. He cares about you, and I'm sick of the excuses." Yelina's voice is devoid of warmth and I'm shocked for a moment.

She's not wrong.

Can I fix them, though? My sins?

My eyes flick back to Lanston and Jericho as they make their way back to our table on swaying legs. The biggest grin I've ever seen is plastered on his lips. His laugh twists inside me.

"You're right," I say. Yelina sighs and tilts her drink back, finishing it off. A mischievous grin spreads over my lips. "What about you and Jericho? You two have eyes for each other, don't you?"

She spits her drink all over the table and starts cough-choking. I laugh as the boys slide into the booth, their faces bright with joy.

Jericho looks between the two of us. "What'd we miss? You two look like you're up to trouble." He's trying to hide his laugh beneath his hand as Yelina tries to clear her airways.

She shoots me a death glare and mouths, "*Not a word.*"

I shrug. "Oh, nothing, just some girl talk."

Lanston presses close to me, wrapping his arms around my center and resting his head on my shoulder. He nuzzles into my neck and says on a whiskey breath, "I missed you."

I lift my hand and press my palm to his cheek. He turns his face to my hand and adorns my skin with kisses. Oh, how I'll cherish these nights forever. An eternity with him would never tire my soul.

"How can phantoms be drunk?" I laugh, trying not to let his under-the-influence sweet talk get too much to my head.

Jericho wraps his arm around Yelina and her cheeks flush red. She says, "Who knows? Do you have to question everything that's fun?"

Lanston shushes her and straightens beside me. "You wouldn't know what it's like to have a curious mind."

Yelina glowers at him. "I think it's one of my better qualities that I don't."

Jericho chuckles beside her. "Must you two always fight?"

The three of them continue to shoot sarcastic words at each other and I sit silently, enjoying the sound of friendship and lively chatter. It's something that's been absent from my life—friendship and goodwill.

It's not too late to have it now. I remind myself, willing myself to smile and join in on the banter.

The four of us laugh and spill drinks, sharing stories of our adventures so far until the bar closes and every living person vacates the building. We stay long after, singing and talking until the sun rises and we've grown weary.

"Where are you meeting us in Paris?" I ask Yelina in a hushed voice. The two men are leaned over the bar counter, sleeping heavily. The corners of my mouth turn up as I watch Lanston's peaceful expressions. His mind seems so weightless.

Yelina draws in a long breath. "Where did you say you were performing?"

"Palais Garnier."

"We'll be sure to be there. We can pick up where we left off here and drink our ghostly woes away until the dawn comes for us." She smiles playfully. A curl of smoke lingers over her shoulders, wisping away in the ray of sunlight just as quickly as it appeared. I've already seen their traces, and yet it still draws sadness to my heart.

"Do you remember anything about the night you died?" I ask carefully, keeping the expression on my face blank.

Yelina drops her head to look at her feet. Her eyes are bright with memory, and her blonde hair is pulled back into a ponytail that rests over her shoulder.

"I remember everything about that night." She doesn't meet my gaze. "The fire that burned my flesh and the pain that hollowed out my thoughts. Smoke killed most of us before the flames did. A small grace." Her voice is stony. Then she looks at me. "I remember reading about you... Does he know?"

My veins fill with ice at her admission. *She knows.*

I shake my head and glance over to Lanston, still sleeping peacefully.

"Will you tell him?"

I nod. "We are telling our stories slowly… in our own way."

Yelina thinks about that for a few quiet minutes before murmuring, "I hope you tell each other everything you couldn't say when you were alive."

Our goodbyes are brief. We know we'll see them in a week or two in Paris. Still, the sight of them leaving, holding hands and bumping into one another playfully, tugs at my heartstrings. I already miss them.

Lanston looks up to the clouds above, bruised and promising rain. Our bistro table is under a red awning, but if the wind picks up, it won't be enough to keep us from getting wet.

I scoop up the last piece of the scone and chase it with a sip of hot tea, humming with delight at the flavors. They don't make their pastries as sweet as they do in the States, but that doesn't make them less enjoyable.

"What's next on the list?" Lanston asks, sounding far-off in thought as he watches people go about their days.

I grab the list from his bag beside me and hold it up.

<u>*Lanston & Ophelia's Bucket List*</u>
Go to Paris

A Ballad of Phantoms and Hope

~~*Sail a yacht*~~
Ballroom dance
Drink on the beach at night/camp out
~~*Ride a train somewhere new*~~
~~*Visit Ireland's Trinity College Library*~~
Save a stray plant

"Drink on the beach under the stars, Paris, and the ballroom dance." My fingers curl around the page. Is that all that's really left? I don't want our time together to end. I suck my lower lip in and try to stay positive. "And saving a stray plant."

Lanston sips his chai latte before looking at me with ideas springing to his mind, his smile as endearing as it always is.

"Let's camp on the beach next. I know the perfect way to get back across the island too." His smirk is loose and childish. It only takes a few moments for me to figure out what he's alluding to.

"You've found a motorcycle haven't you?"

30

Lanston

Ophelia's thighs are clamped tightly around my hips and her arms are practically keeping air from entering my lungs. The smile on my face is painful at this point, but I can't seem to let my lips fall.

After the first few hours, she loosens her vice grip on me and starts to relax more. Her head turns to look as we pass distant castles on the Irish countryside. We find a beach on the west coast as we're traveling north from Galway: Keem Beach on Achill Island.

It's empty by the time we pull up. On a cold, dreary day such as this, I'm unsurprised.

The stars are already peeking out from the fading

sunset, and we only have our two bags, a blanket, and a wine bottle Ophelia snagged from the pub.

"This is the smallest beach I've ever seen," she says with a laugh. Her black puffer jacket is zipped up to her chin—long purple waves of hair spill over her shoulders.

"Ireland is known for its cliffs, not its beaches." I chuckle, looking up at the hills on each side of the coast. Sheep and rocks are our only neighbors, along with one lone, abandoned building at the top of the slope.

"Yeah, but still, are you sure this is your bucket list beach?"

I lift my shoulders and let them fall. "As long as I'm experiencing it with you, that's all that really matters to me." Her face lights up and her cheeks redden. Then a thought flickers across her gaze and she sullens. I raise a brow but don't ask what's the matter. A silence stretches between us before she bundles up the blanket in her arms.

"I'll get the bed set up," she says as cheerfully as she can and walks down the beach before I can respond. Is she upset with the location? Or maybe because our list is getting shorter... I want to add a thousand things to the bucket list, never wishing for our time together to end.

She pulls away emotionally when I try to let her know how I feel about her. Shit. Jericho makes it sound so easy.

Last night, he drunkenly told me that I need to take the leap like I did with Wynn and just tell her how I feel.

But she's so guarded. I don't want to get hurt again, even if it's my last chance at love.

A stream of light brightens across the sky and draws my attention. Ophelia makes a small gasping sound as she notices it too.

"*A shooting star*," we say simultaneously.

The grin returns to my lips and Ophelia waves me over to the blanket frantically. "Hurry!" she shouts. I trot down the wet sand and lower to my knees beside her.

"Why the hurrying?" I ask with a smirk.

She gets close to me, tucking herself beneath my arm and staring up at the falling star. "I don't want to miss this moment. It's once in a lifetime." Her heart is beating so fast I can feel it where my fingers trace her ribs.

"What will you wish for?" My voice is soft, and though I want to watch the falling star, I find her awe with it much more appealing.

Her eyes flash up to mine. We stay like this for a lovely moment, forgetting the stars and the wishes we'd only just been talking about.

She brushes her finger across my lower lip. "For another life, but this time, you'd be there."

My smile grows. "Yeah? And what would we do in this new life?" She leans forward and rests her arms on her knees. Her head tilts to the side as she stares at me.

"We would laugh... as much as we do now. You'd bring me coffee and I'd sing and dance for you. You're the artist, drawing and painting pictures of me and other somber things. You'd be popular but not famous. It was never what you wanted, you see." Her words are soft-spoken and gentle—a compliment. The vision of the life she speaks out pieces together in my mind. A beautiful life. And quiet. The two of us would grow old, but our souls would remain the same.

"What of you in this life, my rose?" I ask, craving more of her imagination.

"I would dance in only the most renowned theaters amidst the wisest audience. Only for them and only for you." Ophelia's eyes glimmer with the light of the shooting star. "To violins and cellos of the most somber songs."

Only for me.

"I wish for that too." My voice is low. Melancholic.

But another part of me is content, overwhelmed with the feeling that we were meant to meet this way.

"Can I tell you something?"

I blink down at her and smile to encourage her.

She swallows. "Your light is contagious. Bright. I could find you in the depths of the underworld. Through mist and darkness. Through it all."

The blood in my veins warms as I grin. "That bright, huh?" She winces with vulnerability. I take a shallow breath, leaning close and pressing my forehead to hers as I whisper, "I would wait for you if it meant walking the cold castle walls of a cathedral until I lost my own identity. Until all I knew was you." I press my lips to hers.

I kiss her like she's the only person in the entire world. The only soul that walks on the same soil as I do.

A broken soul. A wandering spirit. A sad, lost thing. Now found.

Ophelia lets her head relax, kissing me as fervently as I do her. As if each stroke of our tongues and lips could be the last. She sighs with desire, bringing her hand down my chest.

We go down together. The blanket and sand swallow us whole as our worlds collide.

"Ophelia," I say her name like one would whisper prayers to a goddess.

She straddles me, long hair outlining her lithe features. Her eyes are hooded beneath dark lashes, mouth parting to say something in return before she freezes. Ophelia snaps her eyes up to look at something toward the entrance of the beach. Horror befalls her expression and I watch her entire body tense with fear.

Terror slips inside me, stirring my blood. I twist to look where she does and find darkness moving down the lip of the parking lot toward us.

No. How did they already find us?

"Ophelia, get to the ocean!" I hastily reach for her wrist, but she looks up at me with an anguished frown. I know then that she's planning on doing something foolish. "Ophelia!"

She gives me a caressing look. One that someone only does if they're memorizing the features of your face or the way you would gaze at them with adoration one last time.

"I love you, my darling."

Her words are sorrowful—an unspoken goodbye.

Then she darts across the beach so fast that I don't have even a moment to think before the dark cloud of whispering mist is chasing after her. What looks like an arm shrouded in shadows juts out and strikes me. It hits me so hard that the world falls around me like petals and rain.

Slowly, terribly—my eyes close and everything stops.

My rose. Please, *please*, don't go.

Not without me.

31

LANSTON

"LANSTON, DEAR. IT'S TIME FOR SCHOOL." MY MOTHER called from the living room of our small, shitty house. It's the first day of my junior year in high school.

I grabbed my secret stash of art brushes, charcoal pencils, and drawing notebooks that I secretly bought over the summer. It was dangerous to take this risk, knowing how much my father despised my attraction to artistic things. But he should be asleep already. The night shift always wears him out well before dawn.

My mom knocked gently on my door and peeked in. "Are you almost ready?" she asked kindly. I nodded. Relieved that I could finally go back to school after a long *summer stuck at home. School was the only place I could escape this life of constant fear and uncertainty.*

My smile was short-lived, as my father loomed ominously behind my mom. Her smile was weak and feigned happiness. I would feel betrayed, but this wasn't the first time she'd smiled while he cornered me.

"Good morning, sir," I said as I kept my eyes low and out of his cold sight.

"Lanston, what's the last class on your schedule?" He held up a folded piece of paper with a list of my classes. My heart sank. I knew he was talking about the art class. It must've been mailed. "Well?" he pried.

I tried to think of anything that would take the blame off of me, even though it's an extracurricular that I purposefully signed up for. "Everyone has to take an art class." I lied.

His scowl grew, but it was left at that.

My mom kept her fake smile glued to her face as she dropped me off at school.

A breath of relief flowed through my lungs as I stepped onto the front lawn. Cement steps led up to the school building and many students swarmed in groups with their friends.

I pulled the sleeves of my sweater down into my palms, keeping the scars of the summer tucked away.

This year, I would want to live. I made a small promise to myself.

The day went quickly. New faces, old faces, home-

work. People were friendly and that was something I really missed.

Art class was held outside. It was a nice, sunny September day, but the warm weather was limited, so the teacher encouraged everyone to enjoy it as much as they could. I drew a tree—tall and entirely black and lifeless. Beneath the earth were bones instead of dirt.

I thought of death a lot.

Something about it lured me, the sadness perhaps, or maybe it was the comfort it brought me. It was something undeniable. Something we all face together in the end. No one is the exception.

"Nevers, may I see what you've conjured up today?" Mrs. Bensen asked curiously. She was older, mid-sixties, and probably close to retiring. Her smile was bright and filled with kindness. Still, I hesitated. My drawings were always perceived with bad thoughts.

People just thought I was strange, and I was. But it didn't make me bad, did it?

I showed Mrs. Bensen the picture and she examined it carefully for a few minutes. The wrinkles around her eyes grew with a grin. Then she handed it back to me. I awaited her feedback. For some reason, it felt important. Whatever she had to say, I wanted to hear it.

"You have great talent, Nevers. Your use of multiple forms of shading is impressive, and it's a creative take on the tree assigned," she said kindly.

It confused me for a moment. Surely, she didn't actu-

ally think it was good. But her smile was true and the light in her wise eyes comforted me.

"You don't think it's wicked?" I asked quietly, looking from side to side to ensure no one overheard us. Mrs. Bensen chuckled softly and patted me on the shoulder.

"My sweet boy, a majority of the world's most treasured artists are of similar mind to you. Dark and dreadful things fill their heads. But isn't that what attracts us to them? They are different and stand out. I would rather see a dark, twisted perspective on something than the same old tree over and over." She motioned her hand to the students behind her.

They were all drawing the tree as it was, an exact replica. Green and alive, filled with leaves and sunlight. Mine was the only tortured one.

"You are unique."

A stupid grin was planted on my face for the rest of the afternoon. I was unique? I'd never thought that before. I replayed her words over and over in my head on the car ride home. Feeling the inspiration to draw and take my passion to the next level.

Is this what it felt like for someone to believe in you?

I'd never known. But my chest was lighter than it'd ever been; hope and dreams filled my mind.

When we pulled up to the house, I thanked my mom for picking me up from school. Usually, I had to walk home, but she was actually on time today. I couldn't wait to drive myself soon.

I headed inside and went straight to my room with the intention of grabbing my extra notebooks and pencils and heading to the library so I could draw in peace. The door creaked as I shoved it with my shoulder and my breath caught in my lungs as I saw my father sitting at the edge of my bed, flipping through the artwork I'd hidden all summer.

My eyes widened and fear flooded me.

"What the fuck is this?" he asked quietly, dangerously. When I didn't respond, he shouted, "What the fuck is this, Lanston!" He slammed the notebook on the floor and stood abruptly. I flinched and started to backtrack into the hallway.

Words evaded me. Nothing I could've said would calm him.

"I told you I don't want you drawing this shit! Get the fuck out of my house, you worthless boy." He swung a punch at my face. I leaned back to avoid it and fell backward against the hallway wall, knocking picture frames to the ground as I scrambled to get up quickly.

He kicked me in my ribs and I muffled the groan of pain. I staggered to my feet and ran through the shithole of a house, gasping, crying, clenching my teeth so hard I tasted blood.

My mom's eyes widened as I flew past her. I knew she wouldn't say anything; she never did.

I dared a glance back as I reached the end of our driveway and saw the two of them staring at me like I was *a disappointment. Something that embarrassed them. Something that the neighbors should shake their heads at. Their frowns were heavy with disdain and weariness.*

They were sick of me.

But what did I do wrong? What did I do?

I ran until I reached the library, making sure to pull my hood up so no one saw my puffy eyes. The bottom floor was always vacant, and today was no different. The desk in the corner was dark, and I decided that I would stay there for as long as I could.

There I remained, curled under the particle board with my backpack tucked tightly between my chest and thighs.

I cried loudly. Uncaring. The sobs filled the dark room, and no one heard the words I said.

No one heard me.

"I want to die."

Waves echo somewhere distant. Crashing on the sand and sounding angrier than I've ever heard the sea.

My eyes open dreadfully. Why did I dream of them? I shake my head in an attempt to clear my thoughts of the horrors of my past.

A shudder runs down my spine and I blink a few

times as I try to remember where I am. Sand is cold beneath my fingertips and the sky is bright with clouds separating above. It comes to me like a freight train. Those Who Whisper, the darkness, my rose running away.

Ophelia.

32

Ophelia

The darkness and whispers fade once the dawn breaks the edge of the sea, brightening the sky and signaling safety.

I fall to my knees on the black rocks lining the cliffside. My breaths are labored and hard, pulling air in with raspy, dry inhales.

Tears drip down my nose and I want to scream. *Why? Why have they followed me this far?* Their hunger is stronger than before. They've never chased me with such fever and desperation.

Why can't they just leave me alone?

A cold breeze slips beneath my coat, chilling the

sweat on my skin. I fist my hands in the dirt, gritting my teeth and shutting my eyes.

I don't want to stop our adventure together; it's too soon to go our separate ways. But I can't let him be in danger because of me. A twisting sensation swirls through my stomach and makes me wince.

The beach is visible from this cliff. Lanston has already vanished, searching for me, perhaps.

"You won't find me," I whisper to the open air beneath my bare feet. I stare down at the ocean, dark and foreboding, lapping furiously at the ebony rocks.

I will keep the whispering darkness away from him—away from my love.

My arms spread and the wind lifts the sleeves of my black coat. I've fallen many times into water as dark as this. Darker even.

I lift my foot and step toward the sky. As I fall, I shut my eyes and think of him, always him.

Lanston.

I'm sorry to have to break our promise.

The water consumes me, devouring my soul and hollowing out every thought left inside me. I surrender to the whispers and finally listen to their words.

Until I'm nothing. Until I am darkness.

"Do you love me?" he whispered to me sweetly.

I nodded and smiled, infatuated with him. I'd fallen in love twice in my short life. Once when I was sixteen and another at twenty-five.

His smile was slick, like poison on my skin. I should've known anything as beautiful and cruel as him had teeth to bite—venom to kill.

But what lured me most to him was his ability to make me hate myself as much as I'd grown used to. As if I needed someone to remind me should I stray and think rationally. He'd learned so much from observing the interactions between me and my parents.

The role I played in the family.

The scapegoat never gets away. Everyone seemed to know that except me.

"You know I do," I said back, not meaning it at all but saying it anyway.

He was kind when he wanted something. Tomorrow, his face would change.

We sat placidly at my stepmother's table as she prepared dinner. My father frowned as I told him of the recent dance gig I landed.

"You'll go hungry chasing these silly dreams," he said coldly.

I'd learned just to nod and accept whatever they'd say. But today I wanted them to know how well I was doing. The life I'd created for myself.

"I'm actually making a decent bit. I'll be able to pay

off the lessons and have a good chunk left over to travel. I'll also be starting therapy," I said timidly.

It was going to be my first session and I was terrified. I knew what they thought of it, but I'd heard from so many others that it helps. God, I wanted help. Needed it. Part of me wanted their approval. I knew that was stupid, but I still wanted it.

I picked at my skin nervously waiting for someone to say something.

My stepmother slammed both her fists against the countertop. Cold shot through my body like a bullet. Sweat instantly collected on my forehead. Dishes fell to the floor and shattered. My boyfriend's eyes widened and my father took a deep breath.

"Why? So they'll lock you up? They'll see how fucked up and awful you are! Vile bitch. Do you know how much you ruined our lives?! How much we gave you?" she screamed at me, throwing the pitcher of tea at the sink. Glass went everywhere.

But I couldn't even think. My blood was louder than I'd ever heard it, roaring through my ears like a siren. Telling me to flee and find safety from this place.

"You're the reason I'll die of cancer someday. All the stress you've caused me. Tell them that. Tell them everything you've done to me," my stepmother shouted as she threw her cup of water at me.

Water hit the side of my head and still I blinked numbly. I knew I should move, but I couldn't. I just sat there and pinched my skin so hard it tore.

This will never end. *I thought.* Shhh, don't let them see you cry. Just go. You know how. It will *never* end. You are the problem.

I am the problem.

Slowly, I stood from the table. Everyone was yelling at me now, but their voices and words were deep rumbles. It were as if a veil had fallen over me, shielding against the horror. Somehow this blow up was my fault. I walked steadily toward the front door and walked across the lawn with my bare feet.

"Hey. Where are you going!" My boyfriend called after me. His footsteps were loud against the pavement.

I stopped in the middle of the vacant street, gravel sticking to the soles of my feet, and looked back at him. I wanted him to say something nice. I needed it desperately.

Couldn't they see the pain they were causing? The despair that bubbled over?

I was tired. I was losing myself. More and more with each word.

He stopped and grabbed my wrist. "What? Are you going to go hurt yourself again? Come on, Ophelia. Get back inside and have dinner. Don't make this a big deal."

Am I the only sane person here? Can't anyone else see?

"Go back inside and have dinner? After that traumatizing display of aggression? No. I won't be going back inside." I tore my arm from his grip and he slapped me across the face. Fire spread over my cheek and I stood there, stunned and motionless as my head bobbed with shock.

"Those are your parents, Ophelia. Respect them. No matter what. You respect them."

I glared at him.

"You want me to respect them? That's fucking laughable." I turned and continued to walk. He stomped after me. The rain had started and everything was escalating, boiling inside me.

Wouldn't it be better if I just made this stop?

My emotions were wild, like fire loose in the forest. Burning and raging through the dry and impoverished pines. I wanted to scream and run as far as I could. My hiding place was too far away to walk to on foot and the pounding in my head was too loud.

Please stop. No more. No more.

I hit the side of my head as if the impact could make the voices stop. Don't do anything stupid. Don't. I firmly pounded my fist against my temple.

"Go fucking kill yourself, Ophelia. Do us all the favor." His words were steel in my lungs. My feet ceased and I turned back to look at him. He looked at me with no love. No care.

"You don't mean that," I said, glad that the rain hid my tears.

His face was emotionless and colder than I'd ever seen it. Behind him stood the two people who hated me more than anyone else in this fucked up world. Weren't they supposed to care the most? It hurts. The ultimate betrayal.

"No one likes you. You're mean and irrational. You bring out the worst in people. Go fucking do it. You won't be missed."

He left it at that.

I fell to my knees. The words were crippling.

They all went back inside then. But I remained.

The voice in my head spoke loudly again, as it always had. A snake that promised rest.

You know how to make it stop. I pressed my palms to my eyes, shaking my head. But the whispers didn't stop. They didn't go away.

Not when I walked five miles to the bridge.

Not when I stood on the edge and stared down at the dark, rabid water.

Not when I let go and closed my eyes against the pain of the world.

Not when I walked as a phantom.

33

Lanston

There's no corner of Ireland I leave unscathed. No castle or city I do not scour. *Ophelia, where are you? You cannot leave me behind, not like this.*

I shout into the cosmos until my voice dies. I return to the art park in Dublin, trying to stop people and ask if they've seen her, but nobody hears me.

Not a single head turns.

Not like this.

I can't bear it.

At first, the days pass quickly, with little sleep and urgent searching. Then the weeks drag, hope slipping through my fingers like water.

The weariness tugs at my soul, begging for rest, for

peace. Yet I push on, brushing the tip of my finger across our bucket list for small glimpses of light. But the illumination has faded, the paper now worn and unreadable.

I fall into ruin, searching for my rose.

Even more so when I find her final letter, slipped between the pages of my artbook. She must've stuck it there before I woke up after our night at the pub. My chest aches at the thought of this being the last of her I'll ever know.

"I can't read it without you." I choke back on tears. The knot in my throat is too thick to swallow. I fist her letter in my palm, willing myself to open it with trembling hands.

Lanston,

Hey, you. This is the last letter I'll give you. Well, maybe not the last, but you've shown me that we can talk about the things that happened to us. And I want to share those things with you as easily as you do with me. I want to watch you continue to draw, letting the beauty of your mind infect the pages. But I'll leave you with this until then.

The last part of my tragic story.

My depression grew after high school. The people in my life weren't kind of my illness. They urged it on even. Do you want to know how I died? I'll tell you.

It was me.

My murderer was my illness; it took me young, naive. I

jumped from the bridge and fell to the depths of the world. Where the darkness finally came for me.

I hope you don't hate me... I know what I did was wrong, but what if I told you I fought it really fucking hard and for a long time? What if I told you that I searched for the light but couldn't find it? Would I still be painted as a bad person? The one who only wanted attention?

I'll tell you another secret. I didn't want attention. I just wanted to be gone. I wanted to be away from all the cruel things that made me hate myself. The words that made me hate myself.

The bridge we met on, the bench I stood on and pulled roses from, was the memorial bench the local church placed for me. They didn't put my name on the plaque. My family didn't want their last name muddied with my sin, so roses it was.

Ophelia roses.

I'm stuck on earth because I was taught people who die by suicide are damned to go to hell, for it is the ultimate sin. I run from the darkness in death more than I did in life. I'm not even sure if it's true. I hope it isn't—because, well—it's not fair, is it?

But I still fear it with all my heart.

Do you want to know what they say? Who they are?

It's the voices of my parents and extended family. Each time they utter my name, it's followed by "She killed herself, you know." "That wicked girl." "She's going to hell."

That's what the whispers are, and I'm terrified that they'll catch me one day.
Well? Are you looking at me weirdly now? I hope not. I hope you'll just kiss me and make me laugh like you always do. Like I'm sure you are right now.
I wish I found the cure to my illness.
I wish I had a light like you.

I love you, Lanston. Until the stars die.
Ophelia

The letter falls to my lap as tears crash on the pages. Why didn't I see it before? Her trace—the wet hair.

Footsteps trail up the path leading to the graveyard I'm lingering in. Morbid, I know, but I wanted to be somewhere depressing to sulk.

"There he is," a whisper, followed by another hushed voice and the footsteps get closer.

I needn't turn. I know it's Jericho and Yelina. The text I sent them two weeks ago when we were supposed to meet in Paris was probably enough to make them worried sick about me.

Jericho wraps around my front and kneels slowly in front of me. I keep my head hung low, unwilling to carry the weight of the world any longer.

The emotions that swell inside me when I think of Ophelia are unbearable. She was a part of me that I will never find in another. My very marrow churns in grief for her.

Jericho sets his hand on my knee and Yelina crouches beside him.

"You look like shit," he murmurs in that consoling way of his.

I don't respond. I only stare at the ground and the gravestones before me. All the forgotten people who lie here, sleeping and no longer traversing the world.

Why does everyone leave me behind?

A tingle spreads across my cheek and my head is jerked to the right. I finally look up, startled. Yelina has a fury I've never seen blooming across her cheeks and eyes, tears welling and her breathing uneven.

She slapped me. Delayed, my hand unconsciously drifts to where my skin felt discomfort for only a moment.

"What's wrong with you?! I've never seen you give up like this. Don't you care about her? Don't you care about yourself?!" Yelina screams at me. It triggers me; yelling has always done that. My blood thickens and my heart clammers inside me.

I'm on my feet before I even know what I'm doing. Anger has a hold on me.

"Of course, I care, Yelina!" The raspiness of my voice and sheer volume strikes her, making her shrink back and I instantly see myself in that frightened pose.

I take a deep breath. I won't be *him*.

Calmer, I say, "I care. More than you could ever understand. I've searched everywhere and she's nowhere. I'm tired." My voice cracks. "I'm so, *so* fucking tired. But she chose to leave. What am I supposed to do?"

Jericho and Yelina share a concerned look. "Yelina, why don't you grab us all some hot drinks?" Jericho says with a hint that he'd like to talk to me privately. She stares at me with sorrowful eyes before nodding and leaving us alone in the graveyard.

We're silent until her footsteps can no longer be heard.

"I'm leaving tonight," Jericho finally says.

I look at him and raise a brow. "Heading back to Harlow?"

Jericho shakes his head. A sad smile pulls at the corner of his lips.

"We're going together."

My heart sinks. "You... you found what's keeping you here?" Jericho smiles and nods slowly. He lifts his hand and rubs the back of his head.

"Yeah, it's so stupid how obvious it was."

I stare at him expectantly.

He leans in close and I mirror him. Jericho whispers,

"There's something inside you that still festers. You're going to have to face it. You know what it is, Nevers, I know you do."

My throat tightens.

"You'll figure it out, but do you think you can do it without Miss Rosin?" His tone is knowing.

I lower my head and stare at the ground. "I've searched for her; she cannot be found." An uncomfortable weight settles in my chest. "You know, Wynn and Liam didn't show up last year."

Jericho's brows arch with emotion. He knows I'm talking about my grave, the anniversary of all of our deaths.

I curl my fists against my knees.

"Everyone I care about... everyone I love. They don't stay. Ophelia chose to leave me behind. Even if it was to keep me safe... she's gone." The words come out as a whisper.

Jericho stands and offers me his hand to help me up. I look at him for a moment before clapping my palm to his. He lifts me from the gravestone and turns me to look down upon it.

"Tell me, Nevers, what do you see when you look at this gravestone? Do you see the person? Their phantom?" Jericho says nostalgically. I've watched him many times stare down at his own grave in Bakersville. Though, now it feels like a lifetime ago.

"They aren't here," I murmur.

Jericho nods. "They are not." He bends down and

wipes the moss from over the name on the headstone, which reads *Gregory Briggs*.

My eyes widen as his name sparks my memory. The phantom in the cathedral was looking for a Gregory Briggs. I kneel and wipe the bottom portion of the stone. An image of him is still barely visible along with words that make my heart ache.

Architect of the Landertis Cathedral — made in memory of his sweet Elanor.

"I'd bet my money this guy has either already passed on or is waiting for his lost love at the cathedral he built for her." Jericho grins and I snap my eyes at him. He doesn't even know the faceless phantom that Ophelia and I found weeks ago, dancing to a soundless song, thinking of only this man. Only, she's in a different cathedral, waiting.

"What's your point?" I ask.

Jericho laughs and slaps his hand across my back. "My point is that he's not dwelling around his stone. His mortal bonds. Neither are you. Or Yelina. Even me."

His eyes are calm and patient.

"We are trudging on. Through the pain, through the despair. But we are not forgotten, Nevers. We will never be forgotten. You don't think Wynn and Liam keep you with them every day? They probably see you in the clouds, in the breeze and stars. You are everywhere."

My stomach sinks with guilt. How could I even think for a moment that they'd forgotten me? I lift my head and find reassurance and guidance in Jericho's.

"You know what?"

He smirks. "What?"

"You're a really good fucking counselor."

Jericho throws his head back and laughs. The sound is rich and circles me. "You're just now realizing it?"

I shake my head. "No, but I thought I ought to tell you at least once." That earns me a slight grin.

We share the silence that follows, taking deep breaths and enjoying the crisp, foggy morning, our last together.

Yelina appears a few minutes later with three coffee cups. When she sees our relaxed shoulders and calm expressions, she smiles.

We sit amongst the gravestones as we sip our drinks, sharing stories of our time at Harlow and all the times after. Yelina leans into Jericho and presses a kiss to his lips. Warmth spreads between them and I can't help but miss Ophelia.

Our love was made for this life and the next.

"What will you do now, Lan?" Yelina has her arms wrapped around Jericho's chest, cheek resting on his shoulder.

The two of them wait for me to respond.

I let my gaze find a murder of crows, watching us quietly from the next row of gravestones over. Crows always fall silent when phantoms are near. It's a subtle sign for anyone who dares to seek us.

"I've decided to find her. No matter how long it takes," I say and as I do, hope soars in my heart. I won't let her become like the phantom at the cathedral. Faceless and somber. Left to haunt her opera house alone.

Not my rose.

"Good. And then what will you do?" Jericho pushes.

"Then I'm going to take her with me to the other side."

Yelina stands and runs to me, knocking me off the gravestone and hugging me tightly. "It's about time, you idiot," she whispers, her voice sounding strained. "I can't bear the thought of you being here alone."

I hug her just as tight. "You don't need to worry about me. I promise I'll be okay." She leans back and wipes her tears. Jericho helps us back up and we walk to the pier as rain begins pelting down on us.

We stay until the sun reaches mid-sky, and then we say our goodbyes. It makes me nervous to think about what's on the other side. Will I see them again? What if we don't cross paths like we're hoping? What if nothing awaits us?

I bury those thoughts, trying to look happy for my friends as they turn to leave.

I reach out and grab Jericho's wrist. He stops and turns his head back at me lazily; kindness beams softly in his gaze. His soul feels tired, ready for the embarkment.

"*Jericho,*" I say with emotion rising in my throat.

He only smiles more endearingly and says, "Do not be afraid."

"But I am."

"That's a good sign. You're ready to move on."

"What if we don't get to meet again?"

Jericho chuckles and turns to hug me, pulling me in close one final time. I shut my eyes and embrace the care that rolls off him so easily. He's been like a father to me for so much longer than before I died. He's always shown me kindness and warmth, wisdom and advice. I know he was my counselor, but he's always been more.

He whispers, "I know in my heart that we'll meet again."

We separate and I stare at him, biting my lower lip to quell the heartache. "See you soon then?" My smile is broken.

Jericho takes my baseball hat and puts it on his own head; I feel entirely vulnerable without it.

"After a while, crocodile. I'm going to borrow this hat —I'll give it back to you when we meet again, kay?" Those are the last words he says to me before turning and taking Yelina's hand. Together, they walk slowly out across the docks. A trail of embers follows in their wake; I'd not noticed them before. I think of my rose's wet hair from the river in which she perished.

I watch in silence until the two of them disperse into the mist; their soft voices and laughter fade until I'm alone again, but this time I'm smiling and hope reignites inside my soul.

34

Lanston

The world seems darker without my friends from Harlow. But I keep their words knitted in my heart. Hope surrounds me. The letters Ophelia wrote for me are tucked in my bag and the bucket list we didn't finish remains folded in my pocket.

I look up at the cathedral, where I hope to find Gregory. It's in a small village outside Dublin. There isn't even a sign for it, but the town is busy with people herding sheep and gathering vegetables for their suppers.

The stones pillaring the stairs up to the arched doors are like ice on my fingertips. I step carefully, keeping an eye out for the phantom. Even though finding this guy didn't top my list of things I wanted to do, I knew it was important to Ophelia. And that makes it important to me.

I didn't just stumble upon his grave by chance. This is a sign. Well, I guess if you believe in those sorts of things. I'm starting to.

As I enter the cathedral the air becomes sweet and warm. The scent of burning candles and old pews fills my senses. Elderly people sit and pray, while others walk through the building, observing the historic structure with awe on their faces.

My eyes lift to the balcony above, and I spot a phantom. He wears a long cloak that reaches down to his feet. It's a drab and muddled burgundy color. His skin is as pale as a dead man's. Dark eyes stare down at me. For a moment, I think I'll turn and run, but I dig my heels into the ground and swallow my fears. If Ophelia were here, she'd say not to judge him by his frightening appearance, just like the faceless phantom.

I find the spiral staircase that leads up and I trail my fingers along the stone as I ascend to the balcony.

"Who are you?" he asks, his voice deep and sharp.

He's young, from a different time. It's almost like I'm in one of those old Victorian movies.

I clear my throat. "Lanston Nevers."

He inspects me from head to toe with a disapproving look. "A tourist, I presume?" I nod with a hesitant smile, trying my best to remain cordial. "I am Gregory Briggs," he says with a heavy accent.

My grin grows wide. I found him, and if I can find

someone this old, there isn't a universe in which I cannot find my Ophelia.

"Gregory, I've been searching for you. Your Elanor, she waits."

His eyes widen and he seems to come to life at the mention of her. Those dark eyes are no longer so black; they lift into a light brown. His skin regains some pink and his clothes a bright maroon.

"Elanor? My darling Elanor?" The desperation and pain in his voice sting me. His love for her is palpable. And here he waited for her—as she did him.

Refusing to leave this world without the other.

"Yeah, I'll take you to her."

Gregory smiles as tears brim in his eyes and he nods.

We walk slowly through the countryside, in hours of silence. By the time we make it back to the city, night has fallen and the lights of pubs and shops illuminate the way.

I take him to St. Patrick's cathedral, where the hush of the evening feels ominous and lovely at the same time. Gregory looks at me, yearning in his eyes.

"She's inside," I say quietly.

He practically runs to the doors and through the silent corridors. I follow slowly, remaining far behind so they can have a moment to themselves. Like a true phantom, I spectate, lingering and admiring their love from afar.

I crest the top of the stairs in time to see them standing five feet apart. They seem stunned by the moment. I was expecting to see Elanor's haunting face again, but her features have returned. Soft skin, blue eyes, and red curly hair that drops down to her mid-back. Her smile is that of an angel.

"Gregory," she says as tears fall.

He closes the distance between them in a few big steps and scoops her into his arms. "My Ellie. Here you are." Gregory twirls with her in his arms. Their foreheads are pressed together with heartache, anguish, and love.

"I've waited lifetimes for you, my love. You are just as you were." Elanor kisses him, and together, they laugh.

Something deep in my chest settles with their union. Love never truly dies. Time cannot steal everything away from us. Not this. Not the soft kisses and whispers in the dusk of the world. Not the ache that nestles inside our chests and blooms when our eyes catch. Love, in its purest form—our ghosts.

Elanor notices me leaning against the wall at the end of the corridor and smiles brightly at me. Then, the smile quickly fades.

"Where is the woman who accompanied you?"

I bite the inside of my cheek to keep from getting emotional. "I seem to have lost her as you lost your Gregory." My voice breaks.

Her eyes soften and she walks toward me.

"Even then, you kept her promise to me?" Elanor asks sadly, thoughtfully. "I'll give you this, young ghost." I raise my eyes to hers as she extends her hand out to mine. I expose my palm to her and she drops a small stone into the center of my hand. It's black and smooth... it looks familiar, but I can't place it.

"What is it?"

Elanor smiles. "It is onyx. A symbol of strength and hope. May you find her."

Liam used to have tons of these. My hand closes over the stone. "Thank you."

The two phantoms meet in the dark halls of the cathedral, their hands enveloping each other. Together, they walk toward something I cannot see. Then, just as Yelina and Jericho had, they disappear, leaving behind traces of gilded dust.

I may be the only phantom left here on the darkest of nights, but my soul has never emanated so much hope.

Clutching the stone, I whisper, "I'm not afraid of your darkness, Ophelia. We are the light."

35

Ophelia

Is there a reality of being that is neither here nor there?

I think perhaps that is where I am. Cocooned in blankets that smell of pages and coffee. Lanston's drawings are crumpled in my hands, pressed tightly against my chest.

He is my only comfort, my only thought. Even when I'm at war within myself, he's here. *I love you*, I want to whisper to him even though I know he will not hear it, cuddled in sheets. *I've loved you all along.*

A small voice whispers above me from outside the blankets. It doesn't sound like the darkness that chases me, it's someone else; someone familiar.

"Ophelia."

My eyes slowly open and I lift my head to the voice. "Yelina?"

The blanket unfolds and delicate hands reach for me, pulling me from the misery and dark. A dull pain throbs through my chest as I stare at the four people before me.

Jericho, Yelina, and two phantoms I don't recognize.

I survey the female's dress and recall seeing it on Elanor, dancing mournfully through the cathedral halls. "Elanor?"

She smiles, a beautiful thing to behold. Her hair is red with tight curls and freckles spread across her fair skin. "Hello, Ophelia." She follows my eyes as I look at the young man beside her. Elanor slips her hand into his and she says cheerfully, "Lanston found my love—my Gregory."

Tears brim in my eyes. "How did the four of you find me?"

Jericho grins and folds his arms thoughtfully as he says, "We couldn't leave one of our own behind. He's searching for you. His heart breaks more each day you're not with him."

The tears fall freely, crashing against the back of my hands.

"He'll never let you go, Ophelia. And he'll never find you here," Yelina adds softly.

My voice is choked with emotion. "I love him. But the darkness... it won't leave me. I fear it will hurt him."

Elanor brushes my hair back behind my ear and

presses a warm kiss to my cheek. "You must return; you cannot stay in this purgatory you've created for yourself. That darkness you speak of, I'd not seen it at first, but I do now. It is *your* fear that gives it life. Your own agony that feeds the beast and gives it power. You have to let it go, sweet one."

"My fear?"

She nods, eyes looking past me toward the dark they pulled me from. I turn my head and find three shadows standing behind me. Father. My stepmother. *Him*.

"You are the phantom, my dear, but still they haunt you. Chasing you with their poison. It's time to stop them. Time to say *enough*." Elanor takes my hands and for the first time I see the shadows for what they really are. Three pitiful memories.

All this time. This is all they were?

"We create our own whispering darkness, don't we?" I say sadly as I meet all four of their gazes. Yelina gives me a somber nod. "No more then. Not when he waits for me." I blink the tears away and wipe my eyes.

"He loves you unbearably," Jericho adds, tipping his hat. I notice it's Lanston's and my smile grows. The four of them look at me with kindness and warmth, and in this moment I feel something shift inside my heart.

"He loves me?"

Yelina rolls her eyes and Jericho chuckles as she says, "You two are the biggest idiots. Find him, and once you do, never let go. We'll be waiting for you two."

She hugs me and I return the tight embrace.

"Are you leaving?" I ask, crying still.

Jericho nods. "But it's not goodbye forever. I'm just borrowing this hat, you see."

I watch as the four of them walk away, leaving me behind, but not forgotten. They found me for Lanston... and I won't make him endure the world alone any longer. We'll banish our demons. Together.

A deep breath coils in my lungs as I take a step out into the void. I shut my eyes and focus on Lanston. *Take me to him. Please.* The next moment, I'm standing atop a skyscraper, far above the city lights. My eyes widen with the explosion of stars and cold air that stings my skin.

He stands at the edge, his light brown hair blowing in the wind without his baseball hat, his hands tucked into his pockets. His head is lifted to the sky.

"Lanston," I say breathlessly. Chills spread across my arms.

He turns his head quickly. The most heart wrenching expression is painted across his lovely features. His hazel eyes take me in. And the universe rejoices loudly, silently, colorfully.

He runs to me. "*Ophelia.*"

Together we collide. The stars our witness as he lifts me into his arms and presses feverish kisses to my cheeks, my lips. Our laughter warms my chest, and his tears mix with my own.

Lanston lowers us, still gripping me tightly in his arms, "I searched for you until there were no corners left to be sought. Until my heart ached and sores grew on the bottom of my feet."

I thread my fingers through his hair, memorizing his sullen, handsome face. Beauty such as his should be framed, stared upon, for he is of the gods.

The sob in my throat threatens to blur out my words as I sputter, "I'm so sorry, Lanston." I bury my face into his chest and cling to him like the reaper himself will tear me away. "I'm so selfish for leaving you. The thought of the Those Who Whisper catching you was too much to bear. I-I—" My weeping gets the better of me.

"Shh." Lanston presses his lips to my head, stroking my hair in long, languid motions. His soft touch is enough to put me on the edge of madness. No person should ever be deprived of love as pure as his. "I'm just happy you've returned to me. I think I would've suffered for the remainder of time, alone and wandering, walking this plane of sorrow, until I reunited with you."

I lift my eyes to his. Both of us are sobbing.

"I don't deserve your affection."

"You do. So deserving, yet you don't even know it." Lanston nuzzles his nose to mine. The warmth of his breath makes my heart yearn to beat alongside his for an eternity. "I want my love to haunt you. Until the stars die—until all the water in the ocean dries and we're all that's left in this cruel, dark world."

The constellations shine through his eyes, the celestial light that is Lanston Nevers.

"I love you, Lanston." I sniffle past the tears, a

wavering smile pulling at my lips. "Together we stand, two phantoms amidst the dark, the cruel. Our love is damaged but healed with unbreakable bonds. We will light the way."

Lanston presses his forehead to mine, letting his tears fall as the sky dances around us this close to the veil. "For all those who stray."

"For all those who stray," I confirm.

An endless night brings upon the dawn.

Our lips meet, hands gliding over each other's hearts, chests, hips, and thighs. His fingers smooth over my hip bones, following the curvature and dipping where flesh meets bone.

"Jericho and Yelina found me. Elanor and Gregory too," I admit, pulling back from our kiss and his eyes widen a fraction before pooling with more tears. "They said they'll wait for us. Wherever that may be."

He grins, a hopeful, charming smile.

"They'll have to wait a bit longer; we still have a ballroom dance to finish and a few more stops." Lanston tilts me back and kisses my neck, sending warmth through my body.

"Elanor told me what you did for them." My voice breaks. "And in return, she helped me see what the darkness that chased me truly was."

Lanston pulls back and searches my eyes. "Really?"

I nod. "It was my fear. All this time, it was me." My voice breaks at that. It's hard to admit that I've been the one causing all the despair. All the heartache.

He brushes my hair back and hushes me softly.

"I found your last letter," he finally says. I take a sharp breath and hold it. Fear itching close by. *Please don't look at me differently.* "I wish I could've been there for you. To be the one to comfort you when you needed it most. To tell you that they were wrong."

There are no words to say. I bury my face into his shoulder and find that all my tears have already fallen.

"I won't let them continue to hurt me anymore," I say with finality.

Lanston pulls back and grins before spinning me to face the city. "Camp with me? We didn't exactly get to finish our beach night." He laughs, letting his fingers fall to my sides and tickling me.

"Lanston!" I shout-laugh and break free from his grasp.

He chases me around the roof until we're winded and cannot laugh any longer. We steal blankets and sheets from the hotel's penthouse suite and lay them out over the roof.

He pulls me in close and points at the stars, telling me all he knows about them, which isn't much, but I still listen with a warm heart and bright smile.

Lanston falls quiet and all I can hear is his heartbeat against mine. Curious, I look up at him. His eyes are already on me, endearment and heat burning where they trace over my face. His soft lips beg to be kissed.

He pulls me close, threading his fingers through my hair and kisses me. They are small ones at first, then our mouths open, searching and yearning for the dance we're so familiar with.

"I missed you so much," he says between breaths.

I let my fingers glide down his neck, over the flexed muscles that meet his collarbone. "You were all I knew as I fell into the dark."

He breaks our connection and bestows kisses to my neck. I fist his short hair and let my head fall back, a soft moan on my lips. He presses his lips to my neck, then my sternum. His fingers trail down my spine and his other hand smooths over my ribs up to my breast.

The thin black dress I wear falls over my shoulders easily, exposing my chest to him. Lanston braces my back and pushes me against his chest as he lifts us into a sitting position. He pulls me into his lap, returning his attention to my breasts.

His erection is evident beneath me. My core heats, urgent for him.

He senses my growing need and starts kissing up my chest. When he reaches the vulnerable skin of my throat, he strokes his tongue up the center, drawing a gasp from my lips. Lanston silences that gasp with his crushing kiss.

He leads me down until my back rests on the ground.

As he rises to his knees to remove his pants, I murmur, "I like you best in the light of the universe."

Lanston chuckles; it's a low, seductive sound that sends a throb through my core.

"Tell me why," he says, freeing his cock and returning to me.

Our lips connect and I whisper to him, "You look like a god. The constellations behind you."

His smile against my lips makes me weak.

"And here I thought you were a goddess I worshiped in secret." He breathes and pushes inside me. His groan is deep and reverberates through his chest, sending lust through my veins like a drug.

My back arches instinctively as he slowly thrusts into me. Our legs tangle as we become one soul. Chasing, kissing, biting. There isn't a part of him I don't adore. His half-lidded eyes draw up to mine, sweat keeping his hair to his forehead.

Our eyes lock in this moment, and everything I haven't yet said, and everything he's been wanting to, threads between us. Can you feel the weight of a heart through a man's gaze? I feel it, wholly and entirely.

"I hear you," I say, reaching my fingers up to trace his cheekbone. "Your cry for life is deafening." His motions slow, drawing his hips to mine until they are pressed together.

"You are the butterfly," he says, staring down at me like nothing else matters. "I am the moth."

My tattoo. His brilliant mind finding us as the somber creatures warms my heart.

We don't smile as we stare into each other's souls. It doesn't feel right to.

Lanston lowers his chest to mine. A fresh wave of pleasure rushes through me as he moves in slow tandem.

Our limbs tangle and our hearts cry out until we both cease, still and moaning with our release.

After our breaths calm and the storm in my mind clears, I ask, "Why am I the butterfly?"

Lanston pulls me to his chest, my head resting on his sternum as we stare up at the night sky.

"Because you're colorful and lively, like a butterfly."

"And why are you the moth?"

"Because I'm always chasing your light."

36

Lanston

Ophelia, dressed in the most enchanting dress I've ever seen, runs alongside the bay. Her white sleeves are clad in lace, intertwined with beige, and sewn in wheat embroidery. It's a light and endearing look—so bright and in contrast to her usual dark attire.

Secretly, I pretend this is her wedding dress and the black suit I'm in is my groom's attire.

She smiles back at me, earning her one in return. My hair wisps freely in the breeze. Paris has a crisp wine scent that floats in the air, tasting of rosé and champagne.

As I watch my rose take in the city, I picture what we could have been had we been fated to meet in life. I think of her, eating pastries and begging me to take her to the opera. We would get front-seat tickets that cost a fortune, but we wouldn't care. We'd be frugal with other things. I'd take her to bookstores, the ones that have a dark, gothic feel to them. Then, with our backpacks stuffed with unnecessary things, I'd drive us around a little too fast on a crotch rocket. Enjoying the feel of her arms wrapped tightly around my lungs, squeezing me as though I'll disappear if she doesn't.

A breath leaves my lungs and I chuckle a bit to myself, feeling foolish, because we are already doing all those things. But it would have been sweeter in life, to call Liam and brag about my adventures. To hear Wynn and Lanny's laughs in the background.

It wasn't written in the stars for me. I decide.

I accept that now.

Jericho reminded me that graves don't hold us down. Our ghosts are free, willing and daring. Just as we are.

Ophelia waves me over and I grin, happily meeting her by the water's edge.

"This bridge reminds me of the one back home," she says sadly.

I stare at her with sympathy, curious about the thoughts that may be running through her mind right now.

It comes to me that perhaps it is not appropriate to say, but I do anyway. "All this time I thought someone murdered you. An angry ex, an abusive family member, someone. But I never considered it was your illness that took you."

She stares somberly at the small ripples in the water below us.

"Are you angry?" Her fists clench tightly against the cement rail, trembling with the fear of judgment, I think.

I set my hand over hers and look out into the watery grave below as she does. "Ophelia, it wasn't your fault. You didn't *commit* a crime. You were ill and succumbed to your illness. It isn't your fault your most important organ failed and told you to crave death as a means of escape." She takes a deep breath and looks at me with despair, clinging to each word I say. "Only fools would be angry with you. You were sick, and try as you might, you were unable to find a light. How could one blame another for falling ill to cancer or disease? Your mental illness was a disease of the mind. It was just harder for them to see. I only wish that you could've found help. That you realized you were not alone in your illness."

"I am not hated?" She whispers so low that it hurts my aching soul.

"No. Not by anyone who understands the call of the dark, my rose." I press a kiss to her temple and she hugs me tightly.

"You always know what to say. You're so young but wiser than most," she admits and looks up at me. Her beautiful eyes are hooded by long lashes, and I find myself falling deeper into her.

"Perhaps we have lived many times. Our stories chasing one another permanently. But maybe now we can settle and rest," I say softly against her lips. She tilts her head back and kisses me endearingly.

"There's nothing I would love more than that, my love."

Palais Garnier is grander than any cathedral, library, or architecture I've yet seen. The walls are that of a fortress of the gods. It's honestly a bit overwhelming. More windows than I can count and gold finishes on statues and window frames above.

Ophelia giggles and nudges me, drawing my attention down to her smiling face. "Pretty impressive, isn't it?"

"Yeah, that's an understatement," I say breathlessly, returning my eyes to the white and gold paint.

We'll dance to any music tonight. Whatever show is currently going on doesn't faze us. Ophelia reassured me that the dance she taught me is universal, so long as the song is slow and beautiful.

People gather outside in masses, dressed in their best formal attire for such an event as this. I can't help but smile. The atmosphere is different, but I am reminded so much of the night I met Ophelia, dancing on a small stage without a care in the world.

We enter the grand building and make our way

through the crowds toward the stage, quickly slipping behind the stage curtains and laughing at our mischief.

I enjoy that most about Ophelia, I think—the laughter she draws from me. It's always so easy and pure.

"Tell me again why this is on your bucket list?" I jest, raising my brow at her and earning myself a playful punch to the arm.

"I didn't say shit about the beach and drinking under the stars, now did I?" she shoots back, and I can't fight the grin that spreads across my lips. I unfold the bucket list and cross off a few more things.

<u>Lanston & Ophelia's Bucket List</u>
~~Go to Paris~~
~~Sail a yacht~~
~~Ballroom dance~~
~~Drink on the beach at night/camp out~~
~~Ride a train somewhere new~~
~~Visit Ireland's Trinity College Library~~
Save a stray plant

Save a stray plant is all that remains. I let my eyes linger over Ophelia's lithe shoulders and smile, knowing I'll cross off the last item soon.

"Aw, come on, I know you loved it."

She shrugs cheekily.

My eyes are drawn to her chest, and I think of ravishing her here in front of everyone.

Ophelia's head tilts a bit and she grins. "What are

you thinking? You have the most peculiar look on your face."

I laugh and shake my head. "Nothing, nothing."

"Tell me!" She wraps her arms around my neck and before I mutter anything in return, the curtains lift. A million lights blind us from every conceivable angle and thousands of faces in the crowd stare up at us.

For a moment, I think they can see us, their faces aghast with whimsy. But then a handful of performers take the stage, running, leaping, dancing.

Ophelia's eyes brighten, and I can feel her joy inside my own chest. I knew then that the bucket list was a farce. Finding peace was never going to be about experiencing tangible things or seeing beautiful sights. It is the company in which it is spent, the meaning and love that is sewn into our fabric, the colors and images we keep of the most cherished ones, and experiencing together the dreams never pursued.

With her, I became the artist I always dreamed of being—she's dancing on the stage she always yearned for.

My rose adds every shade of red to my soul.

Happiness such as this, what a pleasure it's been.

She raises her hand, skin delicate and smooth. Our hands meet in the center of the stage and chills spread down my spine as the music starts up.

"Chem Trails" by Lana Del Rey.

My brow raises because I was expecting something old and orchestra-like, and Ophelia laughs, surprised but so delighted.

"Modern music finds its way into an old theater," she says cunningly. Her smirk is a little too sly.

"Did you mess with the music?" I laugh as we start to slow dance, feet moving with the song in long, languid steps.

She nods. "I couldn't help myself. I wanted this to be perfect." Her hands wrap around my neck and we glide across the stage amongst the confused performers. They dance alongside us, sticking to their routine even though the song has changed.

"How did you pull this off? I didn't think we could alter things in the living world." My smile is starting to hurt my cheeks, but I cannot stop. She enchants me in everything she does.

Ophelia proclaims, "If a phantom wishes hard enough, our pleas can be heard. I wanted this dance with you, with this song, and to kiss you. To tell you I love you over and over if you'll hear it."

I dip my head closer to hers, pressing our temples together.

"What else have you wished for, my rose?" I ask in a hushed voice, unwilling to disturb the music or this moment with her. One of my hands is clasped tightly with hers, the other lingering low on her back.

"I've wished for the plants I've stored in my opera house to find life again one day. For the weary darlings out in the world to find their hope." She pauses and looks at me, her eyes flickering with the lights around us. I only see her. "I've wished most of all for you. To find your reasons, to find happiness and love. To find your missing pieces."

Her purple hair glows beneath the lighting; her eyes have never been so colorful; they are easy to get lost in. Her skin is a beautiful olive, radiant, *alive*.

"I've wished for us," I say finally. And it feels as though I've waited such a long time to say these words. "I've longed for a soul like yours. And here you've been all this time. Ophelia, even if we are stuck on this earth forever, I would find solace in knowing we are together."

The song comes to an end. We stop dancing and stare at each other with endearment.

And then the darkness comes again.

The electricity sparks and shuts off; the crowd screams and panicked murmurs spread like smoke through the room. Ophelia's head whirls toward me, and mine toward hers.

We say simultaneously, "Those Who Whisper."

Our hands join and something wondrous happens. Light seeps from between us, and our breaths become one.

"Cast them away, Ophelia. Only you can do it," I shout above the loud whispers that surround us as if they are the next ensemble. Dark and cryptic.

Her hair lashes around her, our light flickering. "I don't know how! I thought they were gone. Lanston, I'm afraid."

My eyes narrow through the dark that caves around us. "You know the truth now. You know what they tell you are lies. I'm never leaving your side again; set yourself free."

Ophelia's fingers tighten around mine and her jaw flexes with determination.

Their voices suddenly become very clear to me, and I assume I'm hearing what she has all along.

"You are a sinner. You're going to hell. The ultimate sin. You've committed the worst crime. Your soul is damned. Selfish. Evil."

The anger and the hatred in the voices cause tears to roll down my cheeks. Voices of men and women, people who I'm sure she knew well.

My heart clenches and I grind my jaw, unable to keep my words inside my head. I shout, "She was sick! How dare you speak such horrible things to a soul such as her? Ophelia Rosin is the most beautiful creature to walk this earth. The kindest soul. Enough. ENOUGH!"

Like a breath extinguished, the whispers stop as if aghast. As if they've never heard anyone else speak against them.

Ophelia stares at me, silent tears falling from her eyes and then a small smile. The light between us grows until the darkness is cast away, until the room is completely encased with illumination and the stars hear us. Until the only thing the frightened audience stares at is the stage, at us, one might think.

Silence.

Then a small whisper from my rose, *"Lanston."*

I whisper back, "Yes?"

"I've waited my entire life and then some, to hear those words. Even if I knew them myself. To hear you say them..." She looks at me, entirely at peace. "Thank you."

I realize we've fallen to our knees in the chaos. Our hands clutching the other, safe. At a loss for words, I just look at her for as long as I can, not knowing when we might fade.

It feels close now, like a tug from deep within my chest. A call from within.

"I think it's almost time," she murmurs, pressing her hand to her chest, surely feeling it too.

I nod slowly, leaning in for a kiss. "Almost. But not yet."

37

Lanston

Boston is dreary, much like Seattle or a cold October day in Montana.

I look to the sky, thinking of Paris and Ireland, the train we took across the States, the memories made. Ophelia is wrapped safely in my arms, sleeping, dreaming. We no longer need to run from the whispering dark. It feels nice to take our time, even if the end is near.

The park is full of people.

We decided to wait here beneath a tree. Another world apart from theirs. There is no other story I'd want for myself.

I love her. More than I ever thought possible of a heart, I love her.

Ophelia's lashes are long and caress her delicate features as she stirs awake. She looks up at me and smiles, lifting her hand to my cheek; I lean into it.

"Have they come?"

"Not yet," I say.

She sits up slowly, our bodies close, comforting and warm.

We chat quietly for hours to come, without a care in the world, without time to drag at us. Then Ophelia straightens, startling me.

"What is it?" I ask, giving her a quizzical look.

Her lips are parted just enough to catch my eyes.

"I feel it. In the air, in my own heart."

"Feel what?" I laugh at her, brushing a stray strand of hair from her face.

Ophelia stares ahead, unshaken, and says, *"Your heart."*

My eyes widen and I look out across the park. Two familiar souls cross the grass, one small soul between them.

My cure.

I stand as if in a trance, desperate to run to them and tell them my stories. How happy I am. That I have found peace. I want to tell them about Ophelia and have them meet her and love her as much as I do. My hand rises, reaching for them and the visions I had for all of us.

But I know none of that can happen. And oddly enough, I'm no longer bothered by it. A strange feeling flutters through me as if carried on the wings of moths and butterflies. Peace.

My hand lowers and I remain standing by the tree, beside my love. Ophelia rises next to me, observing my expression carefully.

"Will you go to them?" she says softly.

A trembling smile spreads across my face, but my voice is smooth.

"No. I will not."

"Why?"

I watch the three of them happily living their lives. Part of my soul will always be with them, but it's time to say goodbye.

For good this time.

"Because we've all found our acceptance. We'll meet again someday. And besides"—I shoot her a daring look—"I've got a train to catch with the most beautiful ghost I know."

Ophelia smiles sadly at me, with eyes that are my home. "You're sure? We came all this way."

I take one last look at them, older now but as much the two best friends I've ever known. I no longer feel the need to linger.

"I'm sure."

38

Lanston

Harlow Sanctum, now gone along with all the phantoms it once held, takes new life in the form of Never Haven. Stones meet neatly and the fresh gardens are bright with life around it.

It's the first time I've properly seen it. The first time I've walked through the halls and watched the new patients cause trouble as I once had. The staff is caring, and the grounds are as beautiful as Harlow's once were.

There is only one thing left I wish to do.

Ophelia wanders the halls beside me, our hands clasped, awe in her eyes. We stop by the greenhouse, where so many horrors occurred not but seven years ago. How far that seems now.

She picks a handful of poppies and roses, baby's breath and mums.

I tilt my head and offer her my hand. She takes it and smiles up at me.

"Who are those for?" I ask.

"For all of us."

We walk to the memorial, flowers and wishes in hand. A man sits alone, the sun at his back and the forest breeze whispering around him.

He stares at the stone pillar with engraved names, mine upon them.

Ophelia sets the flowers beside the man. He doesn't notice because, of course, we are phantoms. She looks from his face to mine and realization dawns upon her.

"Lanston, do you know this man?"

I firm my mouth and walk around so I can see his face.

His gray hair is mixed with light brown strands. He has a scruffy beard and weary, baggy eyes, darkened by sleepless nights. His coat is black, matched with dark jeans and black boots. A cigarette between his lips, smoke curling in the air.

Father.

I stare for a moment, unsure why he is here, and emotions swell inside me—unknown and painful.

"He's my father."

Ophelia's brows gather and she looks from me to him a few times before finally grimacing. "Do you need a moment?"

I think about that. It wouldn't be harder if she stayed, but the things I want to say to him... they need to be private. I don't want her to hear what I need to let off my chest.

She sets her hand on my shoulder and presses a kiss to my cheek. "I'll be up front watching the sunset." I nod and watch her walk back up the path, disappearing behind the trees.

For a while, I just observe the tired soul before me. He doesn't look like the man I remember. It's been several years since I've seen him, after all.

They say time heals wounds. Of all kinds. But I don't think that's true. I think time only buries things into depths that are no longer so easily stared upon.

Although, I'm certainly not as angry as I once was.

"Hey, Dad," I say softly, knowing he cannot hear me. That somehow gives me strength, knowing he can't talk back and say hurtful things. "It's been a while, hasn't it?"

I take a deep breath and sigh, staring at the memorial stone as he does.

After a few seconds of silence, I turn to look at him. Even after all this time, I struggle to face him. His face is one that will haunt me forever, I think. My mind cannot erase those hateful glares and spiteful frowns.

Finally, I force myself to meet his tired eyes.

And the ugly, old pain in my heart falters.

His hazel eyes are filled with tears and his hands are clasped tightly together. His jacket is pressed like he had a tailor sharpen it up just to visit me. Shoes polished. Watch secured around his wrist.

The knot in my throat swells and an unknown feeling consumes me. It's not sadness or relief, but it isn't anger or resentment either.

My tears fall before his do—he finally came to see me.

He remains silent and I wonder how long he'll stay. My dad was never a man of many words. Why should he start now?

I decide I'll tell him what I've been holding onto my entire life.

"You know, you were a terrible person. Not someone who has bad days or is going through a hard time. You genuinely were one of the bad ones. I didn't deserve the things you did. The things you said." I pause, looking away from his blank expression and back to the field of flowers. "Even though you hated me... I want you to know that I still loved you. Through all the vicious beatings and emotional abuse, I still sought your approval, your love. I only wish you could've seen that."

He wipes his eyes and stands. *Leaving already?*

I bite back my emotions and say callously, "You couldn't even fucking show up to bury me? Why have you come now? Why!" I shout and fall to my knees, pounding my fists against the earth. "And you don't have anything to say to me?"

My father halts as if he's heard a voice in the wind and turns his head back, looking at the memorial stone.

I freeze, finding myself waiting, holding my breath, wishing. Wishing he would say—

"I know you have no use for these now—" He pulls out a drawing notebook from beneath his coat and a fresh set of acrylic paint, setting them down next to the stone. "—but I see now... how wrong I was. How cruel." My father's eyes narrow with anguish and his lip quivers.

My eyes widen as my fingers curl deeper into the earth.

He doesn't say anything else. After several moments, he walks back up the path and leaves. I stare at the notebook and paint, tears falling from my chin.

Why did it take me dying for him to finally accept me as I was?

Footsteps against the gravel path grow closer and a warm hand gently spreads over my back.

"Did he make amends?" she asks hesitantly. I look up at her and wipe the tears from my eyes.

"In his own way."

39

Ophelia

Lanston smiles brighter tonight. I don't tell him about the secret letter I left behind at Never Haven while he spoke with his father. It isn't meant for him, but I hope the person I did write it for finds it one day.

The very energy in the air has shifted. The universe pushes us toward the after. Tonight is the night.

I feel it in my marrow.

A small band plays a happy tune on the corner of where the bridge meets my street. We stop and listen for a while, smiling and clapping along with the music. After they grow tired, they take their instruments and leave.

"Do you feel it?" Lanston asks, a wondrous grin

making him more handsome than I've ever seen him. His high cheek bones are rosy, and weariness doesn't ache in his soul any longer.

I slip my fingers between his and press my cheek to his shoulder. "It's like a soft wind, beckoning for me. You'll come with me, won't you?" I ask, even though I already know he is. Yet I still get a wave of nerves.

Lanston opens the door to my opera house and bends at the knee, pressing a kiss to the back of my hand and looking up at me like prince charming.

"I'll love you until the stars die. I'd follow you into the darkest night," he says with a lovely lift of his lips. My cheeks warm.

"Such a poet," I say cheekily.

"And you, the inspiration."

I laugh as he scoops me up in his arms and carries me across the veil of my opera house. He chuckles; the sound reverberates through me.

"Do you think we'll laugh like this forever?" I ask.

He raises a brow as if seriously considering it. "I don't see how we wouldn't. I'm far too funny and you're much too easy to please."

We chuckle until he reaches the stage and sets me down.

Everything is as it was when we left. The rafters are still dusty, moonlight dripping through like beaded silk strings. Plants keep the space filled and green. Sadness invades me; I wish they could've found new life. I know they appear to me as alive, but on the living side they must be dead and weeping.

Lanston hops up beside me on the stage handing me a dancing ribbon. It's long and mauve, the same color as my hair. A smile curls at the end of my lips as I hand him a baseball hat I picked up for him at our last train stop.

"You're too thoughtful for your own good," Lanston says as his brows knit with endearment. He puts it on, letting the tips of his fingers glide at the rim.

"And you're too charming," I shoot back.

Lanston's smile breaks my heart. No one looks at me like he does.

He offers me his hand, warm and glowing with life beneath a dappling of moonlight. The universe has chosen to illuminate us in pale blue light, a farewell too bright and dreary even for us phantoms.

Our hands meet, and our breaths jump in unison as we feel the rush of the wind, of the earth, of everything that ever existed and took up space beneath the stars.

Lanston starts chuckling first, tears streaming down his face. Then I burst into laughter, because... well, because I've never felt so fucking happy. I never thought I'd have peace.

Our laughter ceases as we begin to fade.

Lanston pulls me in close, tilting my chin up and pressing our lips together as we slowly dance as if suspended in time. In space. In death.

Then a small whisper.

"I love you, Ophelia. Fiercely, unconditionally, until the stars die."

I know this isn't goodbye, our journey has just begun, yet I find myself memorizing the curve of his jaw, the softness of his lips, and the depth of his eyes.

"Until the ocean dries."

Epilogue

Wynn

The rafters of the abandoned opera house are riddled with holes. Rain dribbles down onto the old pews and fills the air with musk and mildew. Tables oddly fill the space here—angled in nonsensical ways, some even stacked—placed by ghosts, one might think.

Pothos, English ivy, Boston ferns—so many plants in an assortment of containers: terracotta, hanging baskets, cement planters. Roses, succulents, and cacti.

Alive. Thriving in this forgotten place.

Quite the collection, watered by the drops of rain that fall through the holes in the roof. *Someone saved these plants.*

A smile begins to grow across my lips. A wish.

"Mommy, who put all these plants here?" Lanny asks, his face lit up with curiosity. Liam stands at my other side, hands in his pockets, staring at the one beam of light that dapples through the dust and lands on the other end of the room. He's crying silently, with a large smile pulling at his lips.

Tears fall from my eyes too as I stare at the empty stage of the opera house.

A baseball cap and a long mauve ribbon rest at its center. A crumpled piece of paper that looks like a list of sorts. Perhaps forgotten by a passerby, or maybe a monument.

But something in the air is heavy. My mind is mischievous with hope.

Lanston.

"I knew you were up to something," I whisper to any ghosts who will listen.

Liam meets my eyes with the silence he's always had in them. His gaze is knowing. "I didn't pin him for a crazy plant lady type of guy," he jests.

I burst into laughter and the tears fall just as fiercely.

"The Night We Met" by Lord Huron plays on a radio outside the building. It's a slowed version, and the singer's voice is lower and more somber.

We stay for a while, quiet and still. Soaking in the atmosphere, for I fear it will be the last time I'll feel it.

Lanny tugs on Liam's sleeve and begs to get ice cream as we promised. I smile that fate brought us here. I'm not sure who left the drawing of this opera house, two lovers dancing in the shadows, pinned on the board at Never Haven, a short letter with beautiful words of dying stars and drying seas.

But somehow I'm certain it was meant for us.

The three of us leave.

As the two most precious people in my life walk ahead of me, I turn for one last glimpse, hopeful to feel his presence. A sign. Anything will do.

The weight of my hand spreads over my chest, my heart stilling.

Two phantoms meet on the stage, hands clasped and lips brushing. They dance as if suspended in time, slowly and to a song never known. And for a fraction of a moment, perhaps caught in the wind, their laughter fills every shadow of the world, casting a ray of hope for all the weary souls. And it's known then, to any who will hear it. *A Ballad of Phantoms and Hope.*

Acknowledgments

Thank you to all my readers, especially the die-hard Fabric of Our Souls fans! This book wouldn't have come to life without you. Lanston has been and always will be, one of my all-time favorite characters.

I'd like to thank my beta readers, Jay and Kenz. You both bring such insight and allow me to look back on the story with new eyes. Without you, my imposter syndrome would run rampant.

Thank you to my proofreader and PA, Cierra! You answer all the questions and are always such a delight in my day-to-day life! I don't know what I'd do without you!

Thank you to my editors, Leanne and Kelsey, for shaping my stories to be the best they can be. I always enjoy the deep dives into what needs to be fleshed out more to make the biggest impact on readers!

I'd also like to thank my husband for always being supportive of my writing. Thank you for listening to me chat about the characters until the sun goes down and sob over them like their my best friends.

www.ingramcontent.com/pod-product-compliance
Ingram Content Group UK Ltd.
Pitfield, Milton Keynes, MK11 3LW, UK
UKHW011007260625
6562UKWH00011B/211